C. R.

Xmas. 1914.

SCHOOLDAYS AT HIGHFIELD HOUSE

EVERY BOY'S BOOKSHELF

(Uniform with this Volume)

In Mortal Peril. By E. E. CRAKE, M.A., F.R.H.S.

Frank Lester's Fortunes. By FREDERICK ARNOLD.

The Young Nor'-Wester. By J. MACDONALD OXLEY.

Under Fire. By H. FREDERICK CHARLES.

Sir Roland Preederoy: a Tale of the Last Plantagenets. By F. C. BRITTEN.

Bush Luck. By W. H. TIMPERLEY.

A Boy's Adventures Round the World. By J. A. HIGGINSON.

George Burley. By G. E. SARGENT.

The Strange Adventures of a Young Sailor. By J. A. HIGGINSON.

Ernest Hepburn. By H. C. ADAMS.

Will Aylmer: a Tale of the Australian Bush. By L. B. LUFFMAN.

Roy of Daisydale. By L. C. REID.

The Captain's Bunk. By M. B. MANWELL.

LONDON: THE RELIGIOUS TRACT SOCIETY

HE COULD NOT HELP SMILING TO SEE HIS FRIEND
EMERGE FROM THE BATH.

SCHOOLDAYS AT HIGHFIELD HOUSE

BY

A. N. MALAN

Author of

'The Wallaby Man,' 'Uncle Towser,' etc.

WITH TWO COLOURED AND

OTHER ILLUSTRATIONS.

LONDON

THE RELIGIOUS TRACT SOCIETY

4 Bouverie Street and 65 St. Paul's Churchyard, E.C.

CONTENTS

Cacus and Hercules

CHAPTER I

IF there is one class of mortals which seem to me more to be pitied than others, it is that of Frenchmen who undertake to teach their language to boys in English schools. I suppose there are exceptions, but as a rule there seems to be a mischievous destiny, which dooms Monsieur to be plagued and tormented in a manner that must make his life a burden. Remember, I don't say there are not exceptions to this rule. No doubt you know several Frenchmen who are most successful masters in English schools. I am only speaking from personal experience. I wish to write what I saw, without any attempt to make a fine story, straight away, putting down the first word that suits my purpose ; and, in fact, I wish you to consider me as I was in the year

18——— No, I won't give the date, because you'll be able to calculate my present age, and that's not fair.

I had been at Highfield House School a term, I remember, when a new boy called Legg came. Highfield House was preparatory for the public schools. It was a grand old Elizabethan mansion, with spacious and lofty rooms. The schoolroom had been built on as a wing. There were iron gates in front and elm trees all round. The garden was behind the house, and beyond it the cricket-field, and beyond that again were pleasant views of woods and meadows undulating away towards a blue line of hills. I always enjoyed that view, and my pleasantest recollections are connected with long walks on summer afternoons through those same woods and meadows.

Our head master, Dr. Porchester, was fond of animals, and possessed a Spanish ass, the most remarkable of his kind that ever came under my knowledge. He was a very large animal—about twelve hands high—white, with extra long ears. His voice was simply terrible—braying is too mild a term. It was the most fearful tumult and turmoil of unearthly noise. It seemed as though all the evil genius of Donkeydom had been concentrated in the vocal organs of this monster.

The doctor seemed very fond of him, but we boys did not entertain much affection or admiration for the animal. He lived in a paddock adjoining the cricket-field, and had a comfortable shed to sleep in and shelter himself when the weather was disagreeable. The only exercise he ever got was when we boys used to make life merry for him by stimulating him to exertion with catapults, stones, sticks, tennis-balls, and other missiles.

On looking back, I fear our treatment towards him savoured of cruelty at times, but 'Cacus,' as we called him, would surely have died of apoplexy if we had not encouraged him periodically to relax his habitual laziness. He certainly had a lively time of it on those occasions.

The performance usually opened with artillery at a distance in the shape of old tennis-balls. These, having been previously used for fives, had all the vice knocked out of them, but, being generally left lying in the mud, they absorbed moisture and increased in weight; and so, when thrown from a distance, they would inflict a blow, not painful perhaps, but calculated to vex and annoy.

The first successful shot generally roused the enemy

to consciousness. He might be grazing peacefully in a corner of the paddock, and a shell would fly over his head unnoticed; another would drop short; a third might cannon against a tree. But sure enough, in time, one would come with an honest thwack against his carcase, leaving an impress of mud upon his shaggy side, and such indignity could not go unnoticed.

He would start with a sudden shiver, utter a squeal indicative of scorn and wrath, and, trotting off for a

few paces, would turn round and give a few savage
kicks. Meanwhile the fire would wax fast and
furious. The tennis-balls would soon fail, but the
small-arms could do effective service. The range of
the catapults was unlimited ; the impact of their
missiles was of stinging force. From a dignified trot
Cacus would break into a vicious plunging gallop,
spurning the sods and scattering them in his rapid
progression up and down the paddock at tearing
speed, snorting, roaring, kicking, plunging, ears back,
tail stiff like a pump-handle.

We thought it fine sport, and there was probably
not more cruelty in it than in fox-hunting, coursing,
pigeon-shooting, and other similar sports, which a
section of our nation regards as ennobling to the
British character, though this may be no excuse for
us.

Remember, therefore, I am but recording veritable
history, not condoning faults.

Certainly two important personages used to look
with disfavour upon our pastime. Cacus himself, to
judge from his conduct, thoroughly disapproved of
it, and Dr. Porchester likewise regarded it with displeasure. He used to come into the schoolroom at
preparation and speak about the practice, and call
upon the offenders to stand up, which we always
did.

I look back with gratification to think that it was
a recognised custom among the boys at Highfield
House to stand up at once when thus called upon.
Never mind how serious the offence might be, or
how certain of severe punishment, we always counted
it a point of honour to surrender ourselves when
guilty. If any boy failed to do this he was invariably
despised by the rest, and given to understand that
he was a 'sneak,' and found things go so hard with
him among his companions that he learnt a lesson
for the future which he was not likely to forget.

Dr. Porchester used to come in of an evening after

one of these escapades, and harangue the assembly
somewhat as follows: 'I am afraid you have been
tormenting the harmless donkey again. I picked up
several tennis-balls this afternoon in the paddock,
and the grass showed unmistakable signs of disturbance. There were some panes of glass, too, broken
in the greenhouse.' And sometimes he would ask
which of us had been guilty of this inexcusable
mischief. At other times he would content himself
with remarking upon the cowardly behaviour, and
put it to our good feeling not to repeat the offence.
Either way he made us feel ashamed, and for some
days Cacus would be suffered to laugh and grow fat
in undisturbed tranquillity.

As a rule it was only six or eight of us who took
part in these invasions. The senior boys always
held aloof. They might enjoy surreptitious glimpses
of the sport, but it was not consistent with the dignity
of the Highfield aristocracy to join in such question-
able amusements.

Then that boy Legg, whom I mentioned before,
though in all other respects one of the idle and
thoughtless, could never be induced to join us in
baiting the ass. He told me the reason in confidence
one day. His mother died a year before he came to
school. She used to ride on a white donkey, and
Legg was always reminded of her when he saw
Cacus.

I remember taking him round the place the first
day he came to school, and how he brightened up
at the sight of old Cacus quietly grazing; and, to
my astonishment, he climbed over the fence, went
up to the animal, and patted him familiarly; when,
instead of resenting his overtures of friendship, Cacus
seemed to appreciate them.

Legg was the only fellow who ever ventured near
the monstrous donkey, and he seemed to exercise
a magic influence over him. Cacus never resented his
familiarities, and Legg got the name of 'Hercules.'

He was a queer-looking chap with a long nose, thick lips, and his head went out in a strange way behind.

He perpetually had a weak throat ; his tonsils were always too large, which peculiarity imparted a thick and husky character to a voice naturally harsh. He was very backward and dull at lessons, invariably at loggerheads with the masters, popular with the boys, a happy-go-lucky sort of fellow who made every one laugh by his quaint antics.

It remains to introduce the French master, and then we shall be fairly on the way to recount the stirring episode which was perhaps the most exciting adventure in which Cacus figured.

Monsieur Delamere was a Frenchman born and bred, short and stout. He wore spectacles and spoke very imperfect English. He had known better days, but having lost his fortune through adverse circumstances he had come to England and settled at Deepwells, which quiet village offered among other attractions opportunities for giving French lessons in three or four wealthy families besides Highfield School.

He used to teach us in the mornings, the first hour after breakfast. He had the schoolroom to himself, and took two classes at a time. One wrote exercises or prepared translations, while the other was taken *vivâ voce*. It was not an arrangement calculated to ensure much real work, and I don't think we ever really learnt any French. In the junior classes there was always a spirit of mischief abroad ; and when in process of time we rose into the upper classes, it was more from the force of circumstances than from any proficiency in the Gallic tongue. The consequence was that French at Highfield was a sad farce, and was certainly the weakest point in the educational system.

I always wondered that the doctor did not take measures to effect a reform in this matter, but he was generally busy at the time with correspondence, and so never looked in before 9.45, when the second lesson began.

Now it may be imagined that on Tuesdays and Fridays, when the fourth and fifth classes came together for French, there was often a very riotous proceeding, and the babel of tongues, the shuffling of feet, the intermingling of scraps of songs, cracking of nuts, laughing, scrimmaging, and every imaginable species of insubordinate conduct, gave to these French lessons a character which may be feebly represented thus :—

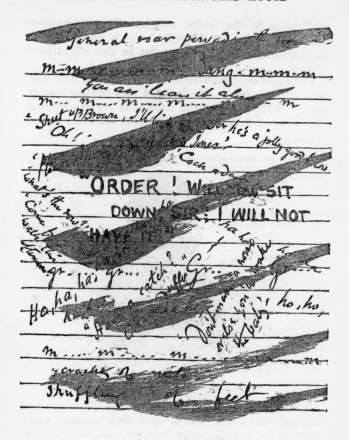

Chapter II

WHAT a shame! 'I should think so!'
'Mossoo has actually reported Jones to
the doctor for behaving badly in school!'
'Oh my, what a joke!' 'What cheek!' 'What will
he do next?' 'We'll pay him out!'

These and similar remarks passed from one to
another of some half-dozen of us one Tuesday morn-

ing in the summer term. It was after school, and we had just rushed out into the playground. If I remember right there were Legg, Jones, Davis junior, Broadly, Burke, and myself.

We formed a scapegrace portion of the fourth class, and on this occasion were loud in denouncing the audacious and unconstitutional behaviour of Mossoo. It was a glorious summer day. The lesson had been hot and drowsy, and we were glad enough to get out of the schoolroom and classrooms into the fresh air. Homer talks of the 'white shining south wind,' and its truth always strikes me on a day like that Tuesday, when everything shone with dazzling brilliancy, and the cool breeze prevented the sun from being oppressive.

We soon ran off to the field for half an hour's cricket before dinner. And while we played in a

remote corner we were devising plots for vengeance against the French master. Suddenly the tremendous voice of Cacus broke upon the serenity of the air; and as its harsh cadences performed their discordant gamut with the accustomed fury, some one suggested, 'What fun it would be if we could get the brute into the schoolroom next French lesson! He'd teach Mossoo to sneak!'

The suggestion was no sooner made than it was taken up. 'Why shouldn't we?' 'Oh, I say, you fellows, it *would* be fun! Think of Cacus kicking and plunging about the schoolroom! It would be glorious! Just the very thing! We'll manage it!'

The scheme certainly found favour with us, and we proceeded to consider ways and means. How could it be managed? Obviously Cacus must be decoyed out of the paddock and led up to the schoolroom door, and then the door must be suddenly opened, and he must be urged forward by a sound whack from behind.

'Now, Legg, old fellow, you must just put your pride in your pocket, and undertake the first part of the job,' said Davis. 'You must contrive to get Cacus up to the schoolroom door by ten minutes or a quarter-past nine. We'll give the fellows time to settle down. Then I'll get leave to come out, and as I open the door you must drive him in with the jolliest crack behind that you can give. Eh?'

'Oh yes, it's all very well for me to do it all,' said Legg; 'but I'm not going to lick old Cacus for any one. If that's the plan, I don't half see it.'

'Oh, it's all right, Legg. You must get him up to the schoolroom door,' said Burke. 'You're the only fellow who could possibly do that part of the business. You needn't get into the row by yourself. We'll share it somehow. What do you say, you fellows?'

We talked it over after dinner, and it was finally resolved as follows. The resolutions were drawn up, and duly recorded in writing :—

'1. Resolved,—That certain members of the fourth class, being dissatisfied with the conduct of Mons.

Delamere, have decided to express their dissatisfaction towards him.

'2. That the means they have resolved to adopt shall be duly carried out by Legg, Davis junior, and Burke. That Broadly, Jones, and Malan shall hold themselves equally responsible for the consequences, as being implicated in the scheme, aiding and abetting the others with their full approval and counsel.

'3. That the method of procedure be strictly carried out as follows: On Friday morning next, when the school-bell rings at 9 a.m., all members of the fourth and fifth classes shall duly assemble in the schoolroom for the French lesson, Legg only excepted. He will repair to the paddock, and, by whatever method his wisdom may recommend, he will proceed to decoy, lead, or drive Cacus up to the schoolroom door which opens into the playground. His arrangements must be so conducted that, without any noise or premonitory warnings, Cacus shall be at the door exactly at twenty minutes after nine. Davis junior and Burke shall at the same time request permission from Mons. Delamere to leave the room. They shall immediately possess themselves each of a cricket-stump, previously concealed within easy reach; and while Legg leads Cacus and opens the door and instantly steps backward six paces, Davis and Burke shall administer respectively on the right and left flank of the donkey a vigorous blow with the stump, calculated to induce him to advance at his fullest speed into the middle of the schoolroom. The door is to be immediately closed, and the subsequent proceedings left to the general discretion of the other members of the fourth and fifth classes.

'(Signed)   'J. BURKE.
'A. N. MALAN.
'E. H. LEGG.
'J. BROADLY.
'F. DAVIS.
'W. JONES.'

B

It may be imagined that we waited for the execution of this exciting programme with no common interest; and if ever a subject deserved a new chapter in any story that has ever been recorded, it was surely this.

CHAPTER III

THE memorable Friday dawned, and Aurora's chariot drove up the great heaven with divine radiance. 'A light wind blew from the gates of the sun,' and nature breathed obeisance to the lord of life. I looked out of window about half-past four, and drew in rich draughts of the pure morning air, fragrant with the ambrosial scent of early summer. The whole matter had been kept a profound secret by the six conspirators, consequently there was no unusual excitement.

Prayers, first school, and breakfast went on as usual, and in the half-hour after breakfast we sang and played fives, and read, and went round the field, and looked at Cacus, and filled up the time with ordinary amusements. We six did not keep together; we felt more or less uncomfortable.

In each of our six throats there was a choking sensation; hearts beat unduly fast. I have since experienced the same sensations before going into

the Oxford schools for examination, and also when
rowing in the college eight, in that period of five
minutes between the first and second guns. It is not
a pleasant sensation; a little of it goes a long way
towards producing a bilious attack, and a prolonged
course of it would not improbably end in jaundice.

When the bell rang at nine I thought my heart
would have burst. I felt as if I was going to be
executed. Some of the boys noticed my pale excitement, and asked ' whatever was the row ? ' and thought
I must have the measles.

The lesson began with the accustomed farce, and
proceeded with the usual accompaniment of irrelevant
noises; but five of the habitual obstructionists seemed
unaccountably demure. My own sensations may be
taken as a sample.

I thought the big hand of the school clock would
never get round to the fatal mark; and yet, as it
slowly verged in that direction, I wished it could
stop altogether. A gulping succession of chokes
seemed needful to keep my heart from getting up
into my mouth.

Five minutes past! Wood junior, put to stand on
the form, managed to exalt himself still farther by
getting on a shelf that formed a canopy over the
master's chair. There he amused himself by chalk-
ing the letters A S S inverted on his French dictionary, with a view to bringing it down smartly on
some friend's back, whereby the ignominious title
would be transferred from the cover of the book to
the covering of the boy.

A quarter-past nine! It could not be fancy;
hark! I distinctly heard the sound of hoofs on the
gravel. Hark! *Quadrupedante putrem.* The conspirators stole furtive glances at each other. A
rubbing as of a donkey's nose against the door smote
distinctly on my ear. Would my heart really burst?

Twenty minutes past nine! ' Please, Mossoo, may
I go out for a minute ? ' simultaneously fell from the

lips of Davis junior and Burke. 'Allez donc,' was the reply, and I thought I must faint. It took them ten paces to reach the door.

Even as upon some lonely mountain-side, where scattered rocks afford safe hiding-places for the venomous rattle-snake, a frolicsome young rabbit, all unconscious of danger, sits on his haunches daintily nibbling a dandelion. Suddenly he espies the cold, terrible eyes of death levelled upon him with unutterable fascination. A cold tremor seizes his limbs; he

cannot fly, though the friendly hole is within easy reach. His will is spellbound, his muscles rigid; he awaits the inexorable doom in abject helplessness.

Or, as a luckless boy sentenced to the extreme penalty of the rod kneels at the command of his preceptor, and with clenched teeth awaits the descent of the judgment which in a brief moment will send a thrill of anguish through his frame. To both of these miserable beings the moments preceding the execution of fatal vengeance seem an age.

Even so, to me, the moments that elapsed after

Davis and Burke had disappeared outside the school-room door, previously to the door being reopened.

* * * * *

Whack! whack!

E-E-e-e-E-E, A W-w-w-w—E-E-E—A W—clatter, clatter—bang, kick, plunge—wild madness—confusion —consternation—amazement—fury—ruin. Ha! ha! ha! Oh! bang, clatter—down goes a form—over goes a desk—boys rushing madly about.

Oh that Apollo would touch my lips with his wand! Oh for all the epithets and deep-mouthed rolling hexameters of Homer! Oh for a moment's power to describe in adequate language the scene that en-sued on the frenzied entrance of the infuriated Cacus!

Ton d'apameibomenos the loud-tongued terrible Cacus
Brayed with Cyclopean din, and the rumbling thunders of
Ætna;
Bristling uprose his mane, as upon the porcupine angry
Bristle the quills, when dogs urged on by the hunter assail
him.
Quadrupedante the floor sonitu quatit ungula schoolroom,
Clattered his hoofs, as clatters the tramp of a horse on a
highway.

In rushed the monstrous donkey, with head down, ears set back, and hind legs flinging out viciously, aiming no doubt at maiming the authors of his pain, like Hannibal's elephant. Then finding himself in an absolutely unknown land, surrounded on all sides by his well-known tormentors, the ass was overcome with surprise and indignation.

He advanced down the room with a rapid suc-cession of plunges, letting out with his hind legs, first to the right, then to the left—short savage kicks they were, such as denoted rancorous spite and mali-cious intent. Meantime he screamed in short un-earthly EEs, forgetting the AWs, or perhaps omitting them for rhetorical effect. Thus he advanced into the middle of the long schoolroom, and no doubt he would have continued his headlong course but for circumstances which diverted his attention to the immediate surroundings.

His career so far had been productive of general alarm.   He looked so enormous and terrible.   A bull in a china-shop is nothing to a four-legged donkey in a schoolroom.   All not initiated in the secret were absolutely so amazed that they stared with open mouths, or sought safety in precipitate flight.

I noticed that Wood junior in the general panic let fall the French dictionary plump on the back of

Mossoo sitting immediately beneath him ; and it further became evident that the impression of the chalked letters was distinctly imparted to his coat.

How strange it is that in presence of stupendous events the most trivial incidents often fix themselves on the mind !   I remember actually laughing at this ludicrous accident, though other and more serious matters were so imminent.

Cacus had reached the middle of the schoolroom, and, as I said before, he doubtless intended prolonging his onward career until what time he should reach the farther end of the apartment.   But here the fourth class were drawn up in line before the master's desk, and the presence of this formidable array caused the ass to consider the propriety of continued advance. He evidently decided upon a halt, for suddenly his fore legs were driven fast down upon the floor, and performed a sliding figure forward, as the hind legs were immediately brought down to correspond. Suddenly then he was brought up on his haunches in front of the fourth class.

Such close proximity to the vicious heels was by

no means pleasant. Some of us backed towards the wall, others turned and fled. Tomkins, a youth of extraordinary learning, well versed in classic lore, adopted the Parthian mode of attack; for while retreating in hot haste he wheeled round and hurled his French grammar with well-directed aim full upon the nose of Cacus. This was the signal for open hostilities. Instantly the air was darkened with grammars, dictionaries, exercise-books, inkpots, caps, tennis-balls, boots, and slippers. Volley after volley flashed from our serried ranks. By this time we had occupied the heights, and drawn up in battle array upon the desks flanking our master's throne.

There he sat, defended in a measure by the rampart of his desk, though in truth it seemed but a poor defence—only a thin board between his shins and the donkey's heels. Verily he had need of stout oak and threefold brass around his heart to sit unconcerned under such threatening danger. But his heart was encouraged as he looked anxiously towards his troops, and saw by their martial demeanour that they were resolved upon doughty deeds. Cacus meanwhile was buffeted right royally by the varied missiles that fell

thickly upon him. At point-blank range it was impossible to miss him ; and so deadly was the hail of shot and shell that he was bound to consider his movements. Advance was dangerous, for having once lost his line of retreat he must have capitulated unconditionally. Prudence therefore suggested retreat ; but here I feel bound to say a word for the sagacious strategy displayed by the ass.

His plans were evidently made with rapidity and keen foresight. He knew that the sooner he got out of the schoolroom the better. He wheeled round, therefore, but instantly saw that all means of escape were cut off by the fact that the door was shut; and furthermore, the fifth class, having rallied their panic-stricken forces, had taken up a strong position on the left flank, which being naturally fortified by a book-shelf and desk, they had further barricaded by two extra forms. Piles of school-books were visible on the ramparts of this fortress, leaden inkpots flashed in the sunlight, ammunition was plentiful and varied.

The keen glance of Cacus instantly grasped the whole difficulty of the situation. He was for a moment undecided. He kept shuffling about the floor and growing more furious every moment. He looked at the windows, but they were too high for escape. He truly seemed in evil case, and the fourth form were beginning to raise a pæan and behave as victors on a hard-fought field, when lo! the firing sud-denly ceased. The whole available stock of their ammunition was spent.

Cacus seemed aware of the fact, for now he showed no inclination to shift his ground, and coolly began to survey the field of battle, and actually had the audacity to rub his back against the French master's desk. This process seemed to afford relief to his troubled spirit, insomuch that he continued to rub other portions of his body, and increased the intensity of the operation, until the weight of his unwieldy carcase caused the desk to shift its position and tilt up on end, thereby forcing Mossoo with much violence to make himself as small as possible. The inkpot was simultaneously jerked backwards, and besides emptying its contents down the learned man's face, it dealt him a blow upon the temples; which blow, if the skull had not been of extraordinary thickness, must inevitably have proved fatal.

Such was the state of affairs at 9.30, and only one short quarter of an hour remained before the certain appearance of the doctor! Monsieur Delamere was not of great bodily strength. His muscles had under-gone much fatty degeneration. He was consequently

unable to free himself from the very uncomfortable
position in which he now found himself. Cacus had
no vicious intentions against him; it was merely the
brute's asinine nature to make himself comfortable at
another's cost. He never reflected that much inconvenience might be caused by his selfishness. But it
was indeed the most ludicrous sight imaginable to see
our Gallic preceptor thus imprisoned.

To say we laughed is too mild a statement; we

shrieked with laughter till the tears dimmed each eye.
The derisive peals roused the indignation of Cacus.
He thought we were laughing at him. It was useless
to apologise; an ass is never open to conviction. He
had made up his mind that we were laughing at him,
and with scorn on his lip, defiance in his eye, he made
for us! Knowing our defenceless condition, and
without further warning, he left off rubbing, took
three steps and a kick to the off, reared himself on
his hind legs, and brought his fore legs down with a
sounding bang upon the desk, where a moment before
we had been collected.

This was a real terror. We fled as best we could.
Some jumped off backwards; some executed a flank

movement, jumping off and doubling to the rear of the
enemy, shot past him and fled to the fortified camp
of the fifth class. Tomkins entirely lost his balance
and precipitated himself like a frog on to the floor,
coming down with such violence on his head that
he was fairly stunned, and lay moaning without any
attempt to rise. This diverted Cacus. He saw his
advantage—one of his enemies within reach. He
jumped down—that is, the upper portion of him

descended from the desk, and, horrible to relate! he
seized up Tomkins by the jacket and commenced
pulling him towards the door!

Luckily, Tomkins was prepared to bathe after
school, and having secreted his towel inside his
jacket, he subsequently informed us that the teeth of
the donkey did not lacerate his flesh. But we did
not know this; we were terrified at the sight. Would
he *eat* him? Palæphatus says in the Delectus that it
is laughable to imagine that a horse could devour a
man, but he doesn't say anything about an ass; and
we didn't know anything against it. Cacus was a

furious monster, and seemed capable of devouring a boy without much effort. Anyhow we couldn't look on and witness the disappearance of the ill-fated Tomkins by whatever method the ass might think fit. It would have been worse than Ulysses and his companions looking on while Polyphemus swallowed one of them after another.

A glance at the clock showed that five minutes of the quarter-hour had gone ! What could we do ?

In the extremity of our distress a deliverer was at hand. True to his name, Legg, our Hercules in very truth, was not far off. He had been watching the stirring scenes from a point of vantage, perched up in a tree outside, which commanded a bird's-eye view through one of the windows. He would not take part in the battle, for he could not bring himself to worry his favourite ; but he had witnessed all that had taken place, and at this terrible juncture he slid down from his perch, rushed to the schoolroom door, threw it open, and advanced quietly but swiftly towards Cacus.

Without a shadow of fear he seized one of the donkey's ears with his left hand, then brought his right hand down with a vigorous slap upon the neck, and made a very alarming guttural noise, which combination of arguments had the desired effect at once. For Cacus relaxed his hold of Tomkins, lifted his head, and seemed to feel that he had made more of an ass of himself than was consistent with his habitual serenity. Without any resistance he suffered old Hercules to lead him right down the schoolroom by the ear. And so the victorious Alcides carried off his captive, and with the utmost expedition led him back to the paddock.

There still remained five minutes of the French lesson. We set to work with a will to try and rectify the mischief and restore order. Tomkins was picked up, and, being the only seriously wounded man, was borne off the field by two members of the ambulance.

and carried bodily to the hospital to have his wounds dressed. Mossoo was extracted from his temporary prison, and the desk replaced. Books, boots, slippers, inkpots, and tennis-balls were gathered up and restored to their several places. The fifth-class fortress was dismantled; every one was seated at his desk apparently occupied with deep study. Only Legg and Tomkins were absent when the well-known step was heard outside, and the doctor entered for the second lesson. Then the other classes began to reassemble from the various classrooms.

It so happened that the doctor had been out between breakfast and school. He was now out of breath, and had evidently had to hurry back in time; so he knew nothing so far of the late stirring events. He did not look about much, but walked straight to his desk. There was the usual shuffling of feet and opening of desks and changing of books, but no one said much.

The fourth class cleared off as soon as possible to their next lesson; the fifth class likewise lost no time in disappearing. Mossoo, who stood in great awe of the doctor, got his hat and went off at once. Oh, how we secretly applauded this heroic conduct on his part! There was a breathing space—time for counsel and discussion—and by three minutes past the quarter the second lesson was commenced throughout the school, to all appearance as though nothing unusual had occurred.

CHAPTER IV

THE French master lived in a small house about ten minutes' walk from the school. It was a pleasant walk across the fields, or you might go by the lane that skirted them. This morning he chose the fields, and seemed to enjoy the bright sun.

It happened that Legg was just returning from the paddock, where he had replaced the ass, and was about to enter the schoolroom when Mossoo came out. They did not meet. Legg was sharp enough to avoid a direct interview by dodging behind a tree.

But the appearance of Mossoo altered the mind of Hercules. He eyed the master warily, and watched him climb over the stile at the end of the garden, and then Hercules dodged across the same space behind the cover of trees and got into the lane. He thought he would see how Mossoo seemed to take the morning's performance, and, if possible, make a timely apology, and get him to forgive us before he reported the matter to the doctor. So Hercules stole along the lane, peering through the hedge every few yards.

Mossoo, all unconscious, walked briskly along, apparently muttering to himself. Hercules could not hear what he said, and would not have understood it if he had ; but it sounded like the menacing growl of a savage dog. Suddenly, to the astonishment of the boy, the Frenchman gave several skips into the air, flung up his hat, kicked it as it came down, burst out into loud laughter, brayed, flung out his hind legs, and, amid much powerful gesticulation, gave evidence of great internal amusement.

He vaulted the next stile, and ran wild through the next field, after which he would have to come out into the lane. Legg waited for this, hidden in the hedge about twenty yards from the gate. He could see everything, and judged with no small satisfaction, from the very unusual vagaries exhibited, that the French master, far from being angry, was as much amused by the joke as the boys had been.

This was an astounding discovery. Could it be indeed true? Hercules was profoundly interested, and resolved to satisfy his mind upon the point somehow. Mossoo was now in the lane, and as he walked on he flicked the nettles in the hedge with his cane, sang fragments of lively airs, laughed occasionally, and gave stray kicks.

This conduct raised him immensely in the eyes of the wondering Legg. He thought after all Mossoo might be a jolly fellow, if one only knew him.

As he went on and turned a corner he espied his small daughter running gaily down the lane with her hoop. Mossoo gave a shout of delight. The child ran to him. He caught her up and kissed her, and began describing, in his broken English, the adventure with the donkey. He always spoke English to his wife and daughter, for the sake of practice.

'Oh, my child, it was droll. The ass, he enter the schoolroom; he kick and gallop up and down; he bray; he bite the boys; he upset my desk; he behave so wild. Oh, but it was droll. Come into the summer-house. I will tell you all about it.'

Legg followed them, keeping well out of sight, and when they entered the small garden he hid in the hedge, and heard a further description of the exploits of Cacus. And Louise was so amused, and looked so charming as she laughed and ran round the gravel path with her hoop, that old Hercules fairly lost his heart.

And when Louise said, 'Oh, my father, it was so droll, I am sure you will not tell Doctor Porchester, for he would be so angry with the boys,' he longed to jump through the hedge. And when with beating heart he listened for the reply to this suggestion, and distinctly heard, as a great puff of smoke came out of the summer-house, the answer, 'No, my dear; I shall not tell the great man. The boys, they are droll creatures, full of fun and mischief. They tease me, but I not mind. They have good hearts, but oh, they are so idle. I do my best to teach, they laugh, they do not attend. Not my fault. They not like boys in France. I make allowance——'

When, I say, Legg heard this noble speech his whole heart was full of thankfulness. He felt a choking sensation of joy. He could not trust himself to hear more. He slid noiselessly down from the hedge, and crept up the lane till he was out of hearing, and then he ran the rest of the way at full speed, bursting with gratitude and eager to tell the fellows what a jolly good fellow old Mossoo really was, and determined not to annoy him any more, and to make the rest of us promise to behave more soberly at the French lessons.

So fast did he run that he got back just as we were coming out of school for a quarter-hour between lessons. We were running off to the field to publish the eventful news, and discuss the probable consequences, when we came across Hercules breathing hard after his run, and he lost no time in telling us of Mossoo's generous magnanimity.

We were amazed beyond measure, and at once drew up a formal apology to be presented to him that afternoon. We deputed Legg and Davis to convey it to him after dinner. We really meant every word of it. We had had our fun, and were actually going to get off any unpleasant consequences. Was it possible? I feel that this is rather an unwise moral, but I undertook to record facts without any

attempt to turn out a fine story, and in its bare, un-
garnished outlines the historian would fain portray
faithfully the noble behaviour of the French master.

The apology was presented in due course. It was
issued in the name of the fourth and fifth classes, and
concluded with a promise in future to pay proper
attention to the French lessons, and a hope that their
thoughtless conduct would be forgiven. It must be
understood that we were actuated simply by admiration for Mossoo's generosity, and intended our
apology to be an expression of this admiration. And
it may be added that a very marked improvement
was visible afterwards in our behaviour at French,
insomuch that Monsieur remarked more than once
that our conduct was commendable and our progress
very satisfactory.

And so it came about that the extraordinary cam-
paign of the four-legged ass in the schoolroom was
productive of beneficial results, and marked a turning-
point for the better in the laborious process of imparting and acquiring a knowledge of the French
language among the refractory members of Highfield
House School.

The End
of
The Tale

A Dunce's Disasters

CHAPTER I

TUESDAY, July 16, 18—, was a day of sincere summer weather at Deepwells. There could be no mistake about that. It was a day to prove the overpowering influence of heat upon school lessons —when boys are unusually disposed to be lazy, and masters are physically incapable of exacting the full tale of work; for on both sides Nature proclaims a truce, and hostilities are suspended from sheer inability to carry on war.

Dawson and Smith occupied adjoining desks in the schoolroom. They were reclining like Roman gentlemen at a banquet; before them were spread dishes of intellectual meat in the shape of *Florilegium Poeticum* and Latin dictionaries. But their fastidious appetites loathed the food, and their spirits sighed for cold water and the shade of spreading trees.

The master, Mr. Fields, was seated on his throne, alternately fanning his heated brow with a red pocket-handkerchief and correcting some Latin exercises. Occasionally he would utter a suppressed growl, and fling some remark of withering sarcasm at the head of a luckless youth who had shown outrageous audacity in blundering through a sentence.

'Dawson, what do you mean by writing such infamous rubbish? The sentence is, "The boy was not fearing the voice of the great ass," and you've got, "*Puer non fuit timens vox ingenti asini.*" What's to be done with you, Dawson? Answer me!'

'I tried to do it, sir.'

'Oh, you *tried* to do it, did you? You dare to tell me you *tried* to do it! You *tried* to write this abominable trash? Well, you've been tolerably successful; and, if you go on steadily as you've begun, by the end of term you'll be able to write such glaring tomfoolery that I shall have to spend my holidays exhibiting you as a rare example of juvenile precocity—only fit to be stuffed and preserved in a glass case!'

A ripple of subdued laughter greeted these remarks, while Dawson blushed and looked undecided whether to laugh or cry. He was a dunce, and no mistake! but withal he was a delightful little dunce. Everybody liked him, including the masters who had to contend with his stupidity.

Mr. Fields heaved a deep sigh and kept furiously digging his pencil into the offending exercise.

Just then a pleasant diversion took place. The schoolroom door opened and in walked the pompous butler bearing a dish of most delicious-looking strawberries.

'The doctor's compliments, sir, and he thought these might refresh you this hot morning.'

Dr. Porchester was fond of devising quaint surprises to vary the burden of lessons in the hot weather.

'Thank you,' said Mr. Fields. 'Pray convey my best thanks to the doctor.'

The strawberries were set down on the master's
desk and the servant withdrew. The boys eyed the
beautiful fruit with reverent and delightful gaze.
Nothing could have presented a more grateful con-
trast to the dusty surroundings. Fresh and fragrant
of summer, that fruit might have been picked in the
garden of the Hesperides for the table of Jove !

'Now, boys,' said the master, 'here's something to
make your mouths water ! How I should like to
divide them among you ! But of course I can't when
you are so disgracefully idle. Just look at Dawson
and Smith ! Do they look like athletes training for
the classical palæstra ? Have any of you attempted
to work this morning ? As for these exercises—why,
boys who can compose such disreputable nonsense
can have no soul above suet-pudding ! the ethereal
juices of this charming fruit would be lost upon you !
So I fear I must make myself ill with them alone.
Dawson, if I promised you this strawberry' (taking
up the finest), 'would you do me one sentence of
Latin without a mistake ? Don't answer. I know
you'd try. Never mind. Time to come up to class.
Sharp ! '

The boys were always more or less amused by the
facetious harangues of Mr. Fields. He had a way of
making his lessons amusing, and enjoyed his little
jokes amazingly. But he was an excellent teacher,
and his ' Repetitions ' were always best in the school
when the boys went up for the weekly examination
to the doctor.

So dictionaries were hastily shoved into desks, and
the boys formed class with promptitude, and just a
trifling ' hot-up ' for a high place to start with.

'Ah ! ' said the master, ' " Care is soothed by song."
A very pleasing title for a beautiful passage from
Tibullus. Let us hope that the spirit of the Muses
will assist our endeavours to translate it into equally
beautiful English.'

The first six lines were bungled through with a

few false quantities, which the master said made his
teeth ache, and it was Dawson's turn to go on at the
lines—

> 'Cantus vicinis fruges deducit ab agris,
>   Cantus et iratæ detinet anguis iter.'

He read them through without disaster, and proceeded to construe thus : '*Cantus*, having sung, *vici-
nis*, to the neighbours, *deducit*, he deducted, *fruges*,
the crops, *agris*, from their fields.'

'And who,' said the master, rising from his chair,
with scorn in his voice, derision in his eye, 'who was
this unprincipled scoundrel who thus, under the disguise of friendship, perpetrated such a thievish trick
upon his unsuspecting neighbours ? Where was the
policeman ? To think of the rascal first singing to
them—no doubt a comic song—and then, while they
were splitting their sides with laughter, he sneaked
off and stole their turnips and mangold-wurzels !
Oh, Dawson ! your genius has drawn for us such a
picture of cold-hearted treachery that the blood is
sent curdling backwards at the thought ! Now let us
parse it—*Cantus ?* '

'*Cantus* is the past participle from *cano, canere,
cecini, cantum*.'

Dawson spoke out with the emphasis of conviction
that this was a true answer.

'Oh, indeed !' said the master. 'Very nice, very
excellent ! What a pity that such a display of grammatical knowledge should be absolutely mistaken !
Next, next, next !'

Surprise was depicted on the boys' faces. They
looked from one to another. Surely there was no
mistake ; it was only one of the master's dodges to
try and extort a ludicrous blunder.

'What !' said he, 'can't we suggest an improvement ? *Cantus ?* Eh ? Can't us try again ? Can't
'um do it ? Can't you do it ? *Cantus, cantum, cantus,
cantui, cantu ?* Oh yes, you see it now—you should

have seen it before. And so, as usual, I must translate it to you. Listen with all your ears, Dawson :—

"Song draws the fruit from my neighbour, Mr. Fields."

What more appropriate line could you have found
for the occasion? Why, Dawson, instead of auda-
ciously creating a participle, and endowing it with a
force altogether alien to its nature, if you had only
stood up and sung that chorus, "Drink, puppy,
drink," as I heard you singing it yesterday in this
very room—why, how could I have done otherwise
than give you all these luscious strawberries? What
a chance you have lost!'

The master's eye twinkled at what he evidently
thought a very happy joke, and Dawson was told
to proceed with the next line, which he rendered to
the master's satisfaction :—

'Song even checks the advance of an angry snake.'

This translation seemed a surprising effort to Mr.
Fields, for it drew forth the remark, 'Bravo, Dawson!
we may yet live to see you senior classic of the
school; and if ever you are confronted by an adder,
bear in mind the precept of the poet, and sing your
loudest, and see if he doesn't get up on his hind legs
and dance.'

But there was no time for further frivolity, and the
remainder of the lesson was solid hard work—not
another jesting word spoken; so that when the
'quarter' came the boys all knew the construing,
and had turned it back *vivâ voce* from English into
Latin, and parsed it, and so done it thoroughly.

As for the strawberries, six of the finest were given
to Saulez, who marked off top, and the remainder
were divided among the rest of the boys by their
good master, who reserved three for himself. And
his eye melted as he saw their keen appreciation of
the dessert, and his heart throbbed as the class broke
up with a joyful cheer, for his soul was full of true

sympathy with the nature of boys. He studied their characters as an artist studies expression in the countenances he paints ; he knew the secret of winning their confidence and respect, and in all his dealings with them he took for his motto these words of Juvenal, 'MAXIMA DEBETUR PUERIS REVERENTIA' (The greatest reverence is due to boys). That is a proud motto for you, boys ; and, as its sentiment is profoundly true, REMEMBER ALWAYS TO DESERVE REVERENCE, by being humble and courteous and respectful and obedient to all who are set in authority over you.

CHAPTER II

THE boys at Highfield House were not surprised that an extra half - holiday should be given that afternoon. It was such a glorious day ; the deepest blue sky was cloudless, and it would have been cruel to spend the afternoon bending over dusty desks and grammars.

Dawson and Smith, companions in work, were no less chums out of school. They were not much of cricketers, and generally tried to get leave for a long walk on fine half-holidays. This was not difficult on that Tuesday ; and immediately after dinner they set off. How delightful it was down the cool lane ! The heat was no longer oppressive.

They ran gently for a quarter of a mile, so as to
get well out of range, and then stopped to rest and
look about, knowing that they should see nothing to
remind them of school. No, it was pure summer,
green and shady. The lane was seldom used by
carts, and was almost entirely carpeted with turf.
The hedges were full of ferns, fox-gloves, honey-
suckles, dog-roses, and lots of other wild flowers.

Butterflies were glancing, and bees humming, and
dragon-flies darting like winged jewels.
'Isn't it glorious!' said Dawson, wallowing in the
long grass. 'How jolly these afternoons are! I wish
it was always summer. But I say, Tom, we must
move on; it's two miles to Darkwood Copse, and the
ruins are a mile farther, and I want to call at old

Punchey's cottage to see if he's got the water-rat.'

So the boys set off again, and now took a path over a common covered with furze and heather and bracken.

'I wonder,' said Smith, 'if we shall come across an adder. I should like to try whether the beast is really fond of music. I believe it's all bosh ; but I've brought my penny whistle, and we could give him a tune. Let's practise.'

Smith played the air of that chorus in the hunting song which Dawson loved to shout at the to of his voice in the echoing schoolroom ; and on they marched to the strains of enlivening music. The copse soon came in sight.

'We'll try that bank where we saw one last year,' said Smith, 'and if possible catch him asleep. I know the dodge. Lay hold of him tight round the neck, he can't bite, and tie your handkerchief over his head. Nothing's easier.'

'Do you think you dare do it, Tom?' asked Dawson. 'I shouldn't like to try, I know; but if you can manage it, I'll sing to him. I know another song, if he doesn't seem to like the one about puppies.'

'Oh, he won't be particular. That's the bank. It was just under that ash-tree. Let us go very softly, so as not to wake him.'

The boys crept cautiously on, and soon reached the bank on the outskirts of the wood. The shadows of the trees threw soft traceries over the grassy slopes. Stepping lightly, they peered into every nook and

mossy corner, but saw nothing, not even a dead stick, that could be mistaken for a reptile.

'Never mind,' said Dawson, 'let's go on to the ruins. I wonder what was the history of the old castle. I wish we could find some treasure hidden there. Let us pretend to be Tom Sawyer and Huck Finn the Red-handed. What a jolly story that is; what splendid adventures they had; and how exciting the doctor makes it when he reads it out loud to us! Oh, Smith, shouldn't you like to have some grand adventure in the old ruins?'

'Rather!' said he; 'let's hurry on; perhaps we shall surprise a robber!'

But the boys were not to reach the ruins that afternoon. Their expedition was doomed to a premature termination, as the remainder of this chapter will explain.

They had turned on to the high-road in order to take Punchey Brown's cottage on the way. This important personage deserves a word of introduction. His importance was mainly recognised by the boys of Highfield House, for he was none other than the authorised purveyor of 'grub' to that establishment. For years he had enjoyed the monopoly of supplying the lads with fruit, buns, ginger-beer, and other delicacies dear to the soul of boys. From a humble beginning he had gradually risen in business; for having been originally but the owner of two baskets, which he stocked from a neighbouring shop, he was now the proprietor of a shop, and had lately started a cart and one—to wit, a donkey.

He called his establishment Wayside Cottage, and had fitted up the room on the right side of the door as a shop wherein to display his wares. A back room had been converted into a bake-room, in which his wife periodically turned her hand to the confection of buns and pies and savoury cakes. These basked habitually in the shop windows, or found their way to the school precincts. The room on the left of the door was devoted to another branch of business—for Mr. Brown had assumed the title of 'general dealer,' and had amassed a motley collection of crockery, ironmongery, and haberdashery; all of which goods were deposited without much regard to scientific classification in the room on the left. Furthermore, in order to extend his connection, he was accustomed often to don his brown velveteen coat with the brass buttons, and envelop his neck with a red handkerchief, and sally forth on a pilgrimage—his donkey-cart stocked with carefully selected goods—to visit outlying hamlets ; only appearing at Highfield, as a rule, in person on Wednesdays and Saturdays, and on other days sending his son with baskets of provisions.

It was about three o'clock when Dawson and Smith reached Wayside Cottage. They found the proprietor leisurely preparing for a drive. He was leaning on the donkey ; and the cart, piled up with crockery, etc., stood by.

' Hullo, Punchey ! '

' Well, young gents, so you've got a 'alf-'oliday, and are out for a bit of a spree. Warm weather, ain't it ? Guess you would like a bottle of ginger-beer, eh ? '

' Rather, Punchey, if you're certain it won't poison us ;' and the boys made haste to invade the refreshment room.

' Go gently,' said the general dealer; ' the old 'ooman's rayther cross —don't tread on her corns.'

Despite the warning, they entered with somewhat more alacrity than ceremony, and encountered Mrs. Brown in the shop, where she had just deposited a consignment of hot buns. The boys pulled off their caps with a profound bow.

' Good-afternoon, missis ; it's awfully hot, and some of your ginger-beer wouldn't be amiss, especially as Mr. B. is going to treat us.'

' Treat you, indeed—what's that about treating ? I'll

trim John's jacket if he talks about treating. Honest
folks have to work early and late, and must live.
Twopence a bottle, young gents, as many as you
please.'

And the old lady bundled out to get the beverage,
for it was kept in a cool corner outside. She returned
with a bottle and tumbler in each hand, which she set
down on the counter, and proceeded to tap one of the
bottles.

Now it happened that the gaseous evolution in the
ginger-beer had been brisk during the heat of the last
few days, and the bottles, though securely fastened
with wire and string, contained the pent-up furies at
such high tension that a pressure of almost irresistible
force was exerted on the corks—in other words, the
ginger-beer was 'up' almost to bursting-point, causing the corks to bulge and lean over sideways.

It was only the night before that the Browns had
been violently roused from sleep and terrified out of
their senses by a tremendous report, followed immediately by another and even another. Mrs. Brown had
shrieked 'Murder!' Mr. Brown imagined dynamite.
He had told her to 'shut her row'; she had taunted
him with being 'afeared to open the door,' and
ordered him downstairs to tackle the thieves and prevent their being murdered in their beds. And it was
not until he had accomplished a tour of the premises
and was on the point of returning to his chamber,
that a frothing and seething in the corner where the
ginger-beer was kept conveyed to his agitated senses
a true suspicion of the cause of the alarm.

Mrs. Brown now began cautiously to untwist the
wire of the cork; and though painfully apprehensive
of an explosion, she was not over-careful about the
direction in which she pointed the bottle. She was no
more to be trusted with that formidable piece of artillery than a nursemaid might be with a Woolwich
infant, as the result proved.

The boys watched the operation with interest and

amusement. The cork was unctuous with saccharine exudations. Mrs. Brown's fingers were fat and clumsy An ominous sizzling portended the approaching release of the imprisoned liquor; and BANG went the cork with a deafening report, hitting Dawson full in the right eye!

'Mussy me!' exclaimed Mrs. Brown, while cataracts of foam welled forth, deluging her gown and splashing on the floor in apparently inexhaustible streams.

The old dame grappled manfully with the engine of destruction, and vainly strove to stem the torrent by inserting her thumb into the orifice. Dawson was yelling with pain. Smith, stunned by the suddenness of the catastrophe, stared open-mouthed; and Punchey stood in the doorway rolling out salvoes of laughter from his stalwart chest.

It was a comical scene. Mrs. Brown, on recovering her presence of mind, informed the company that she was 'all of a tremble and a shake'; yet a woman's instinct prompted her to deeds of mercy, and she was soon engaged in bathing Dawson's eye. The pain he endured was considerable, but gradually subsided under her treatment. The boys were then invited to regale themselves with a jam sandwich and raspberry vinegar. Dawson's handkerchief was tied over his eye, and they essayed to proceed on their walk. But Disaster No. 1 was not yet fully enacted. The boys must needs inspect the contents of the cart, and assist the proprietor in harnessing the donkey. Dawson's spirits were not damped, though his eye was dimmed.

'Hold hard, Punchey, don't put him to just yet; let me show you how a Roman general rode in triumph when he returned from the wars. Smith, play "See the conquering hero comes," and imagine that those sheep coming down the road are the citizens flocking to see the gallant sight.'

So saying, Dawson went up to the donkey, who

had been quietly browsing along the hedge-side, patted him and cajoled him with soft words, laid hold of his hair, bent over his back, and nimbly mounted the shaggy beast. The latter seemed surprised at the liberty, but began to move on.

'Gee up, Neddy!' cried the general, applying inducement with the calves of his legs. Neddy gee-ed up a little, and slightly elevated his heels, while he lowered his head ; and Dawson's equilibrium was dis-

turbed. But he clung valiantly to a tuft of mane, and righted himself in an instant. The course of the hero was undoubtedly erratic. It was hard to make out what direction the triumphant procession was intended to take. It was more like the ride of Silenus in the revels of Bacchus. You remember the lines in Ovid, of course.

The sheep were advancing with acclamations of 'Baa!' There were no lictors with their fasces to keep the lines. The woolly animals, which our Latin Reader declares to be the most stupid of all, paid no regard to propriety in their movements; but covering the whole road with a straggling, clamouring phalanx, they pressed forward to witness the pageant, and encompassed on all sides the ass and his rider. Neddy resolved to bring the matter to a crisis without further delay. Gathering his strength for one supreme effort, he gave such a vigorous plunging kick that Dawson was sent flying.

He fell on the shafts of the rickety cart, which Punchey had propped, for the operation of loading, upon two forked sticks. These were snapped in a moment, and the sudden collapse of the cart caused the contents to be forcibly projected. There was a shock of 'shivering claps and cracks'—a shower of crockery and tin kettles—and Dawson was buried among the ruins.

An old sheep tried to clear the cart in her excitement. She actually succeeded in getting on board, and her weight instantly tilted the cart up on end; but she likewise was involved in discomfiture, being shot out the other way, and landed sprawling on her back in a rut, where she lay helplessly kicking. The rest fled in trepidation.

Smith was in roars of laughter. Punchey was furious with wrath, and stupefied by the portentous calamity. Dawson lay gasping in the wreck. He had received some serious wounds. His right cheek had an ugly cut, from which the blood flowed freely. His hands were scratched. The sheep had knocked out his wind.

'Get up!' cried Punchey, so soon as he recovered sense enough to speak. 'What d'you mean by smashing my china? Get up, will yer?' And the general dealer proceeded to deal with the general in very unmilitary fashion—for instead of fetching a stretcher and bearing him off the field with dignity, he laid hold of his leg and pulled him out. It took all

Smith's eloquence to appease the wrath of Brown. Assurances of pecuniary reimbursement to the full amount of damage at length prevailed ; and Dawson was removed to the cottage, where Mrs. Brown plaistered him up, and the two boys set out to return home as soon as possible. They had promised without fail to bring Punchey twelve shillings on the morrow, being the valuation he set upon the broken crockery. So meditating and conversing ruefully on the vicissitudes of fortune, they wended their way back to Highfield House.

CHAPTER III

DAWSON was in much the same predicament as France at the time I write. He was engaged in unpleasant relations with China. It was hard for him to raise twelve shillings ; in fact, he only possessed half a sovereign, which was being hoarded up for tricycle rides in the holidays. And he had to draw his whole balance from the school bank to pay Punchey.

The doctor had asked about the cut on his face, and so drawn from him an account of the disastrous events which caused it. There was thus no difficulty in obtaining such a large sum as ten shillings ; for without sufficient reason the demand might have created a panic in the money market.

Smith readily contributed the other two shillings, and the boys set off after dinner that Wednesday for Wayside Cottage. They did not loiter over this portion of their walk. It was an unpleasant and irritating thought to have to part with so much bullion. Dawson was thoroughly vexed with himself. It was the most expensive and least agreeable of all the donkey-rides he had ever had. However, 'What can't be cured must be endured.' The money had to

be paid, and the sooner it was done with and forgotten the better. So they hurried on to the cottage,
and paid over the money, which was not very graci-
ously received.

Punchey declared it was not really half enough to
replace the lost property, and grumbled as he lowered
the shillings into his capacious breeches-pocket. But

the boys didn't wait to listen, and once more they ran
for a quarter of a mile along the road, to get out of
sight and remembrance of the ill-omened spot.

'Now for the ruins,' said Dawson, as they climbed
over a gate to take a path across the fields. 'Bother
old Punchey and his wretched donkey. Don't let us
mention them again. Now for Tom Sawyer and
Huck Finn the Red-handed!'

The ivy-covered tower soon appeared to view, ris-

ing above the elms. The boys approached with
stealthy steps, dodging behind trees, treading cautiously, with an occasional 'Hist!' like the heroes in
Mark Twain's romance.

The hope of finding hidden treasure was intensified
to-day by the lamentable
drain on Dawson's ex-
chequer. Some jackdaws
were talking fussily, and

flying out in pairs to perch again upon some point of
vantage, by which omen the boys judged that no
robbers were at home. Nevertheless, they crept up
to the arched doorway and peeped in: then they
entered.

A rabbit, scared at the intrusion, scampered off;

clear proof that no 'humans' had been about lately.
They gave chase through the turf-grown courtyard,
where formerly the pavement echoed to the clank of
steel and the tramp of armed knights; through the
banqueting-hall, where haughty barons once quaffed
goblets of sack. But the rabbit escaped into the ferns,
and the boys returned to rest among the ruins.

They played at being knights, holding high festival
over imaginary wine-cups, while mirth and song re-
sounded through the ancestral hall. The penny-
whistle was in full blow, and Dawson's shrill treble
was exerted to the highest pitch in his favourite
chorus, 'Drink, puppy, drink.' They were seated
back to back on the massive pedestal of a pillar.
And now Dawson's attention was caught by the
movement of something alive in a patch of tall grass
that fringed the castle walls. Without stopping in
his song he sprang from his seat and was at the place
in an instant, kneeling down and rummaging all heedless after the unknown quarry.

So quick was he to do this that Smith had not
noticed it. Suddenly Smith was startled by a loud
yell. He jumped from the pillar in a trice, and saw
Dawson writhing on the ground, while the tail of an
unmistakable adder disappeared in the grass. Horrible to relate, Dawson gradually became quite still.
His eyes shut; his face grew ashy pale. Smith made
sure he was dead, and was distracted with terror. He
had never seen any one faint before.

The thought of water occurred to his mind. He
rushed to a small pond that was near, and returned
with his cap full of water, which he splashed over
Dawson's face, and then tied the dripping cap round
his left hand, which was much swollen, and appeared
to Smith's agonised imagination to be growing black.
This restorative treatment proved effectual, and to
Smith's unspeakable joy Dawson gradually recovered
consciousness. He gave a few deep sighs, opened
one eye and then the other, moaned out that his

left arm was all numb, and he believed he was, dying.

'Never mind, old chap; sit up, you'll soon be all right. You must get on my back, and I'll carry you home.

Dawson was just able to stand, but when he tried to walk the feeling of faintness returned. He tottered and staggered, and would have fallen but for Smith's aid.

'You must sit down a bit more, Harry. Here's a comfortable corner;' and Smith escorted him to a seat in a recess of the wall.

Dawson drank some water out of Smith's cap, rested for ten minutes, and was then able to get on his friend's back.

The homeward march was thus begun; it was a painful and laborious progression. Dawson was no light weight, and he could not hold on with his left hand at all. Smith had to support as well as carry him. A halt was peremptory at the end of the first hundred yards. Dawson was gently lowered on to a couch of growing fern, and a council of war was held. It was evident that they would never reach Highfield unless some more expeditious mode of travelling were devised. At last it was decided to make a detour of about a quarter of a mile to a keeper's cottage, which the boys thought they could manage to reach.

Dawson could now walk a little more comfortably. There were some stiles to be crossed, and also a brook, which the boys had often jumped in places. But there was no alternative. It was resolved, therefore, to make for that cottage, and they got on pretty well until they came to the brook. A tree had been lopped, and made to fall across by way of a bridge; and, as jumping was out of the question for Dawson, the passage must be attempted by means of that precarious contrivance.

Cautiously Dawson proceeded to cross with shuffling footsteps, Smith following close in the rear and supporting his comrade to the best of his ability. What with the pain and exertion already undergone, Dawson was not equal to the effort. Midway his nerves seemed to fail, his head to turn, and losing his balance, he fell with a sousing splash into the muddy water. Smith narrowly escaped being involved in a disastrous partnership, but he managed to reach land in safety, and could not help smiling to see his unfortunate friend emerge from the bath—an operation of no small difficulty.

Dawson now presented a sorry and woe-begone aspect—drenched and bedrabbled with mud. The rest of the march was as gloomy, on a small scale, as that of the Old Guard in the retreat from Moscow. The cottage was at last reached, and the keeper's wife lent a ready ear to the tale of distress. She was fond of the Highfield boys, and at once offered to treat the sufferer with all the medicative resources at her command. She insisted on putting him to bed while she dried his clothes. She bathed his hand with further application of cold water, though Dawson suggested that he had had quite enough of hydropathic treatment already. She rubbed in spirits of hartshorn and oil, and bandaged up the hand with professional skill. She then prepared a cup of strong tea, with a dose of some cordial added, two thick rounds of buttered-toast, and an egg, for she said that the poison must have stuff to work off upon.

Dawson by no means objected to this part of her curative operations. With a little pressing he made a substantial meal, and Smith kept him company. The partner of his sorrows would fain share in his consolations.

The clothes were dried ; the patient was revived by his rest ; the grandfather's clock in the kitchen warned the boys that it was high time to be getting home. So, with grateful expression of thanks to their kind-hearted hostess, they set forth once more upon the homeward journey. They managed the first two miles very comfortably. Dawson's arm did not pain him much, but it had a peculiarly numb sensation, with occasional throbs and shooting spasms. The poison, no doubt, was working, whether 'on' or 'off' he could not tell.

About a mile from Highfield they met Punchey and his cart. The former seemed rather full of ale; the latter was empty of wares. The general dealer had driven over to the village to make arrangements for refurnishing his stock of crockery, and he had perhaps wetted his bargains—as the vulgar expres-

sion is—with unreasonable licence. His face beamed with complaisant good-humour. All traces of displeasure were obliterated, and when he heard of Dawson's serious disaster he insisted on turning round and giving the boys a lift in his cart back to Highfield.

This progress partook more of the nature of a triumphal entry than Dawson's first attempt, for Punchey prevailed on his donkey to put forth his best paces, and sang songs of uncouth but cheerful melody. And thus the two boys were at length deposited safely at the school entrance.

CHAPTER IV

A T the close of the last chapter we saw Smith
and his unfortunate comrade landed at the
gates of Highfield House. The matron was soon
informed of the disaster, and never before having had
experience in the treatment of such a case, she lost
no time in sending for the physician. He came and
prescribed lotions and physic and complete rest.

Dawson was now comfortably tucked up in bed,
and the next day also was spent in bed. The day
after he was allowed to get up and sit in the matron's
room. The adventure had been told over and over
again by Smith to an open-mouthed audience; and
the invalid was visited by several friends from among
the boys, who looked upon him as a hero, and secretly
envied his notoriety.

These receptions were by no means disagreeable to
Dawson. His hand was an object of profound interest, with the veritable marks of the adder's fangs.

Dawson hoped that the scars would never wear out;
and when alone he would gaze with pride upon them.
No boy at Highfield could boast of such marks;
and Dawson resolved to have his photograph taken
as soon as possible with the left hand prominently
displayed.

Mr. Fields was not behind the boys in coming to
see the patient.

'Well, Harry, my boy — what a business it is!
How odd that you should have had the line to construe about the snake only the day before!'

'Yes, sir; and I don't think Mr. Tibullus was
right in what he said about song stopping the
advance of an angry snake; for I was singing my
loudest at the time the adder bit me.'

'Ah, Dawson,' said Mr. Fields, laughing, 'perhaps
it wasn't the right tune; though certainly the poet
is to blame for misleading you. The fact is, I don't

believe they really knew much about natural history in those days. They had no Zoological Gardens, you see. Tibullus wasn't the only one of those old fellows who got hold of strange notions about animals. There was a naturalist whom every one looked up to as the greatest authority of his time, who thought he knew all about elephants. He tells a story or two that I don't put much faith in. He says that there was once a stupid old elephant at Rome who couldn't learn his lessons, and used to sit up half the night meditating upon them! What do you think of that? Some boys might perhaps take a hint from him, eh? He also says that when elephants want to cross a river, they send in the young ones first. If that is really true, it seems to me a very mean trick. For I suppose they do it as an experiment, and if the old ones see that the water is too deep, or the current too strong, they turn up their noses, wag their tails, and trot off to find some more convenient place, leaving the infants to their fate. The same professor also informs us that when a herd of elephants is on the march, the oldest leads the van, and the next in age brings up the rear. But he doesn't tell us how he found this out. Perhaps he got the veterinary surgeon to examine their teeth. None of those old wiseacres had such extraordinary ideas about animals, after all, as the famous Julius Cæsar. And as you are not allowed to talk much, Dawson, I'll give you a short lecture upon a passage from that well-known author. I've just been having a lesson in it with the second class, and have my book here.'

Mr. Fields turned over the pages and found the 25th chapter of Book VI.

'Now, Dawson, you shall see what ridiculous notions the general got hold of. I think he must have been crammed up when he was a new boy at school, or else eaten too much supper and had a nightmare before writing these chapters. But, at any rate, what he actually says is this:—

'"There is a vast forest in Germany, nine days, journey in breadth for one unencumbered with baggage. Rather a vague definition, but the natives do not understand the measuring of distances. None has ever penetrated to the uttermost parts of this forest, even after a journey of sixty days. It is a region of mystery and marvel and measureless extent. Many strange animals inhabit its vast recesses, nowhere else found in the world. The most remarkable are these : a stag-like bison, with an enormous horn in the middle of his head, from the summit of which palm-like tynes branch forth."

'Here, then,' continued Mr. Fields, 'we have the veritable unicorn, the mythical beast so strangely caricatured in the national escutcheon, who in the language of our nursery rhymes once contended with the lion for the crown. Cæsar proceeds to describe another species :—

'"There are likewise animals called alces. In shape, and the variety of their skin, they resemble goats, but are much larger and have not horns. Their legs have no joints, and if ever, in a moment of forgetfulness, they lie down for rest, or fall by any accident, they can never get up again. Their method of going to bed is to lean against trees. The hunters track them out, and cut the trees nearly through, so that when the alces retire to rest their weight upsets the trees, and they all tumble over together."

'From this,' said Mr. Fields, 'I conjecture that Caius Julius once had a Noah's Ark given him when he was a little boy ; and the imaginations of his infantine mind being extraordinarily vivid, left an impression which he could not shake off in after years. He also mentions an enormous species of wild ox, only a trifle smaller than an elephant, of mighty strength and speed, which spared neither man nor beast, and could never be tamed even in its calfhood. I amused myself a few evenings ago by trying to draw these strange animals, and here are the attempts.'

Mr. Fields opened his mark-book and showed Dawson the drawings. And while they were talking, the school-bell's familiar clamour broke upon their ears.

'I say,' cried the master, 'there goes the bell. I must be off. Good-bye, Harry. I suppose you'll be back in school to-morrow to torment me once more ; but I'll come and see you again.'

So saying, he packed up his books and hurried off.

And this seems a good opportunity for closing my story ; for, even as I write, the school-bell breaks in upon the stillness, and I must leave the last words till lessons are over.

*　　*　　*　　*　　*

Lessons are over once more ; and perhaps some one will ask what is the moral of this story ? Well, I cannot say I exactly know. But I gave you one valuable piece of advice, boys, at the close of the first chapter, and here is another to finish up with. We were just talking about the school-bell. Remember, whenever you hear it ring, that its voice calls 'Attention !' Time is a most precious and responsible trust received from God ; but in play-time it is given you for recreation and enjoyment. There is a time for work and a time for play. Most boys are willing enough not to let the demands of the former encroach upon the pleasures of the latter, but some are not so anxious about the reverse. Now, when you hear the bell ring, remember that Time is no longer yours to do what you please in it. The bell rings, and instantly DUTY calls. Every moment of lesson-time must be jealously given to work. The boy who steals some of its precious moments for anything else is not honest and noble and true. There's something wrong with him—something that savours of shuffling and deceit. Don't skip these few last words. Don't fancy that they are the grains of

Gregory powder which the jam has failed to conceal. Not so. I have taken some trouble to amuse you, and you ought to pay me the compliment of reading my story to the end. For there is one thing more to be said about Harry Dawson. He was a dunce, but he was not an idle dunce. He did his best to struggle with his nouns and verbs and sums. But some boys are dunces because they are idle; and others are idle because they are dunces. Never let either accusation apply to you. Never forget that the school-bell calls you to DUTY; and remember the words of the Poet-Laureate:—

> 'Not once nor twice in our rough island's story
> The path of DUTY was the road to glory.'

One of Mother Carey's Chickens

CHAPTER I

'CLUCK! cluck! cluck! cluck! CLUCK! cluck! cluck! cluck!'

From the noise the old Cochin China hen made you might have thought she was the very identical fowl which laid the golden eggs in the fable. She strutted this way and that, proclaiming her proud delight to the world in general, and to Mother Carey in particular, who was looking forward to a brood of chickens. It had been well if she had looked backward also—for she was at that moment engaged in boiling the potatoes for dinner, and turning quickly round to peer out of the window and see which of her hens was raising the triumphant hymn, she forgot all about the bucket of water, and she must needs kick it over in her excitement, thereby producing a small flood in the apartment. This disaster roused the old dame's wrath, and she gave an extra kick to the inoffensive bucket. The result was excruciating anguish to her great-toe with the corn, and genuine cause for the old lady to howl in good earnest.

Mother Carey lived in a cottage adjoining the cricket-field at Highfield House. Her husband had formerly been head-gardener to Dr. Porchester; and now, having passed the time of life in which his energies were equal to the laborious requirements of that situation, he had relapsed into the less dignified position of knife-and-boot boy. As he naïvely expressed it, 'I've a-been in service this fifty years, and I be only a b-u-o-y after all!'

Mother Carey herself washed the socks of the young gentlemen, and turned an honest penny by the produce of her poultry-yard. She had fair reason to be proud of her chickens. It was not that they were of choice extraction or imposing in numbers, for when all hands were piped at feeding time there was but an ill-assorted gathering of some twenty birds, of all shapes and sizes, from the gawky Cochin down to the dainty bantam. But by careful diet and treatment she prevailed upon them to give her a very respectable supply of eggs, and her spring chickens invariably fetched a good price, and were famous far and wide for the flavour and delicacy of their flesh.

Now, any one acquainted with the dame might have been struck by her countenance on this occasion. The habitual serenity of her face was replaced by a frown of unqualified dissatisfaction, as she looked out of window and espied the old Cochin China hen craning her neck with vigorous efforts of intonation. It may have been the smarting corn on the dame's big-toe; it may have been the mess of water on the floor of the kitchen. But probably the cause of her displeasure was otherwise.

That particular hen had lately developed a tendency towards deception highly to be censured in a bird of reputable character. For three days in succession that fowl had trumpeted forth the tidings of an egg laid. Yet, although Mother Carey searched high and low, she could not discover where the canny old fowl had concealed the treasure. She had looked in the copse, in the stable, in the wood-yard, in the barn, in the outhouse, in the peat-stack, in the straw-stack, and in the haystack. In out-of-the-way nooks and corners had Mother Carey hunted, and all to no purpose.

There were eggs unlawfully hidden, and the hen-wife was justly indignant at the insolent deceit. She

could not spend her day dodging the Cochin with incessant surveillance. Time was not long enough. She wished to trust her fowls—to teach them honesty and appeal to their sense of honour by treating them with confidence, and was this to be the return? Mother Carey gave a sniff and wiped her eye with a corner of her apron. It was only yesterday, when that gossiping old crony, Mary Woostford, called and recommended a strict watch to be set upon the movements of the culprit, that Mother C. had said, 'I'd scorn the haction, marm!'

The proprietress of the poultry-yard was visibly irate against this member of her galaxy. The flash of her eye, the impetuosity of her step, betokened hot displeasure. She'd let the rascally old fowl know, and suiting the action to the resolve, she was out in the yard in an instant, armed with a mop. There was a shriek and a scurry of legs and wings, and the Cochin made rapid tracks for cover.

Mother Carey returned to her potatoes.

It behoves me to throw light upon the conduct of this hen.

Know, then, that there was a boy at Highfield whom his sponsors had christened Thomas, while his surname was Bertram. But his schoolfellows, with an eye to the exuberant development of his cheeks, called him 'the Dumpling.'

In the practice of nicknames we may notice a usage of classic antiquity which has defied the vicissitudes of time, and will doubtless continue to future ages. Had not Cicero's grandfather a wart on the top of his nose which got him the cognomen of 'Chick-pea'? Was not Ovid conspicuous above his fellows for the size of that member, wherefore they called him 'Nosey'? And the progenitor of the Scipios was doubtless tall and straight like a walking-stick. Among the celebrated *graffiti* of Pompeii are numerous caricatures and inscriptions savouring strongly of this custom, so that if the Latin prose

E

book is to be believed a boy named Caius was called 'the Cow,' and another with large eyes and a round face was known as 'the Owl.'

Where were we?

Talking of the Dumpling, sir.

To be sure. Well, he was a full-fleshed lad of jocund countenance and a turn for idleness, vanity, and mischief, which often got him into trouble, as it always will to the end of the chapter. But perhaps we must not be too hard upon his all-too-numerous followers, for if it was not for such boys there would be no need of schools to train and correct and drill them into shape. And if there were no schools there would be no holidays, and whatever should we do then?

Without further preamble, let me state at once that this Dumpling was simply and solely to blame for the hen's conduct which so grievously displeased Mother Carey. Yes; so prone was that youth to folly, that, not content with setting a bad example to himself and his companions, as though that were not enough, he must needs lead astray into unseemly conduct a Cochin China hen! And this is how it was.

The Christmas holidays were just over, and the Dumpling had found them hang heavy on his hands. Not being of literary tastes, he did not care for reading stories even of thrilling adventures and hair-breadth escapes. Not having a taste for the fine arts, he would not practise his scales on the pianoforte nor amuse himself with a pencil or a paint-brush. Not caring for bodily exertion, he would not even join the merry company of sliders and skaters, though the ice had been in superb condition for a whole fortnight. The obesity of his carcase prevented him joining with any pleasure in games, and if he was forced by the home authorities to go to a juvenile party he would sulk in a corner and throw a chill over the festal mirth, which even the warmth of his red cheeks failed to dispel.

Seeing then that these things were so, the Dumpling had cast about in those holidays for some diversion which might be congenial to his degenerate tastes, and he had been successful. His brain, so inactive as a rule, had shown extraordinary quickness in devising a remedy for his *ennui*. He had taken a course of lessons in cookery. I use the word *taken* advisedly, for it cannot strictly be said that the lessons were *given*.

The cook was far from pleased at the frequent visits he paid to her domains. He would come rolling into the kitchen at any time, no matter how busy she might be. He was not unpleasant or rude in his manners. Nay, he took care to make himself agreeable to the servants. He had brought the cook a new cap with pink ribbons as a Christmas present; and he had a way with the servants which was quite irresistible. He would smile till his beady eyes twinkled and the dumplings on his cheeks became more pronounced than ever, and the housemaid, at all events, thought him a fine, handsome young fellow.

Thus he would often gain admission to the kitchen, and there inspect the culinary operations. He was specially interested in the manufacture of puddings and pies. Pie-crust he loved. You might see him with his pocket-knife scraping off the remnants of crisp brown flakes that fringed the margin of an emptied pie-dish. He would convey the morsels to his mouth and devour them with a voracity commendable in a prize pig, but not so in a boy never likely to be a prize boy in any competitive examination.

The Dumpling went back to Highfield after those Christmas holidays with fine stories of his achievements in the art of cookery. He boasted to have made mince-pies and cheese-cakes and toffee and all kinds of sweets. He would gather round him a bevy of kindred spirits and dilate upon the glories of his skill with wondrous eloquence, while his hearers licked their lips and smacked their chops, and feasted in imagination upon all the luxuries of Christmas.

'And then, you fellows, my mater one day wanted a trifle, and cook was busy, and I said I'd make it.

So I got the eggs, and sugar, and sponge-cakes, and jam, and cream, and brandy, and sherry, and made such a splendid dish. The white of the eggs I flipped up into foam half a yard deep, and the strawberry jam at the bottom! Oh, it was crackey, I can tell you!'

'I should like some now, I know jolly well,' said a

very skinny, pale-faced boy, who looked as if he had never eaten a dinner of roast beef in his life. 'I wish you'd make us one of your grand dishes, Dumpling, just to show what you can do.'

'I'd make a trifle fast enough if I could only get the things; but how can a fellow get anything good at this beastly place?'

The Dumpling moved off without waiting for any one to answer his question. Most of the boys were playing football in the playground, for it was between 2 and 4 p.m. The gravel was in prime condition —hard and dry. The sun was bright, the air crisp and frosty, and of course the boys as a rule were making the most of it, playing up with that grand energy which is so delightful to watch. If boys would only throw the same determined vigour into their lessons, we should have them all at the top of the class; the bottom would be No Man's Land— Ultima Thule, the other side of the Streams of Ocean.

Most of the boys were hard at play. Only a very few were loafing about, and those were the troublesome, idle, mischievous spirits who break windows, cut the desks, pick mortar out of the walls, break rules on the sly, skulk in twos and threes behind odd corners, and generally give more unnecessary trouble than all the rest. But we cannot stop to consider these uninteresting specimens just now, for the game waxes warm round one of the goals, and who can resist the inclination to look on?

Notice that splendid young fellow with a face which one day will be a type of manly beauty, with a chest that even now makes one feel strong to look at it. That's our friend Harry Stephenson, captain of the games, the most popular boy in the school. See how he defends the goal, with his entire soul thrown into the work, rallying his side around, cheering, directing, charging, shoving his mightiest. He'll ward off defeat if any one can. But, see, that little bit of a chap has hold of the ball, with limbs as lissom as a cat's. His legs seem to flash as he runs and dodges. Why, that's—no, it can't be—yes, it is —that's his small brother, Dickey!

Who could believe it? In spite of his diminutive size he runs like a hare. What a colour he has! Why, he's the picture of health, as different as possible from what he was the last time we saw him on the platform at Ventnor Station. He's getting the ball through! He'll get a goal! Ah, no. Harry has caught him. With one arm encircled round the small body he lifts him clean off his legs, but as tenderly as is compatible with stern duty. Harry's other hand secures the ball in a trice, and depositing Dick with a laugh he punts the ball half-way down the playground, and looks round, now that the danger is past, to see that Dick is none the worse. God bless you, boys!

Hi! stop one moment, Master Puffy-cheeked Dumpling; don't go skulking out of the playground just yet. You want to get round that corner and steal off to the field to potter and loaf after some silly mischief. But do stay one moment and watch the game; for if you did, surely you could not choose but join in yourself, and perhaps dissolve some grains of superfluous fat, and raise in your unwieldy frame a glow of vigorous life which might prevent your yawning and lolling over the desk all through that Latin prose lesson which comes on at four o'clock. No, he has disappeared round the corner, and I have not the heart to follow him just now.

CHAPTER II

THE Dumpling was no more affected by his proximity to that game of football than is Nelson's statue by its proximity to those majestic lions in Trafalgar Square.

The fat boy strolled on with his hands in his

pockets, whistling 'Grandfather's Clock,' and banging at everything he passed with an old cricket stump. He left his marks, like the North American Indian threading a primeval forest. You could trace his progress everywhere. If Dr. Porchester had the railings painted in the holidays, the Dumpling's stump would register its trade-mark on them before he had been back half a day. Things sacred were no more safe against his vandalism than things profane. The spear-headed railings round the chapel were decapitated here and there by his destroying hand.

I think there must have been sad laxity of parental discipline at home. When his mother first brought him to school she had in a measure prepared Dr. Porchester for the worst. She had said, ' I am afraid my boy is not very fond of his books ; but he has a decided turn for mechanical pursuits. He is very clever at taking locks to pieces, and cutting things out with his pocket-knife. I hope he will have an opportunity of keeping up these tastes.' The doctor, with a twinkle of grim sarcasm, had replied, ' Madam, I quite understand you, and I have no doubt your son will find the opportunity. But at Highfield we call these tastes *mischievous*, not *mechanical*, and do not as a rule encourage them.'

The Dumpling sauntered on till he reached the confines of the cricket-field. He banged his stump not once nor twice upon the top wire of the fence, and watched the reverberating thrill pass down to the gate a hundred yards off. He then essayed to surmount the fence, putting one foot on the lowest wire, which bent to the ground, the other foot on the next wire, which gave in proportion. Then by a mighty effort he hoisted a leg over the top wire.

To get the other leg over required him for a moment to poise his unwieldy frame on a wabbling wire about one half-inch in diameter. This Blondin feat was beyond his powers. He lost his balance hopelessly and fell with irretrievable ruin, like a sack of

Portland cement, on the same side of the fence from which he started.

Rendered furious by this failure, he got up and belaboured the wires with his club. A second attempt was then made on different principles. He stooped to conquer. Putting his head and arms and shoulders between the second and third wires, he tried to wriggle the hinder portion of his body through. But this also was a hopeless business. The upper wire was elevated to its full extent, the lower one depressed abnormally ; but no amount of kicking and jerking would enable the broadest and most circumferential portion of his person to get through.

Once upon a time, in Oxford days, I heard a mouse in my cupboard purloining biscuits. I knew of the hole by which the thief gained access, and opened the door to expel him. Like his prototype in the fable, my intruder had eaten himself to repletion, and, foolish Troglodyte ! he tried to escape by that same hole. He got half through, and remained hopelessly stuck ; and his ineffectual efforts for liberty were highly ludicrous.

Even so was it with the Dumpling, who only after grievous labour succeeded in extricating himself on the wrong side of the fence. Baffled a second time, and exasperated into bellowing, he got up, and, like Achilles, shuffled off in mighty wrath to the gate, by which only available entrance he at last achieved his purpose.

There stood an ancient willow tree in a remote corner of the field. Its trunk was hollowed out by time and decay into a cavernous recess, whereof the sides and ceiling were metamorphosed into touchwood. Oftentimes, when the sun was shining brightly, would the Dumpling, like Prometheus, draw down fire from heaven with a burning-glass, and set this tree smoking and smouldering. He now bent his steps towards that goal, with what intent I know not.

He arrived on the sound side, and by force of habit

began to worry the willow with some vigorous blows of the stump. The immediate result was a screaming and a clucking, and the precipitate flight of a Cochin China hen—the same bird which greeted us at the outset of this story.

The Dumpling jumped, and was on the point of hurling his club at the terrified bird. But he did not do that. He went round the tree and peered into the cavern, and there on a heap of touch-wood that had been scraped into the form of a rude nest he espied an egg reposing.

'Hullo,' quoth he ; 'fresh eggs ! Hi cockolorum !' by which cabalistic ejaculations he signified his appreciation of the discovery.

He knelt down and took up the egg, and whistled as he turned it round. It suggested a train of thought. The hen, meanwhile, recovered her scattered wits and came as near as she might venture to see what was going on, with pleadings of anxious expostulation that her property might not be pilfered or destroyed.

The Dumpling replaced the egg, and feeling in his pockets, drew forth some grains of Indian corn. With a 'coopy, coopy, coop,' to attract attention, he threw a few grains to the hen, which were eagerly devoured. By the aid of more corn he decoyed the bird back to the tree, and when once again she was installed in the cavern, he threw her a few more grains as a parting present, and withdrew, pondering many things in his heart, and soliloquising thus :—

'Fresh eggs! I'd be able to get the other things, and just show that young ass Buffles that I can make a trifle.'

The next day, at the same time, the Dumpling repaired to the willow tree, and, after expelling the hen, found, to his delight, two eggs. Of these he selected one, and depositing some corn by way of payment, he went off rejoicing. On three following days he repeated his tactics, only that on the last occasion he abstracted both eggs, thinking that five would be ample for the dish which was to confute the sceptic Buffles.

No wonder Mother Carey had been outwitted!

I said at the commencement of this tale that the Cochin China hen had been led into deceit by the Dumpling, and there were just grounds for the statement; for we have no reason to suppose that the bird was wilfully disposed to fraud ; and, assuredly, had it not been for the fat boy's seductive allurements, she would never have returned to her cavern in the willow after the alarm of her sudden ejectment at the point of the Dumpling's club.

When the eggs were safely stowed away in his desk, the pilferer summoned a council of his boon companions and broached the subject so dear to his soul. He commanded Buffles and Grubbins and Stodge and Guzzling Jim to attend his presence one day at the quarter-hour between morning lessons.

'Look here, you chaps! I vote I make a jolly dish of trifle. I've got some fresh eggs, and if you'll help get the other things you shall have some.'

'Hurray, Dumpling!' said Stodge. 'What do you want us to get?'

'Well, there's sponge-cakes and strawberry jam, and butter and sugar, and sherry and brandy.'

'I'll make young Talbot stump up a pot of jam,' said Grubbins ; 'he's just had a hamper.'

'And I'll spend twopence in sponge-cakes if Punchey brings them this afternoon,' said Jim.

'And I'll ask the cook to give me some butter and sugar,' said Stodge.

'All right, so far,' said the Dumpling. 'So you must get the brandy, Buffles. I think we might perhaps make beer do instead of sherry. I'll manage that ; but we must have brandy ; you can't make it fit to eat without brandy.'

'How can I get it?' asked Buffles. 'Shall I tell one of the day-boys to bring some?'

'No, you ass!' replied the chief. 'You'd better not say a word to any one else. You must get Mrs. Towels to give you some; she has it for fellows when they're æger.'

'Well, all serene!' said Buffles; 'I'll have a try. Where shall you make it?'

'I haven't quite settled that, but I think in the wood-yard out by the stables. Fellows don't often come there.'

It was the Dumpling's orders that all necessary supplies should be procured before evening, so that things should be in readiness for the next day. He also directed that the contributions should be put in a dismantled tea-chest among the lumber of the wood-yard. Furthermore, to add dignity to the proceedings, he consolidated himself and followers into a Society of Friends, to be designated 'The Jolly Guzzlers.' He was to be president; Guzzling Jim, whose sobriquet suggested the title, vice-president; Grubbins, treasurer. Stodge and Buffles had no distinguishing mark beyond the letters 'M.J.G.,' which they might append to their names in all epistolary communications with their superior officers.

The first meeting was fixed for the next day at 6.35 p.m., immediately after tea, in the dismal wood-yard, where, by the light of a dark lantern, they purposed consuming the dish of trifle, which the president announced he should be able to prepare in the wood-yard during the afternoon of the morrow.

The requisite ingredients were procured without any insuperable difficulty. Jim had been kept in for an imposition between two and three, and found all the sponge-cakes gone from Punchey's basket—only two stale currant-buns left. These he purchased and deposited in the tea-chest.

Buffles had been sore puzzled how to get round Mrs. Towels, the matron, for the brandy. I am thankful to say he would not tell a lie about it, and resolved to ask point-blank. Mrs. Towels was very

kind and indulgent to the boys, and seldom had the
heart to refuse them anything asked within the
bounds of reason, and these bounds she set with a
liberal regard for the queer ideas of boys.

So Buffles approached her with winning words and
his most polite air. 'Mrs. Towels, would you be so
kind as to let me have just a little drop of brandy?
I'm not going to drink it, but I want it very particularly. Please do!'

'Oh, my dear! whatever can you want brandy for?
Oh! perhaps you want it to rub your chilblains;—a
very good thing too, which I always recommend it
myself. Yes; to be sure! I'll give you a bit of
flannel. Now, Master Browne, don't you tease the
cat, there's a dear young gentleman! Yes, Master
Dawson, your cap is quite ready; I'll fetch it.'

There were generally three or four boys in the
matron's room requiring small attentions.

Mrs. Towels was going off to fetch the cap.

'The brandy, Mrs. Towels!'

'It's in the cupboard, my dear. You may take a
little. Be sure you take the right bottle.'

Buffles lost no time. He opened the cupboard and
saw a phalanx of bottles of all sizes and shapes. He
had a medicine bottle and cork ready to hand. Three
among the host were black wine-bottles. He un-
corked one of these and applied his nose—not quite
sure. Poured a little into his vial—not the right
colour. Tossed it into the fire. Buffles tried another.
Oh yes; that was brandy all right. He filled the
vial and departed.

Alas, for the frailty of human judgment! This
fluid which Buffles fondly supposed to be brandy was
nothing else than the most abominable of pharma-
ceutical concoctions. It was the stuff known as
'House Mixture,' supplied by the school physician,
and dispensed by the matron to boys suffering from a
bilious attack.

Off hurried the deluded Buffles to the wood-yard,

and found Grubbins just returning from the same errand. The others had all deposited their contributions, and the president was informed with due ceremony. He had borrowed a large earthenware dish of Mrs. Carey.

It was now 2.45 p.m. ; there was a clear hour in which to prepare the trifle before school. The Dumpling would not allow any member of the club to assist in the culinary operations. In solemn and solitary silence he took off his jacket, rolled up his sleeves, arranged the messes in order, and went at it with the no-mistakey air of a professional in the confectioner's craft.

CHAPTER III

'WELL, now, if that ain't enough to drive one mad !' exclaimed Mother Carey as her husband came in to his dinner the day after the Dumpling's last visit to the old willow-tree. 'There's the rascally old hen been a-cackling again, John. She's a-cackled four days running, and where she's hidden the eggs I don't know.'

'Very strange, to be sure, missus,' said John as he took his seat at the table. 'I've seen her with the rest, as innocent as a babe, a score of times, and how she continues to bamboozle us I can't say.'

'It's a myth and a tragical story, John, and I can't make out the pros and poffs of it,' rejoined his wife, who was rather proud of her power of language.

John now turned his attention to dinner, and when it was over he lit his pipe and sat down in the chimney-corner to ponder on the vagaries of poultry in general and the impertinence of this Cochin China hen in particular. His meditations were broken by a rat-tat-tat at the door.

The Dumpling rolled in.

'I say, Mother Carey, could you lend me a dish ? Do. I'll take care not to break it. Oh, I say ! what

a nice smell of dinner! Wish you had invited me.
'Xpect you had something better than everlasting
beef and stickjaw. Hullo! John, I'll bring you back
some baccy next term; better than that old cabbage
stuff you're smoking there.'

'Thank you, sir. Mother, lend Master Bertram a
dish.'

The Dumpling looked round the kitchen, and
espied a large yellow earthenware basin.

'That's the very thing, mother. I'll take great
care of it.'

'Well, sir, mind you bring it back.'

'All right; thanks.'

The Dumpling went off with it. As soon as he
was outside the cottage door he put the dish on his
head and his cap on the top, and made for the wood-
yard, whistling as he went, his trusty club 'dealing
destruction's devastating doom' along the path
wherever anything capable of receiving damage presented itself within range.

And so we find him, as we left him at the close of
the last chapter, with jacket off, succinct and expe-
dite for the important task before him.

He worked away with zeal, and his eyes sparkled
as he mixed the brandy and beer with the yolks of
the eggs, and flogged up the whites with a wisp of an
old broom. He was tempted to taste the mixture—
but no; by a powerful effort he restrained his appetite, for he wished to inform his boon companions
that he hadn't had one mouthful unfairly, thereby to
raise himself still further in their estimation.

The dainty dish was at last finished to his satisfaction, and certainly presented a pleasing appearance.
The strawberry jam, with the rich sauce, looked
rapturously inviting under the snowy mountain which
towered so majestically above it.

The Dumpling eyed his masterpiece with a soft,
approving smile, and turned his head sideways right
and left, to contemplate the dish in all its aspects,

and there was a sense of unqualified complaisance in his heart.

The bell for changing boots at length broke harshly on his ear, and reluctantly consigning the trifle to the recesses of the old tea-chest, he rolled down his sleeves, put on his jacket, and joggled off to the house.

It was not to be expected that much work was to be got out of him that afternoon. His intellect was absorbed in one line of thought, and no allurements of Euclid or Colenso could avail to draw it in another direction. The circles in the figures looked like dishes, and he sighed for the hours to fly.

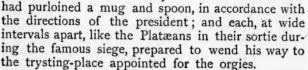

Though time waits for no man, its moments often linger unpleasantly for boys, and it seemed an age to the Dumpling before the opportunity arrived for displaying the triumph of his skill to his admiring clients. However, the hands of the clock did at last point to half - past six. Tea was finished. Each member of the secret society had purloined a mug and spoon, in accordance with the directions of the president; and each, at wide intervals apart, like the Platæans in their sortie during the famous siege, prepared to wend his way to the trysting-place appointed for the orgies.

It was a clear frosty evening. A full moon rode triumphant in the sky. The Jolly Guzzlers had to be careful in picking their way under shadows of walls and trees, for boys were not supposed to be out after tea, and many windows overlooked the ways to the wood-yard.

Buffles was the first to arrive, having performed his journey without danger.

Stodge had started next, but was delayed on the road, for at the outset, while scurrying across a moon-lit space, he had heard a window open, and a voice which no boy could mistake had called out, 'Hullo! who's that?'

Stodge decided that such a question was not worth answering, and had dived into the shadows of a laurel clump, where he crouched for a while before making a dash across some more open ground.

The voice was indeed that of Doctor Porchester, who had been talking to old Carey about putting some hay-ropes round some exposed water-pipes to prevent them bursting by the frost. The doctor had gone to the window of his study to make meteoro-logical observations as to the probability of severe cold that night, and his eagle eye had espied the form of a boy flitting past.

And so the window had been opened, and the words uttered in a severe tone.

Not receiving any answer, and being aware that the suspicious form had vanished into darkness, the doctor had said to his trusty servant, 'John, just go and see who that was, and what mischief he's up to, and don't forget the pipe that supplies the foun-tain.'

Now, old Carey was good at woodcraft, and knew well enough how to stalk a boy. He had already made his own private observations, being naturally of an inquisitive nature, and anxious in this instance to ascertain the object for which his yellow dish had been borrowed. He had taken a sly peep out of his cottage window, and watched the Dumpling enter the wood-yard, and when he went to fetch the boots that afternoon he visited the yard and just 'pro-spected' a bit, and it did not need much ingenuity to discover the dish. Old Carey opened his eyes, and said, 'Who'd a' thought it?' and indulged a long, low, chuckling laugh as he surveyed the confection, for truly it presented a most enticing aspect, and he could not but admire the culinary skill displayed.

Therefore, when the doctor bade him go forth upon his errand, old Carey put two and two together, and having discovered that they made four, he laid his plans accordingly. Proceeding by a route apparently contrary to all rules of warfare, being distinctly in an opposite direction to that of the enemy, John Carey went down the playground and into the field. He even walked to the extreme end, turned half-left, and skirted the wall, which manœuvre brought him under the massive shadow of some ancient ilex-trees. Turning half-left once more, he swiftly stepped out the distance intervening between himself and the vicinity of the wood-yard.

By this masterly stratagem he reached a long red-tiled and ancient stable flanking the yard. Noiselessly opening a door at the farther end, he entered, and passing along, he posted himself opposite a window looking into the yard, a pane of which was broken. Kneeling down at that spot, he could not only see all that went on in the wood-yard, but also hear every word that might be spoken by any persons present therein, being himself meanwhile in safe concealment. To him, then, I am indebted for the information contained in the remainder of this chapter.

He saw Buffles and Stodge seated on two stumps of trees, holding converse together.

'I say, Buffles, I had a terrible shave of being caught. Old Poco saw me from his study window and holloaed out, "Who's that?" I was in an awful funk, and dodged behind the laurels. He couldn't have seen who I was.'

'What an ass you were to go that way!'

'Well, Dumpling told us to go different ways, and none of you fellows would dare to go through the garden. I'm not half such an ass as you.'

F

'Yes, you are. Dumpling says you're the greatest ass in the school. Hark! here comes some one.'

The door of the wood-yard was cautiously opened, and in stole Grubbins. Guzzling Jim soon followed.

'Hullo, you fellows; it's all right. The president will be here in a jiff. I saw him start. He's coming down the playground.'

A minute more and the president's heavy tread was heard outside.

The four subordinates rose to receive him, each with mug and spoon in hand.

Now nothing could have been easier than for the Dumpling to open the door and come in like the other boys had done. But his waggish nature prompted a more difficult method. I remember, at a circus, seeing a clown take up one of those paper hoops through which a fairy equestrian had just bounded. The clown held it out and jumped into it; and in order again to extricate himself he went through a series of the most difficult and ludicrous movements, twisting himself into inconceivable attitudes; whereas, had he been so minded, he might have stepped out as easily as he stepped in.

Some such clownish intention evidently filled the Dumpling's mind. For with prodigious exertion he climbed to the top of the black boarding that formed the barrier of the wood-yard, and reared his gigantic form into prominent view. There he sat grinning.

'Hullo, you chaps; you're all here, I see. Now let me show you an acrobatic performance, just to whet your appetites.'

There was an old tree leaning against the fence, amid a heap of faggots, a broken-down wheelbarrow, a wooden tub for catching rainwater, and a nondescript accumulation of lumber.

The Dumpling, after some difficulty, elevated himself on a fork of this tree. Standing on one leg, he kicked out the other, and set the whole fence vibrating and cracking as he executed a wild, untutored

THE DUMPLING EVENTUALLY CRAWLED OUT OF HIS SHELL.

ballet, whistling a few bars of quaint melody. This was interrupted by occasional grunts, needful to preserve his balance. He then essayed to descend the tree. The footing was precarious, and the Dumpling slipped. Nay, more—he fell beyond all recovery. He subsided gracefully backwards into the wooden tub. He was most effectually jammed into this tub; his legs projecting below the knee, his arms above the shoulder. Luckily there was no water in the tub.

' Here, just come and help me out, and don't stand there gaping like a lot of idiots!'

The faithful four flew to the rescue. They seized each a leg or an arm, and pulled four different ways, ' but not all the king's horses, not all the king's men, could set Humpty Dumpty up again.'

' Shove us over, can't you? What puny imps you are!'

They shoved their mightiest, and succeeded in converting him, for the time as it were, into a gigantic tortoise. If only a cast could have been taken of him in that position, a model might have been executed fit to take its place among the antediluvian animals at the Crystal Palace.

The Dumpling eventually crawled out of his shell. Half the interval between tea and preparation was thus fruitlessly expended. It behoved them not further to waste the precious moments.

' Now then,' said the Dumpling, as he smoothed his ruffled plumes, ' don't play the fool any more. Let us see what the trifle is like. I haven't tasted a mouthful myself, for fear you should think me greedy.'

A murmur of approbation greeted this magnanimous declaration. The trifle was brought forth from its hiding-place, and as the moonlight fell upon its snow-white substance the eyes of the Jolly Guzzlers flashed with delight.

The Dumpling placed the dish on an extemporised table, and invited his friends to hold out their mugs,

which he liberally filled in succession. When all
were helped, he gave the word for the commencement of the feast. Simultaneously the four spoons
were dipped into the four mugs. Not even yet would
the high-souled Dumpling himself partake of the
food. He would enjoy the delight of his guests ere
his own lips touched the sweet confection.

Daintily they began to sip the superincumbent
foam, which melted like nectar in their mouths. Then
they came to the more solid composition and its rich
sauce. Into this dived the four spoons, and portions
were conveyed to the four mouths.

Then with a fourfold groan of amazement and
abhorrence, with a spluttering of disgust, heads were
turned aside, mugs were dropped, spoons were
dashed to the ground, signals of undisguised distress
were rampant, exclamations arose : ' Oh, what beastly
stuff! Ugh! it's poison!' The banquet collapsed,
and from the recesses of the old stable there issued a
prolonged chuckling laugh, as though some hidden
spectre were rejoicing at the discomfiture.

CHAPTER IV

THE banquet was indeed a failure. Its immediate effect on the Dumpling was to make
him unusually irascible, and his club was
employed the next day to the no small tribulation
of sundry small boys. Crestfallen and humiliated in
the eyes of the guzzling fraternity, he felt that his
prestige as a confectioner had suffered irretrievable
disgrace. He had to brook the satirical smile of
Stodge, the gruesome gibes of Grubbins, the banter
of Buffles, and the jeers of Guzzling Jim. And he
was conscious that they discussed the trifle with
language more than a trifle derogatory to his dignity.

It was clear that the Dumpling had considerably
lost caste by the late failure. He could not count
upon the allegiance of his followers. The existence

of the club hovered on a very precarious tenure.
Created with the object of providing from time to
time a dainty repast for its members, it had signally
failed at the outset, and all confidence in future successes was as unsubstantial as the froth of beaten
eggs.

The Dumpling meditated upon these things the
afternoon following his ill-starred feast, as he sauntered aimlessly about the field. He looked at the
hollow in the old willow-tree. No sign of a hen's
domestic details ; the nest was no more ; the wan-
dering winds had made havoc of its substance. The
Dumpling hummed an air and banged the tree with
his club. No rustle of wings, no scuttling of legs, no
agitated cluck sounded in response. The echoing
wall gave back the stroke, and that was all.

The fat boy sighed as he moved off in the direction of the hen-yard. He had a few grains of Indian
corn in his pocket. History often repeats itself. He
leant over the railing and called the attention of the
poultry by the 'Coop, coop!' that brings to their
minds the remembrance of feeding-time. A general
clamour of voices ensued ; the young birds bustled
up, the old ones jerked their heads and peered about,
and comported themselves with the dignity befitting
old birds who were not to be caught by chaff. The
Dumpling threw in two grains, for which there was a
flurry and scuffle. The old Cochin China hen was
there, but, being somewhat stiff in the legs, she was
nowhere in the race for the prize.

The Dumpling watched their manœuvres, and as
he watched he pondered. For full three minutes he
stood in the attitude of one absorbed in thought.
An idea seemed to strike him, for he struck a mighty
blow with his club upon the paling. Then thought
took action.

His last grain of corn was carefully bored through
with a nail. He then took from his pocket a coil of
string, one end of which he fastened securely to the

grain of corn. The other end was made into a loop
and slipped over one of the buttons whereby his
nether garments were braced. He then watched for
the near approach of the particular hen, and threw
the grain to her under the lowest rail. She flew
upon the spoil, mindful, no doubt, of similar delicacies erewhile (njoyed. She swallowed it with a
gulp and cackle (f satisfaction.

The Dumpling then turned his broad back on the
poultry-yard to cross the field in the direction of the
willow.

Now the doctor's garden was separated from the
field by a terrace, with a broad flight of steps leading
up and down. On this terrace the doctor and his
sister would often take a stroll for the benefit of their
health. It so happened that they appeared upon the
scene just as the Dumpling's stout form was crossing
the field. There was nothing suspicious in his progress, but something very unusual soon attracted the
doctor's attention.

'Look, Rachel, at that strange fowl! Whatever
can it be up to ? It must have gone mad ! Did you
ever see a more extraordinary performance ? '

It was indeed strange ! There was the Cochin
China hen, with outstretched neck and ruffled plumage, proceeding rapidly across the field, tumbling at
times, then revolving like a spoon-bait ; scuffling
and flapping, and uttering shrill cries of alarm and
distress.

Miss Porchester put up her glasses as she lowered
her topsail—a blue parasol.

'Why, John, the bird must be bewitched ! I will
go at once and see Mrs. Carey about it.'

The lady marched off to the cottage.

The doctor, in his broad-brimmed hat, stood, with
spectacled nose and hands behind him, gazing at this
infatuated fowl, and the more he gazed the more
astonished did he become.

The bird had now disappeared behind the willow-tree. It was curious that, with all his experience of boys and their vagaries, the doctor did not suspect the Dumpling of any complicity in the bird's eccentric movements. It never occurred to him to imagine such a coincidence. He had been a zealous fisherman in his younger days, and loved dearly to cast a fly upon the dimpling stickles of a fair-flowing stream. Often had he played a fine trout, and exulted in landing it after a difficult contest. But the notion of playing a Cochin China hen with a kite-line had never entered his head, and the idea was altogether so incongruous that the learned man might be excused for failing to entertain it.

So the doctor turned aside to saunter beneath the trees until his sister returned.

She was absent about ten minutes, for Mother Carey was of a talkative disposition, and made the most of every opportunity for gossip. It was not often that she got the chance of conversation with Miss Porchester ; she therefore improved the occasion, and gave that lady a history of the fortunes of her hen-yard during the last few months. She dilated upon the deceitfulness of that hen. Beyond doubt, the bird had for some time past been ailing with softening of the brain, which had developed that tendency to fraud, and had at last culminated in pronounced mania.

'There can't be no shadow of doubt of it, ma'am. The bird's gone stark staring mad. When I lived at the farm years ago, before I married John, we had a sheep took in the same way. And you never, how the poor beast behaved ! If he wanted to walk across this room, say, he'd turn over on his back and kick, and get up and tumble forward, and roll and writhe until it made one cry to watch the innocent creature's struggles. And at last father had him killed, and wouldn't let no one eat him, but just buried him in the orchard out of harm's way. And that's what it is with the hen. I knew there was something wrong, for I never see a fowl practise such deceit, as I says to Mrs. Woostford when she come in and says to me, says she, " Mrs. Carey, why don't you watch that fowl ? " and I said, " I'd scorn the haction, ma'am ! " Them's the words I used, miss, as I might be standing here, and as you might be she, and I had the mop in my hand, and——'

Miss Porchester might have stood there till now, with no prospect of the dame's concluding her speech ; but the lady was fain to stem the torrent of words, and so she interrupted it with the remark, ' Ah, yes ! Well, I suppose it is so. But you had better go and look after the bird, and perhaps you ought to kill it. Good-afternoon.'

So soon as she was gone Mother Carey put on her bonnet and went out to reconnoitre. She could trace the fowl's progress over the dewy grass, and followed it to the willow-tree. But there the tracks ceased. There were only the marks of a boy's footsteps, and Mother Carey could in no wise connect the fowl's vagaries with any boy.

She therefore returned, baffled a second time in her attempt to solve the mystery of her bird's behaviour, in much the same frame of mind as she was when first introduced to the reader. Furthermore, the damp grass had produced an irritability in the corn on her big-toe.

Where was the hen meanwhile ?

She was still alive, and that is saying a good deal, for the toils of inexorable fate were closing around her ; and her life had hung by a thread, not to say a twine cord, before ever we have reached this point in the narrative.

For it must be stated that the Dumpling had left no stone unturned to explain the cause of his failure in the trifle. He had ransacked his brains to find some satisfactory clue to the mystery. He only wished he had tasted the ingredients before using them. After all the bragging about his skill in the

art of cookery, to be thus degraded beyond all recovery in the eyes of his admirers! Oh, if he could
only find out how the trifle had proved such an
abomination! It could not have been the buns or
the brandy; the beer could not have made such a
difference; the jam was sound and good; it must
have been the eggs! Of course! Why hadn't he
thought of it before? One of the eggs must have
been ADDLED! That explained it all.

Thus pondered the Dumpling, and as the idea
flashed upon his mind, he brought down his club
with a sounding thwack upon the paling of the hen-
yard, sending the whole flock into a stampede.

'Hang the old hen!' quoth he. 'I'll teach her to
lay addled eggs!'

And then his brain, so subtle in devising mischief,
suggested that quaint stratagem to capture the
offending fowl. On reaching the shelter of the willow he had drawn in the line. He had clutched and
pinioned the feathered biped. He had fitted a noose
of twine round her neck; he had passed the twine
over a branch of the tree. He was on the point of
exacting lynch law, when a glance at the terrace
had revealed the doctor standing with intent gaze
directed towards the spot. Vengeance must be delayed for the present.

Disconnecting the halter, severing the twine that
protruded from the bird's beak, tying his handkerchief round her head, the Dumpling had hustled the
hen under his jacket. He had watched till the doctor left the terrace, and then he had ambled off at his
best pace to the wood-yard, and hidden the gagged
fowl in the old tea-chest, to await execution at a
more convenient time.

Sad indeed was the position of the unhappy bird.
With legs tied fast and wings compressed by durance
vile, with head, as it were, in a bag, she lay bewildered in darkness; and if a hen is capable of thought,
truly her meditations must have been full of dismal

forebodings. By dint of extreme exertion she was' however, able to move her beak and inflate her lungs to a certain extent, by which means she managed to squeeze out a few disjointed sepulchral squeaks. Her powers increased by practice, and when John Carey passed through the yard on his way to the boot-house, he paused as the faint cries of distress fell on his ear.

Deliverance from that cruel bondage was the prompt result. The fetters were loosed, the hand-kerchief removed, and, after a shake or two, the old hen trotted after her liberator back to Mother Carey's yard, little the worse for her adventure, save that a sensation akin to violent indigestion probably agi-tated her intestinal regions.

John Carey showed more intelligence than the wiser heads in interpreting the matter. He waited till school was over, and then waylaid the doctor, to whom he communicated a detailed account of what he had witnessed the evening before, and gave it as his conviction that Master Bertram had treated the fowl with cruelty and insult.

The Dumpling was sent for, and received a long and impressive lecture from the doctor, and a por-tentous imposition in the shape of twenty proposi-tions of Euclid, to be learnt and repeated within a week, under penalty of chastisement by default. He was also forbidden to enter the field without a master.

There is reason to believe that the fraternity of the Jolly Guzzlers enjoyed, like the fabled butterfly, but an ephemeral existence, and that the Dumpling did not again attempt to gain influence over his com-panions at Highfield House by any performances in the art of confectionery.

Peter's Perplexities in Pursuit of Science

CHAPTER I

'PLEASE let me in, Dobbin ; I won't bear-fight,' and a gentle application of the speaker's toe to Dobbin's study-door accompanied the request.

Charlie Ross was a small boy in the fourth class. Dobbin, *alias* Peter Carruthers, was in the first, and it might be assumed that he was therefore far above his junior in social and political importance. But assumptions are not always reliable, and if we draw a comparison from the poultry-yard, Charlie Ross might represent a spick-and-span young bantam, strutting about with a chirp and a crow for every one, while Peter Carruthers would more nearly resemble a sick and sorry old chanticleer, with plumage always ruffled, pecked and chased from one end of the yard to the other, feeling no respect for himself, and consequently eliciting none from his companions.

Different as these two boys were in disposition, they were nevertheless chums. Ross, in the generous simplicity of his nature, felt compassion for the old booby, and the old booby was glad enough to avail himself of the proffered patronage.

Carruthers had received the nickname 'Dobbin' from some facetious wag, who recognised a distant resemblance between his aristocratic surname and the plebeian word ' carthorse.' Dobbin was an eccentric character. I should not be surprised if some day he were to turn out a genius, and astonish the world by a brilliant discovery or two, for he certainly had a strong bent in the direction of science when at school.

One of his favourite notions has frequently engaged the attention of scientific men, but success has not hitherto crowned attempts to solve its difficulties. Dobbin had an idea that the problem of aerial flight was within the grasp of human ingenuity. He often meditated deeply on this abstruse question. He might be seen at times careering wildly down the playground, spreading out the skirts of his coat to their widest extent, and executing frantic leaps and gyrations. His coats were invariably loose, to allow for growing ; and if a high wind prevailed, his movements were not altogether unlike those of a frolicsome porpoise curveting and gamboling in the sea.

He would occasionally bring in the corpses of rats, found during his walks abroad in the vicinity of wheatricks and farmyards. These were secreted under his bed, to be dissected with his pocket-knife as occasion offered, a custom neither pleasant nor wholesome, and from a master's point of view not to be condoned even under that specious excuse, 'the pursuit of science.'

He once brought home a live snake, which he tied up in the leg of an old pair of trousers, and fed upon worms for two days in his bedroom, unbeknown to his companions. When it was eventually discovered, Dobbin and the reptile were promptly assailed by the other inhabitants of the dormitory, and the offender, habited only in his nightshirt, had to catch up his pet and beat a hasty retreat down the passage, followed by a shower of slippers, gym-shoes, sponges, tooth-brushes, pieces of soap, fives-balls, and whatever other missiles chance put in the way. The renegade was not re-admitted either until by vows of penitence and entreaties, and promises of handsome reward, he had appeased the indignation of his companions.

Dobbin's reward took the shape of stale tarts,

procured from an old apple-and-gingerbread woman who lived near the school. By way of surprise he put one of these tarts in each boy's bed in his dormitory. When, therefore, the boys prepared to retire to rest that night they found the tempting delicacies displayed to view. But, alas for the short-sightedness of the unlucky Dobbin! The tarts were of the kind known to confectioners as 'open,' and the jam had in most cases manifested such 'chemical affinity' for the upper sheet that it had almost entirely parted company from the crust. One boy had unwittingly scrimmaged on his bed, and the general havoc occasioned by the squashed tart may be more easily imagined than described. Suffice it to say that the results of Dobbin's device differed strangely from his expectations. There was a general howl of disgust and clamouring for vengeance. But I draw a veil over the subsequent proceedings, which are really too painful to record.

In consequence of these vagaries Dobbin had what may be termed 'a lively time of it.' He learnt with bitter reflection the melancholy truth that no sympathy with his deep pursuits was to be expected from his comrades. He became moody and depressed, he shunned the society of the other boys, and in the solitude of his study he would meditate gloomily on his blighted hopes, and only practise with extreme caution and secrecy his attempts to pry into the mysteries of Nature.

Such was his frame of mind that afternoon when Charlie Ross stood at his study-door demanding entrance.

Now it must be admitted that there was some excuse for Dobbin's pranks. Doctor Porchester had lately introduced experimental lectures in science, as an attractive feature in the routine of scholastic studies. A learned professor had actually come down from London and sojourned for a fortnight at Highfield House. The boys had been electrified

and magnetised ; they had enjoyed ocular demonstrations of the existence of chemical force ; they
had been delighted with fizzings and explosions, and
half suffocated with the fumes of noxious gases,
which set them coughing like a flock of sheep ; they
had been half blinded by the burning of phosphorus
in oxygen, and witnessed many other marvellous
experiments. In fact, they had been initiated by
pleasant paths into the realms of scientific lore.

This digression must be lengthened a little further
to record that after the last lecture, when the room
was being set to rights for evening prayers, and the
butler was wiping down the table, his dignity had
been completely upset by the behaviour of sundry
portions of that whimsical element sodium. These
had been spilled inadvertently about the table, and
had remained peaceable enough while undisturbed.
But now, as with vigorous sweeps of his cloth the
lord of the pantry began to subject these particles to
friction such as they had never before experienced,
coupled with the presence of abundant water, their
appetite for oxygen became so intensified that they
bubbled and squeaked, and fizzed and exploded, and
spurted and flamed, and ran frantically about in red-
hot balls, tumbling and bursting like shells with fiery
scintillations upon the floor. It was by far the most
effective experiment of the evening !

The bearing of the gallant butler under this trying
ordeal was truly heroic. He winced perceptibly at
each explosion, but did not draw back his hand nor
cease to ply his mighty strokes until the table was
purified, and all danger removed of volcanic outburst.
He might have been Gulliver wiping off an army of
Liliputians, who were bravely contesting every inch
of the ground, and shelling the giant with red-hot
shot.

Now it might well be supposed that under the influence of such stirring scenes as these the youth of
Highfield would not be slow to develop a taste for

chemical investigations. But such is the contrariness of puerile nature that few of the boys were moved to make personal researches. The generality of them loved 'a good stink,' as they irreverently styled the less agreeable odours ; and an unexpected explosion was 'nuts' to them ; but beyond this they cared little to enter into the why and wherefore of what they saw. The entertainments gradually grew flat, and from the Olympian heights of 'jolly fun' (as they were considered at the outset) the lectures subsequently descended into the Tartarean depths of 'awful rot' in the estimation of the majority.

It is needless to state that poor old Dobbin formed an exception. He took the deepest interest in the lectures. He was ever ready in moments of emergency to hold a jar, to warm a retort, to carry off a vessel that might be disgorging offensive fumes ; in fact, he was the professor's right-hand man. Dobbin would take copious notes of the experiments, and compile them afterwards into treatises of an original character, and expressed in language which could not always be considered scientific in accuracy nor grammatical in form. For example : 'If you mix something with sulfuric acid you'll make an awful stink. Warmed stuff like salt and black-lead gives oxejin. Fosphoras burnt in it gives splendid light. Pottasum likes hidrojen.'

Dobbin was engaged with his note-book when the importunate entreaties of Charlie Ross for admittance disturbed his meditations. 'Please let me in, Dobbin !'

'What d'you want ?'

'Oh, I want to speak to you awfully particular. Please let me in.'

'All right ; wait a jiff.'

The jiff having elapsed, during which fraction of time Dobbin hastily concealed a box of fusees, a piece of brimstone lately abstracted from a dog's tub of water, some fragments of glass tube, and a paper of gunpowder, the hero cautiously unfastened the bars of his castle. He feared this might be a dodge practised by some of the other fellows to gain entrance for unlawful ends, so he planted his foot against the door as he opened it two inches, and looked out. Seeing no signs of the enemy, he let Ross in and quickly bolted the door once more.

'I've got to write out my rep. for the doctor, Dobbin, and if you'll let me do it up here I'll be very quiet.'

'All right; there's the ink. I haven't got a pen. Oh! I see you have.'

The pen was soon scratching away, interrupted by periodic sighs and groans, and a hint from Peter the Hermit whenever the fancies of Phædrus presented a formidable aspect, which they seemed to do every second line.

It had been a wet half-holiday in the Easter Term. Most of the boys were in the gymnasium. Ross had a cold and was kept in the house, and his friend cared not for feats of muscular contortion.

At length the rep. was finished, and Ross asked the philosopher as to the nature of his abstruse speculations.

'I'm going to try an experiment. It will be the grandest I've ever done.'

'What's it to be?'

'Will you promise not to say a word to any one about it?'

'Rather!'

'Will you come with me when I do it? I shall probably want an assistant.'

'Oh yes; do tell us.'

'Well, it's a very dangerous job, and may possibly blow us both up!'

'That'll be awful sport, Dobbin!'

'Well, if you'll really promise not to let it out——'

'Oh, I'll promise faithfully.'

'Well then, look here. But I don't believe you can keep a secret, Ross.'

'Oh, bosh! I promise you I can!'

'Well, then, I'll tell you. Professor Stubbs told us the other day that gun-cotton is common wool steeped in sulphuric and nitric acids. I'm going to make some.'

'Jolly! What shall we blow up?'

'It's an experiment which nobody ever made before.'

'You're nobody, and you'd better make it behind, or the doctor will catch us.'

'Don't be an ass, Ross. It misbecomes a rat to be an ass.'

The conversation was broken off at this point by reason of the rat's jumping on the carthorse's back, and riding him round the study three times, which same ride was brought to a conclusion by the cart-horse backing on to a chair, over which he tumbled, and horse, rider, and chair were involved in ruin. Order being restored, the philosopher proceeded:—

'I don't believe any one ever thought of what I am going to do; but if it succeeds it will be very valu-able in time of war, and I shall write to the Govern-ment about it. I expect it will be all right. It may seem rather cruel to you, Ross, but we can't always avoid giving a little pain to animals in making im-portant discoveries.'

'Well, do let us hear what on earth you're going to do.'

'I'm going to make gun-cotton on a large scale. But it's a very dangerous dodge. I shall have to think it over for a long time, and there will be so many things to arrange that I don't suppose it will come off this term. In fact, I think I shall put it off till the holidays.'

'Oh no; we'll do it at once. But do tell a chap what it is!'

'Well, look here. If gun-cotton is only cotton-

G

wool soaked in acids, why shouldn't it be possible to turn the fleece of a live sheep into gun-cotton? And if it could be done to one, it could be done to a whole flock. And only think what that means. If ever England should be invaded, the farmers would have to give up their flocks. I've thought a good deal about it. Say an army of 20,000 men was encamped on Salisbury Plain. The explosion caused by one full-grown gun-cottoned Southdown sheep would be sufficient to kill at least twenty men. Consequently it would require 1,000 sheep to destroy 20,000. Only think of that! A whole army blown up at the cost of only 1,000 sheep! Think what a saving it would be to the Government. The taxes would be let off. The nation would rest secure in the possession of my grand secret, knowing that it had nothing to fear from invasion.'

'I say, that's a grand idea, and no mistake! But how should you let off the sheep?'

'Oh, I've thought of that. I shall invent a sort of cracker, so constructed that you can time its bursting. That's easy enough, you know. Every inventor soon hits upon the small dodges for making his invention answer. The cracker could be tied to the sheep's tail. A harmless-looking shepherd would be told to drive the flock in sight of the enemy. They would rush out to capture it. We read in Latin the other day that they always do that in time of war. Say it would take twenty minutes to get the flock safe into camp. Allow five minutes more for the soldiers to collect round to see it. An hour would be ample from the time the flock was sent out of our lines, so I should make all the crackers to go off an hour after they were lit, and our soldiers would only have to sit still and smoke their pipes and wait for the explosion. Isn't it a splendid idea, Ross?'

'I should just think so! It's all bosh waiting for the holidays when you've already planned it all out. I vote you try the first experiment on Saturday.'

CHAPTER II

CHARLIE ROSS was so urgent in agitating for an immediate execution of the grand scheme, and the interest he evinced in it was so great, that Dobbin thought it impolitic to resist, for fear his friend's zeal should cool down. He therefore promised to make his preparations with all possible dispatch. Ross thought everything might be done by the following Saturday, and argued that the acids could be got from the village chemist and the crackers from the ironmonger; 'and if that's all, why ever shouldn't we have the fun at once?'

Ross was an impetuous and impatient youngster, not gifted with that calm and cautious deliberation with which Carruthers went about his experiments.

'It's all very well for you to talk like that, young rat. You've got nothing to risk, and merely look to the fun of the thing. But it's precious different for me. My reputation is at stake. What should I do if we were both killed? What a jolly row I should get into with old Poco if we didn't come in to tea, and they sent out to look for us and found us blown into ten thousand smithereens!'

'Well, but, you old ass,' replied the rat, grinning at these strange forebodings, 'there's no fear, if the crackers are timed to go off in an hour. We could get miles away. If we caught a sheep down in Miller's Dale, and soused him there, we should have time to get up to the top of Shepherd's Hill and watch the explosion without any danger.'

'Oh, I dare say; and where would Miller's Farm be after it was over? You don't stop to think, Ross. When Professor Stubbs let off a bit of gun-cotton about the size of a Brazil nut, it sent a flame up to the ceiling. What would be the consequence of exploding a whole sheep? Do stop to consider. If, as I tell you, it would kill at least twenty men, what would become of old Miller and Mrs. Miller,

and all the little Millers, to say nothing of the farm-
labourers ?'

'Would it carry so far ?'

'Of course. The farm is only in the next field to
that where the sheep are kept. And what's a field ?
No,' continued the sage; 'we should have to decoy a
sheep away from the rest and drive him off to the
middle of Hangman's Heath. There are no houses
for miles round, so the only danger would be to the
sheep. It's a risky business, and the more I think
of it the more certain I feel that we ought to put it
off till the holidays. I could get the governor to buy
me a sheep, and after it went off we might pick up
a stray leg or two somewhere in the next county,
which would lessen the expense, as we could have it
for dinner.'

'Well, Dobbin, you know best. But couldn't we
try some experiment, at any rate, say on a lamb, next
Saturday ? There's nothing to do on a half-holiday
this term, and it would be so jolly exciting.'

The result of this conversation was that Dobbin
so far gave way as to commission his friend to procure
half a pint of each acid necessary, and a packet of
crackers. But Dobbin's mind was ill at ease, and
tossed on a troubled sea of perplexity. He racked
his brains to find some escape from the dangers that
threatened his undertaking. While deeply anxious
to satisfy the curiosity of Charlie Ross, he was no
less anxious to avoid failure and risk. Convinced
of the grandeur of his discovery, he thought that
some preliminary experiments should be made before
the final issues of the scheme were put to the test.

Some one may suggest that our philosopher might
have purchased a sheet of cotton wool, and tried the
result of ignition after saturating it with the acids,
and thus have avoided the more alarming dangers.
But Dobbin was satisfied that gun-cotton was simply
made as the lecturer had stated. He had seen it go
up with a flame and a smoke of imposing propor-

tions, and with pardonable reliance on the professor's word he was filled with the engrossing idea of going a step further than any one had ever yet dared to go. He was certain that his idea was original, that it was simple, and, like all great discoveries, he believed it to be the outcome of true genius. It was beyond doubt one of those apparent freaks of chance on which hinge the most stupendous results, and which exert such important influence on the progress of civilisation. He set it down on a par with the discovery of printing, steam-power, and the electric telegraph. Visions floated before his eyes of future glory. Leaning his head on his hand, he curled one leg over the other, and wished that some artist could sketch him in that attitude. It would be such a beautiful companion-picture to that of James Watt and the tea-kettle—Peter Carruthers and the gun-cottoned sheep! Dobbin's soul thrilled with excitement.

That night, after the boys were in bed, when the gas was turned out, and silence and sleep gradually had asserted their sway, the philosopher lay awake, deeply pondering over his vast projects. It would positively be too dangerous to make the first experiment on a live sheep. The animal's personal objections would probably thwart the enterprise. He would have to pay for the sheep, if his experiment succeeded, and the expense would be absolutely beyond his means. He scorned to think of anything less, not even a lamb. It was sheep or nothing, and the dangers and difficulties attendant seemed insurmountable.

Dobbin's mental agitation brought bodily disquietude. He heaved a series of gigantic sighs, and rolled about his bed, and lost all desire to sleep. The other boys had one after another succumbed to the influence of that blissful interrupter of care and toil. Measured breathing, varied only by grunts and snores of different tone and intensity, bespoke the reign of sound sleep. Dobbin only was awake, and his restlessness had prevailed to the defiance of sleep. He felt an unwonted desire to go into the gymnasium and pull himself up on the horizontal bar ten times without touching the ground. He who seldom indulged in such exercises except under compulsion now felt that he must do something of the kind or burst. So inconsistent is the nature of boys.

At last, unable to bear the extremity of fidgets into which he had worked himself, Dobbin got out of bed. He moved noiselessly across the room, went to the window and opened it, looked out and breathed deep draughts cf the cold night air. This seemed to give some relief. The moon was shining brilliantly ; the black shadows of adjacent buildings lay upon the playground. Suddenly a cat started out from a dark corner and scurried across the gravel, followed by another in hot pursuit. A screech and a yell of unearthly ferocity followed, as the uncanny creatures bounded up the playground wall and disappeared from view. Dobbin shivered as he hurriedly shut the window and crept back to bed, and this time he managed to fall asleep.

Now whether it was that the visions of his dreams brought a new idea to his mind I know not, but after an hour's sleep he awoke and once more got up, with apparently some definite purpose, for he put on his socks and his trousers, and, as he imagined, his slippers, but one was a gymnasium shoe belonging to Smithers, who had thrown it at him while they were undressing. Then he put on his coat and cap, and thus accoutred he left the dormitory. His mind was evidently set upon some desperate resolve. Cautiously feeling his way along the wall, he crept with the stealth of a burglar down the passage. The school clock struck twelve with solemn strokes. The mystic hour of midnight was upon the world, when boards creak unaccountably, and ghosts are supposed to wander forth.

Dobbin felt his pulses throb as he threaded the dark corridor leading to the stone-hall which communicated with the playground. The door was locked, but he knew that the key was kept on the ledge above, for the convenience of the boot-boy, who had to open it at an early hour in the morning. Dobbin got the key, and unlocked the door and passed out, keeping to the deep shadows, and so made his way through the playground into the field. Across this he ran with all haste, and climbed over the wall at the bottom by some well-known helps in the shape of crevices and nails. Scrambling down the other side he got into a grass-grown lane which led to the common. Having emerged upon a corner of this same common, he made for some cottages on the other side.

It may be as well to divulge at once the secret of this midnight escapade. Across the common, in the direction of Dobbin's route, stood the premises of John Galpin, the butcher. As he killed his own meat, he generally had some fleeces of sheep hanging up in a shed at the back of the slaughter-house. This shed, together with a dilapidated outhouse for the cart, a pigsty, and a hen-house, flanked a portion of the common, separated from it only by a rustic fence ; and these premises were open to view, like the house of Julius Drusus, to any passing wayfarer.

The butcher's yard was an interesting object for a walk to those boys whose taste for bloodshed had been nurtured upon the exciting literature of the *Red-Handed Scalping Chief of the Ojibbewah Indians* type. Dobbin, though not one of these, was nevertheless acquainted with the geography of Mr. Galpin's estate, and his purpose now was none other than to borrow without the owner's permission the loan of a sheepskin. His intention was to possess himself of a fleece, and convey it to a lonely spot in a wood close by, to be used as opportunity might offer in lieu of a living sheep. His prudence admitted this scheme as a dignified compromise, for he was minded to invest a log of wood with the fleece, and so, for all intents and purposes, to construct a faithful model of a sheep on which to elaborate his experiment.

Now this was one of those strangely foolish and unwarrantable acts which, when writing a story for boys, one has some qualms in recording, because certain sensitive critics may cry out aghast at our suggesting such outrageous conduct to that class of animals, prone enough already, in all conscience, to devise and execute acts of mischief and folly. But the veracious historian is loth to distort his work by omitting to interweave the dark threads with the light in the tissues of his narrative. The author will therefore advance, *sans peur et sans reproche*, secure in the assurance that no boy who reads this history to the end will ever be tempted to undertake a nightly adventure with the same object, and if he feels disposed to try a similar course for any other purpose, the author sincerely hopes that he will at the outset tumble over the coal-scuttle and get caught, and be so severely flogged by his master that he will never feel inclined to repeat the performance.

By which digression having somewhat eased his conscience, the author will go on his way.

Dobbin skipped across the common, and arrived out of breath at the paling of the butcher's back premises. Everything was in profound stillness. He could see the grim trophies of slaughtered southdowns hanging like executed criminals from the rafters of the outhouse in grizzly array. He paused a moment, to make sure that no one was moving, and then climbed over the paling and sneaked into the shed.

A passing gust of wind now gently broke the silence of night, causing the fleeces to sway to and fro, and raising, as it were, mysterious moans, which

might well be the plaintive bleatings of spectral
sheep, protesting against desecration of their remains
Ugh! it was a ghastly business, and Dobbin's heart
well-nigh sank into—not his boots, but his slipper
and gymnasium shoe. However, the thought of his
mighty enterprise prevailed against vague superstitions, and even as the wind passed by, Dobbin
mounted on a disused block, such as we see in a
butcher's shop with a few choppers adorning it,
suggestive of the days of Mary, when men's heads
were as often chopped from their bodies as joints
from sheep. On this block mounted the midnight
marauder, and after prodigious exertions he succeeded
in unhitching a fleece, which fell to earth with a dull
flump. Dobbin nearly lost his balance, and narrowly
escaped the doom of 'Fidgety Phil' in the Strewel-
peter.

Carruthers lost no time in dragging the fleece from
the shed to the paling. It was an unwieldy thing
to move, and required his whole strength. It made
a dangerous amount of commotion as it swept along
the ground, and Dobbin was thankful when he had
managed to hustle it over the paling and was himself
once more on the common. He felt that it would
be a most exhausting process to drag the fleece all
the way to the wood ; he therefore adopted the only
other feasible method, which was to envelop himself
in the shaggy covering. This was in no wise a
pleasant course, but necessity knows no law.

Seizing hold of those portions which represented
the forelegs of the animal when alive, he dragged on
to his back the voluminous fleece, the tail and hind
legs trailing on the ground, and so arrayed he commenced his retreat.

Clad in this eminently offensive integument, Dobbin
proceeded at a tangent across the common, towards
the dark prominence of a wood which loomed
athwart the horizon. It took him twenty minutes
to accomplish this part of his nocturnal ramble.

The sheepskin was heavy, and made him very hot, and impeded his progress considerably, so that he could only mount the sloping ground which led up to the wood at a slow and creeping pace. At this point he had to cross the lane which skirted the wall of the school cricket-field higher up, and just as he was crossing it his courage well-nigh forsook him entirely, for he distinctly heard footsteps, and an exclamation of amazement from some human being who was evidently an eye-witness of his progress. Summoning all his strength, Dobbin pressed man-fully up the remainder of the slope, and, almost ready to drop from terror and exhaustion, he disappeared amid the dark shadows of the wood.

He was profoundly relieved to find that he was not followed, and forced his way through the rough undergrowth to a secluded hollow, where formerly gravel had been dug. Here at last he divested him-self of the fleece, which he huddled as best he could into a corner of the pit, and then, taking a short cut through the wood, he reached the lane not very far from the precincts of Highfield House.

Nothing of any moment attended the remainder of his expedition. He climbed over the wall, crossed the field and playground, and found his way safely back to the dormitory without disturbing any one. Quickly undressing himself, he got into bed, and being now thoroughly tired out, he soon fell into a profound, dreamless sleep, only to be awakened by the hoarse clanging of the school-bell.

CHAPTER III

DING—dong—beil!
'What a horrid smell!' exclaimed Dick Browning, a small boy with red hair, as he lazily rolled out of bed on the morning after the events recorded in the preceding chapter; or, to be

more accurate, at a less early hour of the same morning. He was an inmate of Dobbin's dormitory.

'Oh, I say, you fellows,' he continued, 'how fuzzy the room is! I votes I open the window. Pheugh!'

The wind blowing in soon freshened the atmosphere of the apartment sufficiently to pacify the fastidiousness of that young gentleman's olfactory nerves. Not much was said as the boys dressed. Dobbin himself performed that operation with unusual haste. His nose was not over-particular, as he considered it incumbent on a man of science to be callous to disagreeable effluvia; but he was by no means unconscious that his jacket smelt most objectionably, and this made him anxious to go and ventilate himself in the playground before prayers.

So downstairs he hurried, and spreading out his coat, with repeated flaps he took a morning flight down the playground and back again.

'There goes that mad donkey, trying to fly!' cried Smithers, a lad of joyous countenance, looking out of the dormitory window, and hurling a piece of soap with such true aim that it caught the delinquent on the hip, and for the moment brought him to sober paces, for one leg was sorely wounded, and one hand was called into requisition to rub the injured spot.

'Hullo, maniac, here's some hellebore!' cried the prefect of the dormitory, aiming the contents of a jug with no less true effect, for a full half of the water fell upon Dobbin's unlucky head, and deluged him with a chilly cataract.

'Give a dog a bad name and hang him' is a proverb of which many a dull boy can comprehend the meaning without explanation. Dobbin had learnt its truth already, as now, with one additional lesson upon its application, he repaired to the dining-hall for morning prayers.

'Don't sit here, you old stink-pot!'

'Here, get out, badger!'

'Gee up, old Dobbin!'

'Poof! you smell like a menagerie of polecats and pickled monkeys!'

Such were the unseemly remarks which greeted his appearance in hall that morning.

In the lesson after breakfast the first class were with Mr. Dunthorne in one of the class-rooms. That learned gentleman appeared in due time upon the scene, and seated himself at the desk in front of the boys. He took out his Homer and found the place. The lesson contained that description of Thersites in which the immortal bard seems to have ransacked his vocabulary to find terms of adequate opprobrium. His epithets are certainly more forcible than polite. Mr. Dunthorne first endeavoured to rouse the enthusiasm of his class by reading to them Lord Derby's translation of the passage.

He then glanced over the Greek and raised his spectacled eyes to survey the boys.

'What's the matter with you all this morning? Have you taken cold?'

It was a curious fact that eight out of the nine boys were huddling as close together as they could, with their eight noses conspicuously buried in their eight pocket-handkerchiefs. The ninth, none other than the unfortunate Dobbin, was banished to the furthermost limit of the form, and sat leaning his face on his fists, the picture of disorder and discomfort.

'Move down, some of you. Don't crowd up so. Move down, Robinson, d'you hear?'

Robinson moved down some two inches, which did not perceptibly ease the abnormal pressure.

'Dear me,' said the master, 'it's rather close in this room. I suppose the window was not opened last night. Just open it now, one of you.'

The whole class made a dash to execute the order, Dobbin excepted, who remained immovable.

'One of you, I said. Sit down, all of you. Car-

ruthers, will you open the window? **Thank you.**
Now then, let us begin. Go on, Browning.'

Browning went on, and acquitted himself credit-
ably.

'Very good. Carruthers, read the next four lines.'

Dobbin stood up, and straightway the eyes of all
the class were levelled at him, while a more ex-
travagant parade of handkerchiefs, with suggestive
coughs, accompanied their scrutiny.

The woebegone, dishevelled aspect presented by the
luckless lad attracted Mr. Dunthorne's inspection.

Eyeing him sternly, the master said,—

'Carruthers, you are more than usually untidy this
morning, which is saying a great deal. I never like
making personal remarks or in any way wounding a
boy's feelings, but I must say you appear most dis-
reputably untidy. Come here and let me put your
collar outside your coat. Eton collars are part of
the uniform of the house. You must be more particular. Come here. Turn round. Wheugh! What
have you been up to? You're wet through, and your
jacket has a most offensive odour! Pheugh! most
offensive!' (Applying handkerchief to nose, and
continuing the harangue in a far-off ventriloquistic
tone.) 'Have you been anointing yourself with
mutton-fat? You seem to be reeking with grease.
How disgusting! Get out of my sight! Go and
change that offensive garment, and get Mrs. Towels
to give you some eau-de-Cologne.' (Removing the
handkerchief as Dobbin began to retire.) 'Get along
with you! Pheugh! No wonder your companions
found your presence unbearable. Dirty boy! get
out of my sight!'

Dobbin was by this time retreating rapidly.

'And look here' (raising his voice), 'some time
this afternoon write me out that Ode of Horace in
Latin and English about *olentem Mævium.*'

This parting shot was greeted with much laughter
from the other boys, which merged imperceptibly

into a mixture of hisses and groans as Dobbin finally disappeared. This episode attached to him the new nicknames of Thersites and Mævius.

His temporary withdrawal from the scene to change his apparel offers an opportunity for looking in at the butcher's and seeing what went on there about the same time.

John Galpin, jovial and burly, dressed in his blue smock, had finished his two cups of coffee and substantial rounds of buttered toast, and having set the boy Simon his morning task, the portly butcher turned out to have a look at the pigs and chickens in the back yard. His eye twinkled as the plump porkers grunted a morning greeting. He chuckled pleasantly to the pullets, and set them a-clucking in expectation of their morning meal. And then the slaughterer of cattle and sheep turned him about and cast his eye over the outhouse and shed.

John Galpin took a pride in being very particular about all the arrangements of his premises, even so far as to sift cinders every week over the surface of his back yard.

Now it happened that this operation had been performed only the day before, and his eagle eye was not slow to discover a remarkable disturbance in the condition of the yard in question. Instead of presenting a smooth and even surface, the cinder-ashes were conspicuously swept in a broad path between the shed and the paling. John Galpin turned his head one way and then another. He looked up into the sky, and then across the common. He scratched his head and gazed at the pigs, then at the fowls. But look where he might he could find no clue to the mystery. Ah, yes! surely there were footmarks on the cinder surface. 'Curious enough, sure!' said the butcher to himself. 'Two young scamps have been prowling about, I'll be bound. One must have had slippers on, and one of 'em ribbed india-rubber soles. That's as plain as daylight.

Come from the school, too, I'll be bound—the young rascals ! Here, Simon, just come out here a minute. What can have made this curious path in the cinders ? D'you know ? '

Simon came out at his master's bidding and looked at the path, and scratched his head, and proceeded into the shed and looked up at the sheepskins. Then he delivered his views on the subject in the following language :—

' Woll, ef this bain't the most extrordinest thing os oi ever knowed, maister ! Os zure os oi stands 'ere, there was noine o' they shape-skeens a hangin' up yesterday. And os zure os oi stands 'ere, oi zeed one of them there shape-skeens a-walkin' on 'is oind legs at the corner of the lane, os oi cum back from a hevenin' porty at gran'mother's about 'arf-past twelve o'clock last noight ! '

' What d'you mean, Simon ? I suspect your grand-mother gave you an extra pint of ale before you started.'

' It be true, maister, for all that. Oi've a-heerd tell that strange soights is to be zeed after midnoight in Cut-throat Lane, and now oi've zeed one of 'em with my own oyes ; and oi wouldn't go that way again after midnoight, not vor vive vlorins. It's my belief as 'ow that path was made by the shape-skeen as it fluddered along. Ugh ! a shape's ghost be an orful soight ! '

Simon paused, but seemed to have more to say yet, and encouraged by his master he informed him that the moon was shining brightly at the time, and that his head was as clear as the moonlight. He stated that this was not the first time fearful things had been seen at the spot where a certain old pedlar was popularly supposed to have been murdered twenty years ago ; that only a week before a friend of Simon, called Bill Javers, had come along that way shortly after midnight, when a horseman sud-denly galloped past him, ' snortin' and roarin' like a vampire,' and Bill Javers had reported to Simon that the horseman's head had horns like a cow, and that fire seemed to flash from his nose. Furthermore this fearful apparition had manifested itself just at the exact spot where Simon saw the spectral sheep. Consequently there was no shadow of doubt in Simon's mind but that this thoroughly explained the path swept in the cinder-ashes.

The butcher scrutinized his assistant attentively during his oration, which was probably the longest and most eloquent ever delivered by Simon, who was not as a rule celebrated for powerful speech. John Galpin marked the lad's earnestness, which forbade suspicion, and approaching the fence he found a tuft of wool sticking on a nail. This seemed to corroborate the main point of the strange story he had just heard. The sheepskin had to all appearances taken a nocturnal journey, but John Galpin had his doubts as to the ghostly nature of the transaction. The footprints contributed a human element to the problem which could not be lightly disregarded.

'There's been a pair of young rascals prowling about here last night, Simon, who could give an account of the matter, I'll be bound, if we could only catch them. Look at those footmarks. They weren't made by you or me. We don't wear such gimcrack shoes. They just came from Highfield House—that's what I think. One of them had slippers, and the other those india-rubber shoes they use in the gymnasium. You know what they're like, Simon. You've seen them wearing 'em often when you've taken up the meat.'

'Oh yes; oi've a zeed 'em, maister; but as zure as oi stands 'ere, there warn't no boys about last noight when oi zeed the shape.'

'Well, I can't help that,' replied the butcher. 'Just come along and show me where you saw the beast. I fancy we shall find a trace of him.'

The two climbed over the fence and crossed the common to the corner of Cut-throat Lane.

'There be the oidentical spot, maister. Oi was just comin' round the corner, and this bank was in clear moonlight, and the ghost glided up the bank under the trees, and oi shook wi' froight, and could 'ardly 'elp faintin' outroight.'

John Galpin looked up the bank, and then went up it, but no trace or clue to the mystery could he find; and after a brief search he came down, and said,—

'It beats me altogether, Simon, but I shouldn't wonder if some of the young gents at the school have been up to a lark. I'll take the meat up myself this morning and see the doctor about it.'

So saying, he returned to his premises with Simon, man and boy being absorbed in cogitation upon the strange business.

Chapter IV

'HA, good-morning, cook,' said Mr. John Galpin, with a beaming smile, as he deposited his basket of 'top-sides' at the kitchen door of Highfield House. 'A fine morning, Mrs. Jones; and how rosy you look!'

It had been remarked for some time past by the other servants that Mr. Galpin was somewhat pronounced in his attentions towards Mrs. Jones; and that worthy person was by no means displeased at the thought of possibly exchanging her sphere of domestic duties at no distant date for a position in which she might execute the same in a home of her own.

'Good-morning, Mr. Galpin; very glad to see you, sir; and I hope the beef's better to-day than it was last week. The doctor complained of its being tough and stringy; and the young gents be very particular.'

H

'There, Mrs. Jones, it ain't the fault of the meat. The doctor couldn't get better, not if he were to go himself and cut it off the living beasts. It's the oven as wants repairing, I fancy; you can't cook these big joints not what I call thoroughly satisfactory-like unless the oven be constantly looked to.'

Mr. Galpin's brother was the village ironmonger.

'Don't talk to me about my oven, Mr. Galpin. I knows when the oven's right and when it's wrong.'

'Well, Mrs. Jones, I apologise if I said anything rude; and I wouldn't for the world presume to cast a doubt on your professional knowledge. But there's no better meat in the London market than mine, though I say it who shouldn't. But I say, Mrs. Jones; d'you think I could speak to the doctor on a little matter of important business?'

Mrs. Jones blushed and stole a hasty glance at the ruddy face of her admirer. Could it be that he was going to tell her master of his intentions to make a proposal? Less likely things had happened, and the thought caused a flutter of excitement in the worthy woman's mind.

'I dare say you could, Mr. Galpin. Step in, sir, and take a seat. Here, Jane! JANE! Where is the idle hussey? Oh, there you are. Just go and tell Jinks to ask the doctor if he could see Mr. Galpin, who wishes to speak to him on a matter of very important business.'

Doctor Porchester sent word that he would see the butcher at once in his study.

The interview being granted, Mr. Galpin proceeded to narrate the mysterious affairs recorded in the last chapter, omitting the ghostly embellishments furnished by the boy Simon. 'I thought it best to mention it, sir, in case you might be good enough to ask if any of the young gents has been up to a lark. The footmarks in my yard were undoubtedly made by slippers and those india-rubber shoes with lines

across the soles ; and I don't think any of the village
lads ever wear them.'

'Ah,' said the doctor ; 'it looks very suspicious,
and I'm obliged to you for mentioning the matter,
Mr. Galpin. But I cannot imagine any of my boys
perpetrating such an egregious act of folly. What
could they want with a sheep-skin ?'

'There, sir, boys will be boys ; and there's no
telling what they won't be up to when the spirit of
mischief comes upon 'em. I'm sorry to have troubled
you, sir ; but it ain't a thing to be looked over, and
it's very annoying.'

'Quite true, Mr. Galpin. I'll do my best to ascertain if any of my boys have been guilty of the offence.
Good-morning.'

'Good-morning, sir ; and thank you.'

'I hope the interview was satisfactory, Mr. Galpin ?'
asked Mrs. Jones, as the butcher once more made his
appearance in the kitchen.

'Quite so, thank you, Mrs. Jones. Good-day to
you.'

'Good-day, Mr. Galpin ; and I hope we shall see
you rather oftener up here yourself, Mr. Galpin.
That boy of yours has what I call an off-handish way
with him sometimes, which is very disagreeable. I
told him I should mention it to you.'

'Oh, I'll let him hear of it, Mrs. Jones, you may be
sure ; the young imperence !'

With which assurance the butcher took his depar-
ture.

Dr. Porchester pondered over the revelations just
made, and his brow gathered gloom as he marched
up and down his study.

He felt pretty certain that two of his boys must
have perpetrated a nightly adventure, and he was
profoundly vexed to think such a thing should be
practicable in his well-ordered establishment.

He would assuredly find out the culprits and visit
them with such severe retribution as might be calcu-

lated to deter them from ever again attempting such a breach of discipline.

But none the less did the doctor's spirit chafe and burn within the barriers of his deep chest as he hurried on his gown, snatched up his books, and went off to his lesson.

The boys were not slow to notice his irritable demeanour, and instinctively deduced the conclusion that there was something up, and they speculated afterwards in boyish fashion upon the probabilities afloat.

'What a wax the doctor was in!' said one.

'I'm sure I knew my rep. all right; why should he worry me so unmercifully?' said another.

'He told me I was incorrigibly idle, and didn't make the most of my opportunities, and a lot of bosh of that sort!' said a third.

'I expect some one's been getting into a jolly row; and I wouldn't be in his shoes if he's caught!' said a fourth.

It was the 'quarter-hour,' that brief but truly excellent interval which so agreeably divides the solid hours of morning school work.

The doctor had gone to the matron's room.

'Mrs. Towels, did you hear any one moving about the house last night?'

'No, sir, I didn't; and I sleep so light, sir, that I'm sure I should have woken up at the least sound.'

'Well, I have my suspicions that two boys left the house last night. I don't want to ask publicly about it, in case I may be mistaken. Have you noticed anything this morning that might point to suspicion?'

'No, sir; nothing whatever.'

The doctor gave two powerful sniffs.

'It's very stuffy in here, Mrs. Towels. I think you should keep the windows open at the top; nothing like fresh air! There's a very odd smell indeed about the room. What is it?'

'I think it must be from Master Carruthers's jacket,

sir. He was sent up to change it just now. He seems
to have got it covered with grease. I can't think how
he could be so careless ! '

' Let me see the jacket, Mrs. Towels.'

The garment was produced from a cupboard, and
its more immediate presence instantly caused the
unpleasant odour to increase sevenfold. Dr. Porchester armed himself with the tongs, and taking up
the jacket with that instrument, he held it at arm's-
length with his right hand, elevating his double eyeglass into position with his left hand, and thus made
a very deliberate examination of the offensive article.

' Ah,' said the doctor, ' just as I thought. The boy
has contrived to saturate his coat with stale fat in a
most disgusting manner. Thank you, Mrs. Towels.
Have the goodness to see that Jinks hangs this garment on a stout bean-pole in the orchard until I give
further directions about it.'

' Yes, sir, I will see to it immediately.'

Dr. Porchester withdrew, feeling satisfied that he
had discovered one of the offenders at any rate.

We return to Dobbin.

He had managed to take so much time in rectifying
the faults of his toilet that he did not think it worth
while to put in an appearance for the remainder of
the Homer lesson. And Mr. Dunthorne, with a
kindly regard for the boy's feelings, refrained from
sending for him. So that Dobbin watched the clock,
and at a quarter to ten slipped into his place for the
arithmetic lesson.

He had reason to be grateful for the fact that boys
at Highfield were placed in various classes, according
to their capacity for each subject. Dobbin's mathe-
matical powers being not equal to his classical attain-
ments, he was only in the second class for arithmetic.
Thankful indeed was he that none of the boys amongst
whom he now sat had witnessed his late discomfiture
over Homer.

He now looked far more respectable than was his

custom on a week-day. Like a snake that has cast its slough and comes forth with renewed youth, or as a stag, which the classic poets tell us puts off its years annually with its horns, so had Peter Carruthers cast off his old garments and come forth decked in his new. His handkerchief, liberally dosed with eau-de-Cologne, diffused a fragrant aroma round his person. His hair was neatly brushed. He had on a clean collar, and presented generally such a neat appearance that good occasion was found for young Dicky Tozer's remark hat he looked as if he was going to an evening party.

Dobbin had recovered his spirits by the quarter-hour. The first class were privileged in the possession of studies. Dr. Porchester had lately built on a wing to the house for the special purpose of providing a small and cosy apartment for each of the ten senior boys. Dobbin had sped with the fleetness of a roe to his sanctum for a brief fifteen minutes' consolation.

He brought forth from his playbox two glass-stoppered bottles of nitric and sulphuric acid, surreptitiously procured from the chemist's assistant by Charlie Ross. Over these he gloated with the fervour of some ancient alchemist absorbed in his researches for the philosopher's stone.

Dobbin did not understand much about the properties of these dangerous liquids. He took out the stoppers and smelt the contents, and nearly dropped one of the bottles as its pungent fumes caused violent irritation to his nose. He was alarmed at the smoky vapours which ascended from the bottle of nitric acid, and fully expected it to burst into flame on the spot. He got some of the liquid on his fingers, which stung him painfully and produced a yellow stain not to be removed by any amount of licking. He began to feel a dread of the bottles, and noticed with apprehension the strong chemical smell which they imparted to the atmosphere of his study. He resolved that as

soon as ever morning school was over he would take
and hide the 'beastly things' in some safe place out
of doors, so that no harm might come from them to
his study.

Hastily replacing them in his box as the bell rang,
he went off to his lessons.

Dobbin was manifestly agitated during the latter
part of the morning school. His mind was preoccupied with the important events of the last twelve
hours. His heart palpitated as he saw the object of
his hopes and fears apparently within his grasp. He
would be off to the woods that afternoon immediately
after dinner. With Ross to help him he would nail
the fleece round a log of timber that he knew of in a
very secluded glade of the wood. And on the Saturday afternoon, which was actually the next day, he
would make the magnificent experiment.

'What are you mooning after now, Carruthers?
Go on with your work!'

Recalled to sublunary matters from the sublimities
of scientific meditations, Dobbin put on a studious
attitude for the remainder of the lesson.

At last it was over, and he hastened to his study
to convey the bottles to a safer place. Taking them
out of his box, he put them carefully in the pocket of
his jacket, which he buttoned up, and was hurrying
along the passage when he encountered Browning
and Tozer.

'We were just coming to find you, Dobbin. The
doctor wants to see you immediately in the matron's
room. He can't wait a moment. What have you
been up to, Peter, eh? Picking a peck of pickled
pepper? Won't you catch it! Yoicks!'

And Tozer, who was carrying a piece of a broomstick, playfully administered therewith a dig in what
he imagined to be Dobbin's ribs.

Little did he reck the consequences of that reckless deed!

I once remember making a chemical experiment

with all due caution in following the directions given in the book. I was told to add sulphuric acid to a solution *while hot*. Now the author of that treatise has much to answer for, in thus deluding the unwary student. Had he written such instructions in these days, we might have connected him with the dynamite fraternity. For experience has stamped it on my memory that one might as well sit down upon a barrel of gunpowder, and stir up the contents with a red-hot poker.

But who can imagine the direful catastrophe that resulted from Tozer's heedless jest ?

For the broomstick alighted upon the two bottles in Dobbin's pocket, and broke them both. The terrible liquids thus liberated mingled together with most frightful vehemence ; surging and seething with relentless fury, like the fiery floods of Mauna Loa, or the flaming whirlpools of the fabled Phlegethon.

For a few moments Dobbin was hardly aware of the disaster. Then shriek after shriek burst from the lips of the miserable victim. He pulled at the buttons, and with frantic energy tore off his jacket. But the acids had eaten their way through, and seized upon his waistcoat. They dropped in frothing clots down his trousers. They seized and devoured the substance of his garments. Yelling with terror and pain he tore at his waistcoat and rent it off. But his shirt was contaminated. His trousers were rotting away under his very eyes. Screaming for help, he rushed to the matron's room, shedding fragments of clothing in his mad career. Into the very arms of Dr. Porchester rushed the frenzied Dobbin, startling that worthy pedagogue as though a maniac had burst upon him.

'I'm burning, sir, oh save me ! I'm killed, oh-h-h-h !'

Mrs. Towels gave one scream, and fainted away.

The doctor saw that some terrible mischief had seized the boy. Catching him by the collar, he rent his shirt down, and tore it off, likewise his nether apparel, by almost superhuman power. He then called a boy and sent him off with all haste for Dr. Clark ; and another was set to throw water in Mrs. Towel's face to bring her round.

Meantime Dr. Porchester had thrown a sheet round Dobbin, and was hustling him off to his dormitory. Arrived there, the doctor took a wet sponge and washed the injured parts to remove the tainting acids, and having so done he bundled the unfortunate boy into bed. Dobbin all this time had been shrieking and moaning and writhing with pain—and so he continued until Dr. Clark applied copious ointment to the wounds, and otherwise soothed the patient by medical treatment. There was a great discoloured patch upon Dobbin's left side and left shin, his hands were badly burnt, and the pain was almost insupportable.

For many days Dobbin's state gave cause for considerable anxiety, during which time Dr. Porchester of course refrained from exciting the boy by any questions.

And I have reason to believe that the shock to Dobbin's system was so great that he partially forgot the circumstances which led to his terrible suffering. Whether or not Dr. Porchester learnt the whole story I have not been able to ascertain. But one thing is certain, that when Dobbin was well enough to be moved he was sent home, and never again appeared at Highfield. And probably to this day his stupendous discovery, which was to electrify the world, remains an unsolved problem.

The Gold Fish

CHAPTER I

EDWIN ASTON was a day boy at Highfield House. His parents were in India, and he lived with a maiden aunt. She rented a fine Elizabethan mansion standing in a grand old-fashioned garden, with terraces and steps and statues, and yew hedges cut into fantastic caricatures of beasts and birds.

Not least among the attractions of that garden was a fountain in the middle of the lawn, with a commodious basin, in which had lived for many years a red carp. This fish was the pride and delight of the maiden aunt. She did not care for pets as a rule; not a pug, nor a poodle, nor a parrot ever found sufficient favour in her eyes to merit adoption. But this carp was very dear to her heart. She had found him in the basin ten years before when she first came to live in Chesterton House. Perhaps he was the last of a family. He was a burly fish when she first knew him, and looked as if he might have grown fat upon other members of his race, the last by natural selection because the strongest. And ten years' careful feeding at the hand of his mistress had increased his burliness in due proportion.

Now, on the day marking the commencement of this story Miss Davis had occasion to pay a visit at a distance of some seven or eight miles. Her chariot and horses were ordered for 2.30 p.m. She was standing, clad in robes of state, on the broad steps of

her porch. Her nephew was at her side, receiving her
parting instructions. She was cautioning him against
the temptation of angling for the red carp during her
absence.

I know not what could have suggested the necessity of such a caution. Edwin was a well-disposed
lad, by no means addicted to mischief, and had never
shown the slightest inclination to meddle with the
carp. Miss Davis may have noticed an unusual twinkle
in his eye, and deemed it to portend angling intentions. Or she may have read the Billingsgate announcement in the paper that morning, or something
else might have roused her suspicions. I cannot tell.
But as she had never before hinted at the possible
perpetration of such an outrage, and as it had never
entered Edwin's mind to plot the capture of that fish,
it was odd that Miss Davis should have called the
boy and said to him, in a solemn and impressive
voice, 'Edwin, I am going for a drive this afternoon.
Now mind, I forbid you to try and catch the gold
fish!'

Edwin opened his mouth with astonishment,
stared at her a moment, and answered, 'All square,
aunt.'

'Edwin, I don't like that expression. You must be
more careful of your words. I am afraid the Highfield boys teach you bad language.'

Edwin looked even more astonished, not to say hurt,
and as his aunt turned to ascend into her chariot, a
casual observer might have noticed that he pursed
up his lips as though to whistle.

When left to his own devices Edwin Aston reflected
for a few moments, and his thoughts, if put into words,
would have been, 'What does aunt mean? I don't
want to catch the carp; I'm going for a walk with
Dawson. He's coming round at three o'clock. It's
nearly that now. There he comes down the road!
Hullo, Jackdaw! Come in. Aunt's gone for a drive.
Let's have some gooseberries!'

'Jolly!' cried Dawson. 'Don't she mind?'

'Mind? No! She's an old brick, and lets me have as many as I like.'

This was literally true. Miss Davis showed her wisdom in allowing her nephew to help himself to fruit at his discretion. She often said, 'Edwin, you may take what fruit you please, only promise me that you will not be greedy, nor pick it unripe, nor eat the skins and stones.' Was not she a sensible person? And Edwin obeyed her commands; and because he could at any time enjoy himself in the kitchen garden, he never abused the privilege. He cared not to fall upon the spoil like a starved lion. Oh no. He was fastidious in his tastes, and would select the reddest in preference to the biggest strawberry, and preferred the small ripe yellow gooseberries to the large unripe green ones.

The two boys therefore made for the gooseberry bushes. Dawson was but little accustomed to such a treat, and Edwin was amused at the voraciousness of his appetite.

'Why, Jack, you gulp them down like an ant-eater!'

'Rather! If your *aunt* was a gooseberry I'd *eat her!*'

Dawson's gluttonous appetite was at length appeased, and the boys walked round the well-stocked beds of cabbages and beans and peas and looked at the young apples and pears, and speculated on their destiny when ripe next term, and wandered off to the pigsty and stirred up the old sow with a bean-pole and made her snort. Talking and laughing merrily, they then repaired to the lawn and extemporised a game of cricket with a croquet-mallet and a tennis-ball, and played till they were hot.

'I say, Aston, it's awfully warm! Do you think we might bathe in the fountain? Hullo, what a fat fish! Let me find him a bluebottle!'

This was soon done. The carp lifted his nose and

deftly sipped in the bluebottle, and seemed to ask for another.

'How jolly the water looks! I may bathe, mayn't I, Aston?'

'I don't mind. It's not very deep, and I don't suppose you'll be drowned.'

Dawson soon disrobed and stepped in. The water was up to his waist. He flopped about, and began to flounder around the basin.

'Ha, ha! See if you can catch the carp, Jack! I'll stop him. Here, old fellow, not so fast! Steady! Wo, ho, my boy!'

On came the puffing Dawson like a white grampus. The carp grew alarmed, and exerted himself to escape, lashing the water with his broad tail as though he were a screw steamer. Edwin strove to check the monster's progress with the croquet-mallet. The chase grew exciting.

'Now, quick! Here! Got him? Hold tight! What a slippery old curmudgeon he is! Ha, ha, ha!'

The sport waxed hot. The carp, unused to such violent exercise, gasped and puffed and put forth all his energies in the struggle to elude capture. Dawson continued manfully floundering round the basin, and more than once seemed on the verge of success, but the slippery fish invariably escaped. How long this aquatic entertainment might have lasted under uniformity of circumstances I cannot say. But at length it was summarily cut short by an unexpected manœuvre on the part of the carp, who made a prodigious leap when opposite the overflow pipe, and fell head downwards into it, disappearing all but his tail. This *début* was entirely unforeseen by the boys.

'I say,' cried Edwin, 'the carp has taken a header down the pipe! Stop him, Harry! Catch him by the tail. Oh, what a go! Can't you pull him out?'

Harry valiantly tried to seize the fish by his tail. A super-piscine wriggle enabled the carp to get completely out of reach, and the boys were put *hors de combat.*

'What will aunt say? Shan't I catch it!' cried Edwin.

'You duffer, Aston! if you catch it you can put it back in the fountain, and it will be all right. But I know! Happy thought! You run down to the pond, where the pipe comes out, and I'll pour a bucket or two of water down the pipe, and swill him out, and you can easily catch him.'

'Oh yes; we'll have him. Wait—let me get a couple of buckets.'

These were soon fetched from the stables. One was given to Harry Dawson. Edwin took the other and scampered through the laurel hedge down to the pond, where the overflow pipe discharged the super-fluous water. Planting his feet firmly, he held the bucket under the mouth of the pipe, and shouted,—

'All serene; fire away, Jack!'

Dawson at once poured a bucket of water down the pipe, and then another, and even a third.

Edwin heard the subterranean gurglings which indicated the progress of the water, and anxiously waited for the appearance of the carp. Gurglings continued, and grew more pronounced. Water slowly trickled. Edwin's heart beat fast. There was a sudden commotion, a bursting report. Fish and water came out with a rush, and filled the bucket so suddenly that the weight of it was too much for Edwin. His feet slid on the treacherous clay, and in the flash of a moment bucket, water, fish, and boy fell with a promiscuous splash into the pond.

'Hasn't he come out yet?' shouted Harry. 'What a time he is! I must give him another dose.'

Two more bucketfuls were poured in. Just as Edwin's head appeared out of the muddy water, the clean cataract burst in his face and sent him back again into the mud.

Harry, hearing no answer to his inquiry, thought he

had better see what was going on down below. Clad
in the garb of a young Dyak of Borneo, he threaded
the mazes of the laurel hedge, and emerged to see the
results of the direful catastrophe.'

'What are you up to, Aston?'

'Up to! Come and help me out, you donkey!
Don't stand there gaping like an owl. Oh, this horrid
mud!'

The Dyak slipped nimbly down to the water's edge,
and Edwin was soon rescued. Poor Edwin! Mis-
fortunes seldom come singly. The carp was at large
in the pond. He himself, encased in mud, resembled an Egyptian mummy. The clouds of his
aunt's displeasure gathered gloomily on the horizon.

'Look here, Harry, you must make haste and dress
and get my Sunday clothes. You know my room.
Bring a shirt as well and some socks and boots.'

'However did you manage to tumble in?'

'Never mind how I managed it. Look sharp and
get my things.'

While Harry was gone Edwin lay down in the sun,
thoroughly disgusted with fortune. He naturally
dreaded his aunt's wrath. He was vexed that the
awkwardness of the carp should have brought such
trouble upon him. His muddy clothes would be sure
to betray him, to say nothing of the absconding carp.
Edwin did not see that it was his fault. Who could
have imagined that the fish would try such a desperate
venture as to escape through the overflow pipe? What
could he say when his aunt questioned him? He
was not going to get Harry into a row. He should
simply say he had not caught the carp. She had told
him not to, and he had obeyed her. She could not
blame him. His tumbling into the mud was an
accident, and accidents will happen in the best regu-
lated family.

Edwin was not in a good humour when Harry
returned with the dry clothes. During the operation
of changing dress, Harry suggested that they should

get a rod and bait a hook with a bluebottle and try and catch the carp.

'There's a rod in the stable,' said Edwin, 'but I won't try. Aunt said I wasn't to catch the brute.'

'Well, but she didn't mean that you were not to try and catch him if he was mad enough to jump down the pipe into the pond. If a man was going to leap off London Bridge and I caught him by the coat-tails I don't suppose it would be an assault [Harry's father was a solicitor]; though if he were walking along the road and I did so he might lick me with his walking-stick, and I couldn't say a word.'

'Yes, you could, and you would; you'd howl like a maniac. But I'm not going to disobey. Aunt said, "Edwin, you're not to try and catch the gold fish," and she blew me up when I said, "All square." '

'Well, she'll blow you up a lot more when she knows that you drove him down the pipe.'

'I didn't drive him down; you did.'

'No, I'm sure I didn't.'

'Yes, you did; quite as much as me, and more.'

'Well, I'm not going to argue about it. If you like to sneak I can't help it.'

'I'm not going to sneak, but you're just as much to blame as I am.'

'All right; I don't care.'

'No, but I do. That's the difference.'

Harry soon afterwards took his leave without further ceremony. And Edwin ruefully gathered up his soiled garments, and as he wended his way towards the house he heard the sound of carriage wheels coming up the drive. He knew that his aunt had returned, and with that knowledge came an oozing away of all hope.

CHAPTER II

EDWIN ASTON made for the kitchen, where he
delivered up his muddy clothes to the cook,
with sundry regrets and apologies. He then
walked as quietly as possible upstairs to his room, and
paid much attention to his toilet, resolved to make
himself unusually tidy, in hopes of creating a favour-
able impression at the tea-table. He was minded to
be particularly talkative during that meal on every
subject he could think of that steered clear of fish.

The tea was laid out invitingly on the spotless
tablecloth in the dining-room of Chesterton House
as Edwin entered. Miss Davis was already seated
at the teapot end of the table, and was pouring out
a cup of the fragrant beverage. He took his seat
with a forced smile, and at once began the conversation.

'Well, aunt, I hope you had a pleasant drive. It
was such a beautiful afternoon. What did you see?'

'Thank you, Edwin; I like to hear you open conversation in that agreeable manner. I had an enjoy-
able drive, and found the Skipworths at home. They
are very pleasant, clever, and well-informed people.'

'Aunt, I should like to read that volume of Alison's
history with the account of Napoleon's invasion of
Russia. May I take it from the library?'

'Certainly, Edwin; I am always glad to encourage
you in literary tasks. Historical study is of great
value in forming the mind.'

'Thank you, aunt. Do you think the old sow will
have any little pigs this year? They were such jolly
little rascals last time.'

'I really cannot tell, Edwin. That topic is hardly
suited to the refinement of the tea-table. You must
be more careful and not so abrupt in passing from
one subject to another. Your conversation should be
more sustained. I had expected you to make further
remarks upon your love of historical reading.'

I

'Oh, I'm very sorry, aunt. The egg I had for breakfast this morning wasn't very nice. May I have some jam?'

The connection between the last statement and the request which followed it was not altogether clear to the aunt's well-balanced mind, but she gave consent; and as Edwin helped himself to the condiment he continued his conversation.

'I say, aunt, why don't you do your hair like Miss Trevor, who plays the organ in church? She had such a lovely chignon last Sunday, all plaited up with ribbons.'

'Edwin, how often have I told you that personal remarks must never be heard in polite society! It is not good manners to draw attention to any peculiarity of another's dress or appearance. Besides which, I would sooner hear you comment upon the sermon you heard last Sunday than on the way the young person who presides at the organ arranges her hair. You distress me very much at times by the thoughtless and trivial character of your remarks. You must try and remember what I tell you.'

Edwin put on an air of offended innocence, and answered, 'I do try, aunt, but I think you are sometimes very hard upon me. I'm sure I didn't mean to be rude. You often make remarks on the way I do *my* hair.'

'That's quite another thing, Edwin. It is my duty to take your mother's place in correcting your faults. But you would be more accurate in saying that I occasionally remark upon the way you do *not* do your hair. Whenever it is *done*, I never make a remark upon it.'

Edwin plumed himself with the idea that so far he had been eminently successful in keeping up the conversation, which had not flagged for a moment. He was now aware that in his anxiety to keep it up he had paid but little attention to the important matter of eating. His aunt showed evident signs of having pretty well finished her repast, and it was incumbent upon him to put his best leg foremost, so to speak, in the race, if he did not wish to be hopelessly left behind. So for some minutes he devoted his entire energies to the business of ladling in tea and munching bread and jam. His aunt's falcon eye was upon him. He knew it, but pretended to be callous, though all the time he was inwardly apprehensive.

'Edwin, there are points about your way of eating and drinking which require improvement. You should not sip your tea with the spoon, and make such vulgar noises during the process. Take the cup in your right hand by the handle, thus, and drink without any sound. You should not bite but cut your bread, nor put jam into your mouth with the knife.'

'All right, aunt, I'll try and remember in future. But isn't it wrong to waste food? There's half a pat of butter on your plate and all the crust of two bits of toast.'

'Edwin, you forget yourself sadly, and are impertinent. My teeth are not so strong as they were. I am reserving these crusts for the gold fish.'

The boy gave an involuntary start and blushed crimson, and in his confusion choked over a mouthful of bread, and made matters worse by swallowing his hot tea too fast. His aunt looked sternly at him, and was on the verge of administering a severe rebuke, but the boy decided that as she had spoken last it was his turn to go on. Restraining his convulsions with much difficulty, he continued the conversation as best he could from the point at which it had dropped, and said :—

'Why don't you have some false ones, aunt? Old Pincers, the dentist, pulls them out at the first wrench, and he's got whole rows of teeth in his shop window. Do you know the fable about the old crab and its young one, aunt? I did it in Latin the other day, and got up top of the class.'

'I am glad to hear you talk about your studies,

Edwin. You know what an interest I take in your progress. I am delighted to hear that you have already advanced so far in the classics as to be reading the fables in the original language.'

' It isn't the original language, aunt. Æsop wrote in Greek, and that cheat Phædrus cribbed them from him. Mr. Fields said so.'

This last remark was too much for Miss Davis's nerves. To be flatly contradicted by her nephew was enough. To hear that a master of Highfield House deliberately encouraged his pupils in dishonesty by the fraudulent writings of ancient authors was absolutely insupportable. She resolved to write to Dr. Porchester at once on the subject. Mr. Fields was evidently not to be trusted to superintend the education of young and innocent boys. Rising from her chair, Miss Davis only said, ' Edwin, if you have done your tea I think we had better go out into the garden.'

' I'm rather tired, aunt. May I take the history book up to my room and read quietly ? I'd sooner not go out any more this evening.'

' Very well, Edwin.' The nephew began to beat a retreat from the room.

' Stay, Edwin ; it is not good manners to bounce out of the room in that violent haste. Open the door gently for me, and wait till I have passed.'

Miss Davis took up her parasol, and sailed majestically forth into the garden through the open bay window of the library. Edwin disappeared to his room without another thought of Napoleon. He was too nervous about the matter of the lost carp to care about the destruction of imperial armies. From the window of his room he could see the lawn. Ensconced behind the curtain he watched his aunt's progress in the garden.

Sure enough, after a turn or two up and down the broad gravel pathway, she stepped on to the lawn and made straight towards the fountain. The crusts

were in her hand. She did not see the carp at first.
She did not see it at last; no, not though she bent
her head and brought her double eyeglass into focus
and made a tour of the basin, peering closely into the
water. Nay, more, she could not discover any signs
of the pet carp, even though she closed her parasol
and commenced operations of diving and dredging
on an extensive scale among the ornamental stones
at the bottom of the basin. She thought it possible
that the carp might be taking an evening siesta in
the seclusion of some subaqueous cave. But no
success rewarded her search. Her brow darkened;
ominous forebodings gathered in her soul. Where
was the carp? What could have happened to it?

Miss Davis turned away from the fountain, holding
her dripping parasol in the attitude of a nervous
female confronted by a strange cow. Miss Davis
passed across the lawn, curiously scrutinized by her
nephew's eye. He read her intention at a glance—
beyond doubt bound for his room, and with all her
canvas set.

Edwin grew red with excitement, and indulged in
quaint antics akin to the movements of a Highland
schottische as it ought not to be danced. He heard
her steps deliberately ascending the stairs. He
heard her heave a deep sigh when she reached the
top, whether from the effects of physical exertion or
mental distress he could not tell, but he delivered
himself of the opinion that 'the old lady was wheezing
like a steam-roller.' It is needless for me to remind
you again that Edwin was a very unmannerly little
boy, whose example is quoted to be avoided, you
understand, like that of all the other unmannerly little
boys that figure in other school stories. I quite agree
with his aunt that he was often not particular about
his language. He now emphasized his last remark
by reference to one of the zodiacal signs, 'Oh,
Gemini! she's on the war-trail and no mistake!'

With all his mock bravado, accompanied by pan

tomimic action, Edwin—to use another of his expressions—was in a ' blue funk.' Nearer came the dreaded step, and he crept with extreme caution under the bed.

A knock at the door.   No answer.

A louder knock.   No answer.

The door was opened.

' Edwin, are you in your room ? '

No answer.

Miss Davis put her head inside the door.   Not seeing her nephew, she might have been expected to withdraw.   But she didn't.   She went and opened a cupboard, and shut it.   She examined the window curtains.   She pulled up the muslin hangings of the dressing-table.   She didn't look under the bed, because it would have been a laborious and undignified operation.   But she did not feel at all certain that Edwin was not there.   In fact, she was so confident on the matter that she went to the door and opened it, and called to the housemaid, ' Jane ! Jane ! '   She took three steps along the passage to call down the back stairs, leaving the door of Edwin's room open, and keeping an eye upon it all the time.   ' Jane, come here a moment, please.'

The faithful domestic was at her mistress's side in a trice.

Preceding her to Master Edwin's room, the mistress said, ' Jane, just see if Master Edwin is under the bed.   I fancy he is trying to hide from me.'

' Oh, miss, how shocking ! '

The housemaid knelt down to obey the command.

' No, miss, he's not there.'

Certainly not ; for while his aunt was in the passage Edwin, rightly conjecturing probabilities, had emerged from his hiding-place and removed himself to the shelter of the cupboard, holding tight to the tongue of the fastening inside, resolved to hold on till he fainted, should any attempt be made to storm his castle.

' Perhaps he's in the cupboard, miss ?'

' No, Jane ; I have looked already.'

Mistress and maid left the room and went their respective ways down the front and back stairs.

Edwin, reassured that the coast was clear, came out of the cupboard, undressed, said his prayers, and went to bed.

CHAPTER III

MISS DAVIS had resolved not to question her nephew immediately about the lost fish. She knew enough of his character to believe that, if he had committed an act of disobedience, his guilty conscience would drive him to unburden himself before long of the heavy secret ; so, when Edwin made his appearance in the breakfast-room next morning with an anxious heart, he found his anxiety groundless. His aunt never alluded to the cause of his apprehension. Her only question in any way connected with it was, ' Edwin, where were you last evening when I came to your room ?' To which question the answer was returned, ' Please, aunt, I would rather not say.'

Breakfast was soon over. Edwin got his books and went off to Highfield House. Miss Davis, having attended to her domestic duties, settled herself at her davenport. A look of stern resolution was stamped upon her face. She had thought deeply upon Edwin's last words at tea the evening before. They had harassed her dreams and made hideous her waking thoughts. And the result of her cerebration was the grim conviction that Mr. Fields was a thoroughly unprincipled man, intentionally undermining the morality of the Highfield boys by countenancing—nay, more—encouraging dishonesty in the use of ' cribs.'

Now Miss Davis had a dreadful horror of the word ' crib,' and ' quite right too,' you will surely say. It is to be hoped that every boy who reads this story has the same dreadful horror of the word 'crib.' If you ever degrade yourself so miserably as to cheat in lessons, please stop reading this story. I am not writing for you. I should not like to have anything more to do with you until you first learn the infamy of such a practice. Cheats, swindlers, and forgers are of one class.

Miss Davis very properly detested the word 'crib.' She had good cause so to do. For her favourite brother, I regret to say, once got into desperate trouble at school through using cribs. Detected and denounced, he ran away in terror of the consequences, and brought indelible disgrace upon himself and his family.

The maiden aunt, therefore, sat down, determined at once to bring the imaginary culprit to justice. She mended her pen and wrote the following letter to Dr. Porchester :—

'DEAR SIR,—I feel it my painful duty to inform you that I have strong reasons to believe that Mr. Fields is encouraging dishonesty in work among the boys entrusted to your care. I have no doubt you will know how to deal with the matter discreetly. Regretting the necessity of this information, I remain, yours truly,

'M. DAVIS.'

This letter, dispatched by special messenger, was delivered to Dr. Porchester in the schoolroom while he was enjoying what he called a 'field-day' of spelling and dictation with the junior classes. He had just delivered the following sentence to be written down : 'The soldiers were a prey to the miseries of gnawing hunger.' And he was standing on the form looking over the curly head of an audacious youngster who had spelt the word 'gnawing' thus—'kngnagh-ning.' This is no invention, mind, but a positive fact, and so interesting in its ingenuity that it deserves to be recorded.

The doctor was always prepared for eccentricities of orthography, and kept a book in which any worthy of special notice were entered. This specimen was like a magnum-bonum plum, and was duly recorded with his best embellishments of penmanship.

At such a juncture was Miss Davis's note received by the head master of Highfield House. He read it forthwith, in case it might require an immediate answer. His amazement was only equalled by his amusement. He found the accused in the quarter-hour, and taking him familiarly by the arm, marched him off to the cricket-field, where he thus disclosed the extraordinary information :—

'Look here, Fields. I have received a letter from Aston's aunt, bringing a serious charge against you. Just read it!'

Mr. Fields read it ; and as he read his eyes opened wider, his eyebrows were elevated, the corners of his mouth quivered with twinkling undulations. He looked up at Dr. Porchester and burst into a fit of uncontrollable laughter.

'Well,' said the doctor, likewise laughing, 'what have you to say in your defence? What explanation can you give?'

'None, doctor! The lady is not sufficiently explicit. What in the world has she got hold of?'

'I can't tell. The best way will be to call upon her this afternoon and ask. Shall you be agreeable to a walk that way?'

'Certainly, doctor ; thank you. I shall be delighted.'

Accordingly, as soon as dinner was over, Dr. Porchester and Mr. Fields proceeded on their visit to Chesterton House, and rang at the house-door bell about 2.30.

Miss Davis had not calculated upon this move in the problem. For once her sagacity was at fault. She was eminently of a nervous temperament. She fondled herself upon the notion of her extreme sensitiveness. In many a skirmish with her nephew she would clench the matter, and prevent all further parley, by a prominent display of pocket-handkerchief, and a whimpering, pathetic appeal that he would 'consider her weak nerves.' This was unanswerable. Edwin had always to capitulate unconditionally.

Miss Davis was reposing after the fatigue of lunch when the bell rang. The sound startled her. She jumped up, flew to the window, peeped through a slide of the Venetian blind. The prospect of visitors was always agitating. Two gentlemen! Horrible! How inconsiderate of them! Who could they be? What could they want? Being short-sighted, and not having her spectacles at hand, she could not recognise them.

The man-servant soon afterwards knocked at the door of her room, and announced that Dr. Porchester and Mr. Fields were waiting below.

Miss Davis, flurried and excited, declared that she positively could not see them.

'It's quite out of the question, James. My nerves are so upset this afternoon. I must decline to see any one. Present my compliments to the gentlemen, and make my excuse with suitable apologies.'

James retired, but shortly returned with a very polite expostulation. Dr. Porchester was extremely sorry to be importunate, but would esteem it a great favour if Miss Davis would kindly grant him a few moments' interview.

'Oh, well, I suppose I must consent, James. Come in and find my salts-bottle. It's somewhere about the room, or else in the library, or possibly in the drawing-room. And tell Jane to fetch me another handkerchief, and let the coachman know that I shall take a drive at four o'clock. And then show Dr. Porchester upstairs. Request Mr. Fields to remain below. Oh, my poor nerves!'

James retired, to execute as much or as little of his mistress's injunctions as he deemed the occasion to demand. He was accustomed to her vagaries, and knew how to treat them.

A brief interval, and Dr. Porchester was ushered into the lady's presence.

'Good afternoon, Miss Davis. I am sorry to hear you are somewhat indisposed. The hot weather is very trying. I thought it best to——'

'Thank you, Dr. Porchester; it's very kind of you to call. Don't come any nearer; please take a seat. I'm in rather a nervous state. I'm not so strong as I used to be—I have had some painful anxiety about my nephew—since yesterday' (Dr. Porchester fondly hoped she was coming to the point at once). 'I have reason to fear he has been guilty of an act of dis-obedience—I should like to confide in you—may I? —You take such kind interest in the boy—I think he is well-disposed and honest as a rule—but I fear he yielded to temptation yesterday.'

Miss Davis had a way of delivering her sentences with a peculiar punctuation, inserting between each a little tremulous gasp, apparently on the point of pausing for a reply, but always continuing the con-versation just as her listener was about to take it up. It is no easy task to converse with such a person. It is a matter requiring tact and delicacy and self-control, and imperturbable patience. In all these elements of social politeness Dr. Porchester flattered himself that he excelled. But he was sorely tried on this occasion, and before the interview closed he half-doubted his title to rank as a man of unquestionable patience and self-restraint.

Miss Davis was compelled through physical ex-haustion to pause for breath. Now was the doctor's chance. He saw that she was launching forth upon a dangerous digression. His time was precious. School at four. He grudged each moment not spent under the blue firmament of heaven. He therefore seized the opportunity to hint in the broadest manner that he had called specially to ask on what grounds Miss Davis had reason to suspect Mr. Fields of dishonest inclinations.

'Oh yes, to be sure, Dr. Porchester. It was very kind of you to call—Mr. Fields is undoubtedly a very pleasant young man with boys—my nephew always speaks of him with regard; I may say, admiration. He's a very dear man.'

'But, may I ask'—the doctor forced himself to the front—'what reasons you have, Miss Davis, for throwing such grave suspicions upon his character?'

Surely Miss Davis must be brought to bay by such a point-blank question. *Varium et mutabile semper femina*, says the poet; and the doctor found this specimen as difficult to lay hold of as Harry Dawson found the tail of the gold fish.

'Oh, Dr. Porchester, I was conversing with Edwin at the tea-table. He is a very thoughtful child, and I hope you find him diligent and attentive in his studies; he was talking to me upon historical and classical subjects; really, for so young a boy, his conversation is considerably beyond his years—yes—beyond his years. I anticipate for him a brilliant future.'

Again the worthy doctor leapt in at the breach.

'I sincerely hope so, Miss Davis. But I have very little time to spare this afternoon' (taking out his watch ostentatiously), 'and if you would kindly tell me what grounds——'

'Oh, certainly, Dr. Porchester; certainly. Yesterday afternoon I had occasion to take a drive. Before starting I called my nephew, and said to him distinctly—without any irritability of voice or gesture—Edwin——'

As has been previously intimated, Dr. Porchester was a man of polished and courteous manners at all times. His respect for the female sex was absolutely unimpeachable. Was it his fault that at this particular moment he should be seized with a spasm of bronchial catarrh, under the influence of which he gave vent to a somewhat violent guttural noise, the immediate effect of which was to startle Miss Davis into an abrupt pause in the course of her speech, and to elicit from her the exclamation,—

'Oh, my poor nerves!'

Now it was indeed sad that a man so well trained in bearing with the idiosyncrasies of parents and guardians of the young lambs committed to his care— that a man who prided himself upon never being taken off his guard—should ever be betrayed into any unceremonious conduct. True that his time was precious, that his soul was vexed with indignation at the consciousness of being thwarted in his purpose; but should he have risen from his seat so hastily? Should he have taken two steps towards the lady with hat in hand and walking-stick unnecessarily brought to the front? No, he certainly should not. But man is only mortal after all, and a schoolmaster is so accustomed to receive instant obedience to his wishes that we must make some allowance for the worthy man's behaviour.

'Really, Miss Davis,' said he, with some warmth, 'I have hardly five minutes to spare. I must beg you to postpone other matters for another occasion, and let me know the plain truth about your accusation against——'

'Oh, don't come nearer me, please! My nerves are very sensitive, Dr. Porchester. I assure you I hardly know sometimes how I shall get through the day. Edwin is a very dear——'

'I must apologise for interrupting you, Miss Davis, but as you are unable to inform me upon the extraordinary information conveyed in your letter of this morning, I see no need to intrude further upon your time, and——'

'Not at all, I assure you, Dr. Porchester. You are so sympathetic and considerate——'

'Well, good afternoon, Miss Davis. I hope you will soon recover your sen—I mean, I hope to-morrow you will be not quite such—that is—hm—hm. Good-bye, Miss Davis!'

'Good-bye, Dr. Porchester; it was so kind of you to call, it does me so much good to talk to you about my dear nephew. I hope he will always——'

But Dr. Porchester was half-way down the stairs, and only heard the distant echoes of the last remark.

CHAPTER IV

'WELL, doctor,' said Mr. Fields, as the two pedagogues left Chesterton House, 'I am naturally anxious to hear the result of your interview.'

'Oh, I could get nothing out of the old lady; absolutely nothing. Charity must make allowances for her eccentricities, I suppose; but either you are a deep-dyed villain, Fields, or your accuser has a bee in her bonnet. I suppose you prefer to accept the latter alternative?'

'Well, I certainly don't like the notion of the former. But it would be satisfactory to clear up the matter. Suppose we examine Aston?'

'Ah, we might possibly get something definite out of him. Bring him to my study after school.'

The masters now set themselves to make up for lost time, trudging briskly through the fragrant meadows and shady lanes.

Afternoon school passed away, and Edwin Aston was invited by Mr. Fields to accompany him on a visit to the head master's study. Such an invitation was not altogether agreeable, but it admitted no refusal. Edwin was alarmed indeed, and as he stood in that august presence-chamber he fidgeted nervously, and looked at the carpet and then from one to the other of his preceptors, wondering what particular scrape could necessitate such an interview. His apprehensions were, however, partially allayed by the kind and cheerful way in which his examination proceeded.

'Look here, my boy,' began the doctor, laying his massive hand affectionately upon Aston's shoulder, and feeling his way confidently into the boy's heart by a peculiar pressure. 'I received a letter from your aunt this morning, in which she says something about Mr. Fields encouraging dishonesty among the boys. Can you tell me anything about it? Try and think now.'

Edwin stood open-mouthed and tried to think, at all times a difficult matter to a boy. But no words gave substance to his thoughts. He was dumb with astonishment.

'Have you been saying anything,' continued the doctor, 'which could make your aunt imagine such a thing as Mr. Fields cheating? Don't be afraid to speak out. I don't want to frighten you. Come, say something, my boy.'

'No, sir, I don't remember saying anything.'

'What did you talk about with your aunt at tea last evening?'

'I don't remember, sir.'

'Oh, you must try to remember. Didn't you say something about your work—history, or Latin and Greek?'

'Yes, sir, I remember now. I asked her to lend me a volume of Alison's *History of Europe* to read about Napoleon in Russia.'

'Very good. Well, what then?'

'She said I might take it from the library.'

Well, all right; and what about the Latin and Greek?'

'I don't think I said anything, sir—at least, I think I said something, sir, about the fables; but I don't remember what it was.'

'Did you mention Mr. Fields' name at all? Were you thinking about him?'

'I don't think I was, sir. I may have been, but I don't think it's likely. I don't often think much about him.'

'Oh,' said the doctor, 'I'm sorry to hear that. But could you possibly have said anything about his acting unfairly or allowing you to work dishonestly?'

'No, sir; I'm perfectly certain I never said such a thing, sir. Of course I couldn't.'

'No, my boy, I never for a moment supposed you could. But have you no idea what your aunt means? Look here, read what she says.'

Edwin read. His fears had all fled, and he was able to understand what was written.

'I don't know what she means at all, sir. I don't think it's fair of her to write like that. I'm sure Mr. Fields is a jolly—I mean—I shouldn't have thought my aunt could have been such a sn—could have written such a letter, sir.'

'I understand you, boy. And you can't tell me anything more about it? You're quite sure?'

'Quite certain, sir. I don't know what she means at all.'

'Well, that will do; you may go. Good evening.'

Edwin went off as fast as he could, relieved at escaping unscathed from such a perilous interview. He hurried home, determined to ask his aunt what she meant by writing such a letter to the doctor.

He threw down his books with a bang and bounced into the dining-room, where he was surprised to find his aunt already seated at the tea-table.

She bade him go quietly upstairs and make himself tidy.

When he returned she said, 'Edwin, you are later than usual this evening.'

'Yes, aunt; I had a jaw from the doctor.'

'A what? Edwin, I don't understand you.'

'A *jaw*, aunt!'

'What do you mean by a "jaw," Edwin?'

'Oh, I don't know; there's no other word for it. He had me into his study and blew me up about your writing to him that Mr. Fields cheated.'

Edwin spoke with a flush on his cheek and a flash in his eye, betokening proud indignation.

'After our conversation last evening, Edwin, I could not do otherwise than acquaint Dr. Porchester with what you said.'

'What I said, aunt? I never said anything, I'm sure I didn't!'

'Stop, Edwin! Never be hasty in your statements. Let me recall to your memory what seems to have escaped it. You were talking about your classical fables, and you distinctly spoke of Mr. Fields acknowledging that the boys cribbed and cheated.'

'What a horrid cram, aunt!—I mean, I'm certain I never said such a thing!'

'Edwin, I am astonished at you! I cannot express the pain your words and behaviour cause me.'

Poor Edwin! he could not analyse the conflicting emotions which filled his heart, but his pride was sorely wounded.

He blushed and stammered, and a rush of tears burst from his eyes as he choked out in broken syllables, 'It's a horrid shame, aunt! I remember now using the words "crib" and "cheat," but I know I never said we cheated. I couldn't believe you were such a sneak!'

The aunt was moved at the sight of her nephew's evident distress; she had never seen him cry before. She might have added further fuel to his disquietude by rebuking his unseemly language, but she thought it discreet to refrain; and laying her hand gently on his arm, she only said, 'Edwin, you must calm yourself. Let us say no more upon the subject now. Finish your tea, my dear.'

Tea was diluted by tears, and ended uncomfortably for both without further conversation.

* * * * *

K

In the early hours of the following morning, when Miss Davis awoke from sleep, she employed the time in meditating how best to solve the mystery of the carp's disappearance. The conclusion to which she arrived was that, since Edwin had not chosen to volunteer any information upon the subject, duty demanded that she should not let the day pass without questioning him upon it. Whenever duty's demands were plain Miss Davis never hesitated to obey them. And the more unpleasant the operation the sooner was she anxious to get it over. Therefore she would ask him at breakfast.

That meal had not proceeded far before Miss Davis opened the attack.

'Edwin, I noticed with surprise last evening that the gold fish was not in the pond. Is it possible that you could have disobeyed my orders and caught it? Stay, do not reply till I have finished. However terrible may be the consequences of telling the truth '— ('Would the old lady give me a whacking?' thought Edwin)—'I feel certain that you cannot tell me a falsehood.

Edwin grew very red and uncomfortable, and answered, 'I didn't catch it, aunt, because you told me not to.'

'I am very glad indeed to hear that,' said his aunt. 'Did your friend Harry Dawson catch it?'

'I'm not a sneak, aunt; but I'm sure he didn't.' Edwin mentally added, 'He was such an ass he couldn't hold the slippery thing!'

'Well, it is an extraordinary matter. I must ask the gardener. Do you think, Edwin, it could have been the boy who comes in to weed the garden? Did you see him anywhere near the fountain while I was out?'

'I told you I am not a sneak, aunt; but I didn't see him anywhere about all the afternoon.'

*　　　*　　　*　　　*　　　*

The following Saturday would be Edwin's birthday. He had been long looking forward to the occasion with glad anticipations. His aunt always made the anniversary as happy for him as she could. She let him invite any of his friends at Highfield to spend the afternoon, and she meant this time to invite some youthful members of the fair sex to meet them.

The privilege of asking his friends was much valued by Edwin. It was a potent engine with which he wrought for himself no small advantage in social politics. Boys at preparatory schools (for whom these Highfield stories are specially intended) enjoy being asked out for an *exeat* beyond everything. Afterwards when they pass on to a public school and become 'men' by one gigantic leap, and develop perhaps into 'mashers,' they are apt to take a different view of such pleasures. It is wonderful how the climate of some public schools assists this sudden development of manhood. Like as tadpoles suddenly find themselves frogs, so do boys suddenly find themselves men. Little Tommy Tucker leaves his preparatory school at the end of a term, and enters his public school after the holidays, and has not been there a week before he writes to his bosom friend Hop-o'-my-thumb: 'I like Winchester awfully. We have jolly fun. Last remedy I and another man went a long walk, and had no end of grub.'

Edwin was very particular about the boys whom he should favour with a birthday invitation. You may be sure that every one who thought he had a ghost of a chance did his utmost to secure the treat. For weeks beforehand Edwin was courted with marked deference by many a companion who at other times gave no special heed to make himself agreeable. The great Dumpling, for example, would come up to him patronisingly in the playground, and lay his great fat hand round Edwin's neck, and smear and crumple his clean Eton collar with greasy, dirty fingers, and say,—

' Aston, you're a jolly fellow. I like you awfully. Come on. I'll give you a cake from Punchey's basket.'

Buffles and Guzzling Jim too would ' suck up ' to him with cringing pertinacity. By varied methods, equally obvious in their intention, many a companion competed vigorously for the longed-for favour.

But Edwin received their overtures with scornful contempt, and set his face like a heathen idol against all such undisguised demonstrations of cupboard love. His genuine friends, of course, made no difference in their behaviour, and reposed secure in the assurance of an invitation. The list of favoured guests was known beforehand only to the happy initiated. And this time three boys were basking in the delightful prospect of the next Saturday afternoon. These were Harry Dawson, Dickey Stephenson—his brother had left, or he too would certainly have been asked— and who was the third ? None other than our old friend Hercules !

Yes, Hercules, the hero of that escapade with the donkey Cacus which has rendered Highfield House School famous all the world over. It is no presumption to assert that the fame of that celebrated episode has spread in all the four quarters of the globe ! *The Boy's Own Paper* is not read in a corner ! It is nothing for the author to be proud of. Virgil draws such a picture of FAME as should make few persons anxious to have much to do with her.

He describes her as a monster hideous and huge, swift-footed, many-tongued, all-seeing, growing as she runs, rearing her gigantic form from earth to heaven, terrifying cities, shrieking in the darkness, never closing her eyes in sleep ! Ugh ! we should not like to have much to do with her, boys !

The wished-for day at last arrived, and a glorious summer day it was, without a cloud upon the sunny skies. But such an occasion deserves another chapter

CHAPTER V

THE excitement about who were going to share in the enjoyment of Edwin's birthday festivities was only finally allayed on Saturday morning, when the three boys, Harry, Dickey, and Hercules, alone appeared decked in their Sunday clothes. Admired by all, envied by most, for these were now among the influential of the Highfield boys, the trio waited for Edwin Aston after school, and accompanied him to the home of his spinster aunt. Full of spirits at the prospect of the holiday, they laughed and chaffed and experienced the keen delight of freedom.

Miss Davis received them at the door of her mansion with a smile of genial, open-hearted hospitality. With all her crotchets and vagaries, she was a most charming old lady when concerned in the entertainment of young people.

Edwin was delighted at his aunt's gracious reception of his friends. The luncheon was spread with substantial elegance, the table garnished with fair flowers and fruits. Mirth and good-humour flowed apace. The boys discussed their school doings, and never an ill-omened word was spoken to mar the harmony of the feast. Miss Davis entered with lively interest into the details of cricket matches, which she understood about as well as a tortoiseshell cat understands the merits of Dresden china. She followed them in the history of woodland rambles and bathing adventures. She affected horror at the mark of the adder's fangs on Harry's wrist. She laughed for the twentieth time over the ludicrous conduct of Cacus in the schoolroom.

Then after lunch was over they went and sat under the verandah to enjoy the cool western breezes that were wafted through clustering traceries of clematis and jessamine and honeysuckle and vine. Miss Davis issued orders to James to bring out a table, and on it was placed an imposing square parcel carefully concealed by paper. This was her birthday present to Edwin, and proved when unpacked to be a handsome 'Compendium of Games,' containing chess, backgammon, draughts, steeplechase, and a host of other games, all turned out in the highest class of workmanship, such as a boy cannot fail to admire. Edwin's delight knew no bounds. The boys examined every item of the contents of the box, and played a game of steeplechase with all the zest that attends the use of a new toy, and were so engrossed in the exciting sport that they were loth to leave it when the sound of carriage wheels announced the arrival of the young ladies.

Then there were shy shakings of hands, and tongues that before had seemed incapable of ever growing tired became on a sudden slow of speech and awkward in utterance, and it needed the full force of Miss Davis's arts to dispel the shyness of the boys and the coyness of the girls. But that good lady was equal to the emergency. Croquet, la grace, and battledore upon the lawn gradually prevailed to remove all embarrassment.

And when they were tired of these amusements it was time for tea; which repast, in honour of the auspicious occasion, was to take the form of a picnic under the beech-trees by the pond. It was to be a genuine picnic, with no nonsense about it—as much a picnic as if the guests were on the wild slopes of a Welsh mountain or among the banks and braes of bonnie Scotland.

Baskets of provisions were brought out upon the lawn, and the boys carried them down to a grassy slope near the pond, where beech and elm trees overshadowed the ground. The young ladies bore the teapots and kettle and lighter articles of the furniture of the feast. Two of the softer sex laid the cloth and set out the delicacies in appetising array, while two were told off to gather sticks for the fire.

These were Molly Stephenson and Louise Delamere. Hercules was squire to the latter upon this occasion, and showed her assiduous attentions. Kitty Brown, the blonde, and Edith Grey, the brunette, presided over the teapots, and a blazing fire was soon crackling and sputtering beneath a gipsy tripod of stakes. It was a period of thorough enjoyment to all concerned, not least so to Miss Davis, who seemed to live over again one of her own sunny birthdays in the days long ago of her childhood. The happiness of the children around her brought back memories of the past. To quote the beautiful words of Charles Dickens—which of you boys can tell me where they are found ?— ' The tear which starts unbidden to the eye, when the recollection of old times and the happiness of many years ago is suddenly recalled, stole down the old lady's face as she shook her head with a melancholy smile.'

Merely a passing cloud to dim for a moment the sunny scene.

Tea could not last for ever, and some one suggested a row on the pond. The old punt was soon manned—a craft warranted, if needs were, to carry a brood of young elephants. Harry Dawson and jolly old Hercules rowed three or four of the girls up the deep and shallow reaches, where perch and tench lurked through the hot summer afternoons, as cool as cucumbers, enjoying life while weary masters and boys labour at lessons.

And now we are approaching the crisis of this tale.

' Oh, do let us fish !' cried Edith Grey. ' May we, Miss Davis ? We can put what we catch into the basin of the fountain.'

(You think, my boy, that you can guess what's going to happen, don't you ? Not exactly, though !)

' To be sure, my love,' answered the kind old lady. ' Edwin, dear, fetch the fishing-rods from the stables, and ask cook to make you some dough paste. We will not use worms, it is so cruel.'

The tackle was soon procured, and two of the girls began to angle. Mademoiselle Louise was not slow to capture a perch, which Hercules gallantly took off the hook for her, and got his hand well pricked by the back fin during the operation.

Then the young ladies declared that Miss Davis must come upon the water—a thing she had never dreamed of during all the years she had been at Chesterton House. A garden-chair was placed in the punt, and a chorus of silvery voices begged their kind hostess to embark. Edwin insisted on being captain of the vessel on that voyage. He declared he could not trust his aunt on the water alone. Miss Davis's nerves seemed inspired with supernatural strength that afternoon. 'The old lady stuck at nothing,' as Edwin expressed it, when afterwards talking over the glorious birthday festivities with Harry Dawson.

She actually stepped into the punt and sat in the chair, and suffered herself to be rowed about ; and when the oarsmen rested for a while, and Edwin put a fishing-rod into his aunt's hand, it seemed to her the most natural thing in the world that she should hold it ! Miss Davis fishing in a punt ! Such a wonder had never been known ! It was the first and last time she ever fished in all her life.

    *   *   *   *   *

Miss Davis did not find her patience long taxed. See, the float bobs—ducks its white head—dives— furiously disappears. The fisherwoman nearly lets go the rod.

'Hold hard, aunt ! don't give in ! you've got something grand !'

Miss Davis holds hard with both hands. The hazel wand bends like a shepherd's crook ! Crack ! the top joint has sprung a leak—that's not quite the correct expression, but the excitement is so intense that we cannot stop to alter it. She grasps the line. She hauls it in hand over hand ! She refuses all assistance! Victory is hers! There lies gasping and floundering at the bottom of the punt

THE GOLD FISH!

*   *   *   *   *

All things must have an end.

The shadows of evening had lengthened. The sun had set. The cool, calm, holy twilight had followed. The guests at last were gone. Edwin and his aunt stood alone upon the lawn.

'Well, aunt, you have given me the best birthday I ever had. I do thank you with all my heart. And it was *you* who caught the gold fish after all!'

'Edwin, I must beg your pardon. I have mis-judged you. In spite of your telling me you had not disobeyed me, I could not help having some misgivings about the disappearance of the fish. I think now it must have found its way into the pond down the overflow-pipe.'

'You're right, aunt. I'll tell you all how it hap-pened.'

And the boy told the whole story, which need not be repeated here.

In his latter days the burly fish once more reigned supreme in the fountain basin, monarch of all he surveyed; and never again did he escape; for a piece of wire gauze was fastened over the mouth of the pipe. He may have sometimes sighed for the deeper waters and broader pastures of the pond, but, at any rate, he had little to complain of in his de-clining years, and continued as of yore to be his mistress's only animal pet.

And as for the question of cribbing and cheating, like many a similar misunderstanding, it was soon forgotten by all concerned; and, somehow, from that day forward, Edwin and his aunt seemed to understand each other better; and so, like the hero and heroine in the dear old children's stories, they lived happily ever afterwards.

The Last Straw

CHAPTER I

IT was a dull, rainy day in February. There had
been a brief spell of frost previously, four days
of unclouded sky, when the air seemed keen
enough almost to cut glass.

The ponds had been skimmed over by the first
night's frost. After the second the ice looked tempting ; after the third excitement was rife among the
boys at Highfield House.

Skates were brought out, or hired of John Carey,
who for twenty years past had been making a collection of these articles, obtained in various ways. They
were let out for the afternoon at a high rate. If you
hired a pair before the ice bore, you might get them
at half-charge for every day you kept them ; but then
the speculation was serious and liable to disappointment ; so they were mostly hired on the morning
when skating seemed certain in the afternoon.

On the fourth day of frost Dr. Porchester had felt
anxious. The ice certainly bore ; village boys were
sliding on the ponds ; a few of the village mashers
were plunging about on skates with their arms working like the sails of a windmill, and performing
spread-eagles with untutored grace.

The doctor had gone down to the pond above
Hook Mill, which was reserved on such occasions for
our particular use. He had stood upon the ice, and
the ice had made unmistakable protest against his
solid weight of thirteen stone six. A sounding crack
ran across the pond. In the immediate vicinity of

his feet stars of spangled cracks shot out like lightnings from the hand of Jove. Dr. Porchester had retreated as though the Mahdi were after him, and had returned to bring us the gloomy intelligence that it wasn't quite safe—we must wait one more day. And then the wind changed, and a muggy, drizzling rain set in; and our hopes were extinguished as by a wet blanket.

I do not think Dr. Porchester regretted the change of weather. Whenever skating was imminent his habitual complaisance gave place to an anxious expression of countenance. He had never forgotten a terrible accident that once occurred on that same Hook Pond, when two boys had fallen through the ice and been drowned; and though the doctor never denied us skating afterwards when the ice was unquestionably safe, still it was always a grave anxiety to him; and so it was but natural that he should be glad of the thaw.

Others of the household took a different view of the matter. It was a very grievous disappointment to many of us boys. We had made so certain of the enjoyment overnight. The mugs of water put outside the bedroom windows at four o'clock were frozen at bed-time. The air was no less crisp and bitter. We had been furbishing up our skates. John Carey had done a brisker business than he ever remembered doing before. Everything was in readiness; we had only to sleep through the night and dream of the exhilarating exercise, and rise in the morning to enjoy the realization of our dreams. And now, to think of the weather suddenly changing without any warning—jumping at one bound from sharp frost to sudden thaw! It was too bad!

Dismal were our looks that morning, as dull and cheerless and chilly as the weather. The very smoke from the chimneys seemed to share in the general depression, coming down in whirling wreaths, as if to smother the last ray of hope in our hearts.

We wandered aimlessly about the schoolroom, muttering ill-omened words of disappointment. The lessons were a wearisome drudgery. When dinner was over we had no taste for the common avocations of a wet afternoon. The attractions of 'Gym' were nowhere. Library-books, chess, and draughts were utterly stale.

The Dumpling, of whom the reader already knows something, had been foremost in expressing his disgust. It was just an example of the inconsistency of boys. The Christmas holidays a year ago had yielded a fortnight's unexceptionable opportunity for skating, and he had utterly eschewed the exercise ; but on this occasion he was bent upon it. This may be accounted for in some measure by the fact that his uncle had lately given him a pair of skates, and he was anxious to prove them. He had been showing them to the boys and swaggering to no small extent about the use he would make of them if it only froze. He took it as a personal insult that the wind should have changed, and sought to wreak his vengeance upon that fickle element by forcibly abstracting it from the chests of his companions. When this pastime became monotonous he had shuffled up to the matron's room to seek any stray consolation that might be going there.

'What a horrid nuisance this thaw is, Mrs. Towels!'

'Oh, my dear Master Bertram, you shouldn't say that. Think of the poor creatures at the North Pole, who can't ever get near a fire in the cold weather. How thankful they must be that it's thawing !'

'Why don't the fools skate till they are warm ? I'd show them, I know !'

'Ah, my dear, it's right for active young gentlemen like you to be fond of athletic sports ; but you must make allowance for those who can't do the same, and bear the disappointment like a man. We all have our trials.'

'What are you going to do with that bundle, Mrs. Towels?'

'That's some linen for the washerwoman, my dear. Jinks will take it round by-and-by.'

'Oh, I say, let me take it. I've got an umbrella. It's so slow stopping in all day. I know where she lives.'

'It's very polite of you, Master Bertram, to wish to save the domestics trouble; and as I know Jinks is busy, I am sure Dr. Porchester would not mind your going. Now, can I trust you, my dear, to go straight to Mrs. Bugler's, and not get into any mischief?

'Oh, rather! I'll be back again in no time!'

So saying, the Dumpling caught up the bundle and disappeared.

He fetched his umbrella from his bedroom, and also slipped his skates inside the bundle. Then he sallied forth and ran in the direction of Mrs. Bugler's for some way down the road;—her cottage was about half a mile off;—but instead of keeping in the right direction, he branched off into a certain lane, and then took to the fields, and arrived at the margin of a piece of water known as Higham's Pond. It was his intention to enjoy a little surreptitious skating if the condition of things admitted it.

The pond was shallow enough near the banks, and possibly seven or eight feet deep in the middle. The ice was just covered with water, but firm enough to the foot. The Dumpling tested it gingerly at first, and walked close to the edge. Then he got bolder and found it to be reliable. He had skated once or twice before some years back, and could get along pretty comfortably the last time he tried. He therefore bound on his skates, and with a view to the protection of his person he fastened the bundle of linen round his waist with string, in such a way that should he unfortunately fall backwards the force of concussion might be broken by the bundle. He was, as we

know, a lad of ready resource, and it further occurred
to him that the linen buffer might materially lessen
the chances of his breaking the ice by a fall.

Cautiously enough did he first begin, like a monkey
stealing roasted chestnuts. The ice was the perfec-
tion of smoothness, just softened by the rain to the
finest nicety, so that his skates travelled over it with
delectable ease, and even his natural clumsiness could
not prevent the execution of some graceful curves,
which brought satisfaction to his heart and a flush to
his chubby cheeks.

He had twice made a tour round the pond, keeping
close to the sides, and now felt confident that the ice
was firm enough to bear an elephant. Therefore he
determined no longer to hug the shore, but strike
across boldly.

' Oh, isn't this crackey, just!   Hi cockolorum ! '

Such prosperity might fain arouse apprehensions
of Nemesis.

The Dumpling had been beating up against the
wind towards the place where he had stuck his umbrella in the bank. He now took up and opened
that instrument, and catching the wind, proceeded at
a rapid rate towards the middle of the pond.

I am not going to drown my hero, because it
would not be in strict accordance with historical
truth ; neither am I going to make him tumble
through the ice and be hardly rescued from a watery
grave ; because, if ever I let him get below the surface, I don't think I should be able to get him up
again. But a very disagreeable situation awaits him
as he sails majestically onwards.

The whole surface of the pond was covered with
half an inch of rain, which rendered it uniform in
appearance. The keenest scrutiny could not have
detected any variation in the character of the ice.
But towards the middle of the pond the process of
freezing had been partially arrested by the wind.
The ice had been rendered uneven ; sundry floating

pieces of stick had become entangled as it froze. There were patches of very thin ice interspersed with the firmer substance about this region, and it came about that as the fat boy sailed on, his right skate went wrong over a stick, whereby his equilibrium was rudely disturbed.

His first inclination was to fall head foremost into his open umbrella ; then by a violent effort of recovery, even as one pulls up a stumbling horse, the Dumpling gathered himself together, and threw himself back with such emphasis that his balance in the opposite direction was irrecoverably lost ; his legs flew up from under him ; his umbrella was turned inside out, and he fell with a crash. The bundle of linen was not exactly where it should have been to break the fall. The fall instead broke the ice. There was a great cracking commotion ; angular fragments of ice rose up like figures of Euclid around him. The Dumpling's whole system sustained a very alarming shock. The foundations of earth seemed shaken.

With the instinct of self-preservation he threw out his legs and arms to their full reach, and providentially found them more or less upon firm ice ; but the bundle now became immersed in water where he had broken through. Thus he was held prisoner in the sternest bondage. It was absolutely impossible for him to escape. If he ventured to shift his position, an ominous sound warned him that he was forfeiting the precarious support afforded to his extremities by trustworthy ice. He dared not even employ one hand and arm in getting out his pocket-knife to sever the string and release the bundle. For had he so done, the risk would have been great of his subsiding entirely through the aperture.

CHAPTER II

'WOULD you buy an orange, sir? They're good oranges.'

'I haven't got any money with me.'

'Thank you, sir.'

The first of the speakers was a shabby-looking individual in threadbare coat of blue serge, who carried a reed basket containing perhaps twenty oranges. The other was Dr. Porchester. It was the same afternoon described in the last chapter.

The doctor went on his way, taking long strides, like the ghost of Achilles in the asphodel meadows of Hades. He walked to a given goal, and then turned and walked back again. He had an hour for exercise, and got as much as he could out of it. On his homeward march he again overtook the shabby individual, who looked up and said, as the doctor passed, 'It's not much to be made of this kind of business, sir.'

There was something in the man's face which pleaded for further notice. The doctor moderated his pace, and said, 'No, I suppose not; and your coat looks thin for this sort of weather.'

'Yes, sir; I had to pawn my waistcoat yesterday. It is chilly work, but a man must live.'

'Where do you live?'

'I don't live anywhere, sir; I've no home. My parents died when I was eleven years old, and I was brought up at the plough's tail. I'm fifty-four years old, and never had a home. I'm lodging just now at a cottage the other end of the village. I've been fourteen weeks in the hospital with asthma, and only came out last week. I suppose you couldn't give me a job in the garden, sir?'

'No; I'm afraid not. But you could get something to do in the neighbourhood, I dare say.'

The man said he had tried all about without success. He had bought the oranges, a quarter of a hundred, for tenpence halfpenny, and was trying to sell them.

'This rain must be bad for you, if you're just recovering from asthma. If I gave you a waistcoat would you pawn it to-morrow?'

'No, sir. I've made some money to-day; I've made eightpence; that will be fourpence for a night's lodging and fourpence over.'

'What have you had to eat to-day?'

'Nothing since breakfast, sir; then I had a ha'porth of tea and a ha'porth of sugar and some dripping toast.'

'As much as you could eat?'

'Well, no, sir; but when you can't get as much as you can eat, you must eat as much as you can get.'

'Do you ever have any meat?'

'Sometimes, sir. I had a bit of a fag-end of a mutton-bone one day last week. I mostly sop bread in tea, with a little sugar.'

'When was the last time any one gave you a shilling?'

'I don't remember, sir; it must have been a long time ago. The workmen sometimes give me a halfpenny, or even a penny; but I don't know that I ever had a shilling given me.'

'Do you drink?—I mean, if I gave you a shilling should you spend it on gin or beer?'

'No, sir; I haven't been inside a public-house for two years.'

'Are you sure? Do you ever say your prayers?'

'Well, sir, I speak to God in a prayerful way; I ask Him to keep me, and He does. One door opens and another shuts. He sent me here to-day to meet you.'

'There's no doubt about that,' said the doctor. 'If you will walk back to my house I will give you a waistcoat; and mind, if ever I meet you again I shall expect to see it on you.'

'So you shall, sir; and I'm very thankful to you, sir.'

They walked back to Highfield House. The man stood in the porch, and the doctor went indoors and rummaged about in his bedroom, and then went and performed a similar operation in a drawer of his writing-table. He then saw the shabby individual put on the waistcoat, and when that was accomplished the doctor put a half-crown into each of the begrimed hands of his new acquaintance. Perhaps you can imagine the man's gratitude and amazement, but I do not think you can. At any rate, Dr. Porchester thought it a fair return for his kindness, and watched a man pass out of his gates who was for the moment probably as happy as any one in the world.

Now, boys, I have been making use of the worthy doctor on this occasion because I wanted to weave this episode into my story; but understand that it is word for word a conversation which I had with a man yesterday (as I write), and I wish you to know how that man lived. Curiously enough, that very day at dinner I had occasion to rebuke a young gentleman who was reported by one of the servants for continually refusing to eat his slices of the best mutton. Boys are sometimes guilty of despising their food at school. I remember once seeing a plate of scraps left by boys at the dinner-table of a great public school. It was being carried by a servant across the road to the headquarters of the poultry department. A poor boy was passing. The servant asked him for a joke if he would like some. The boy's eye glistened, and he just fell upon the plate like a famished animal, and devoured the scraps as though he had never before enjoyed such a treat. Facts like these should make us realize the blessing of always having plenty of good food. I dare say some of us are no more deserving than that shabby individual and that famished boy. The least we can do is to eat our meat with thankfulness and without dainty waste, and join in the Grace without hypocrisy.

The shabby individual hardly knew what to make

of the doctor's generosity. He shuffled on at his best pace, until a glow of warmth pervaded his body such as he had not felt since last summer. He rubbed his chest and sides, to enhance the comfort of sufficient clothing, and enjoy the satisfaction of realizing that the heat he developed was not radiated into space. He paid a visit to the grocer's establishment for some necessary supplies, and then started for Stringer's cottage, where he was lodging, with a view to spending a pleasant evening in the chimney corner.

Now every one who knows the neighbourhood of Highfield House must be aware that nearly half a mile is saved by going across the fields from the church to Stringer's cottage instead of going round by the road. The shabby individual would therefore naturally choose that way, and as the path led past Higham's Pond, why, of course his attention was attracted by the shouts of the Dumpling. That ill-starred youth, lying like a water-logged vessel in the trough of the sea, was not likely to let a chance sail pass without an effort to signal his distress. And so the shabby individual arrived at the margin of the pond.

'I say, you chap, come and help me out, there's a good fellow.'

The basket of oranges was at once put down, and the owner began hobbling over the ice till he reached the prostrate Dumpling.

'Got a knife? Just cut that string, and then give us a hand.'

The string was soon cut, and the bundle of linen sank to the bottom of the pond.

After laborious exertion the shabby one succeeded in towing the fat boy from his moorings and landing him on firm ground. Bertram was stiff and numbed with cold; and had it not been for the solid accumulation of fat with which his bones were clothed it would have gone badly with him. As it was he felt half frozen, and could with difficulty take off his skates. When, however, this was accomplished, and he had taken a brisk run round the pond, his circulation was restored, and his native spirit recovered strength. His eyes now fell upon the basket of oranges which the man of shabby raiment was preparing to remove from the scene. The prospect of 'grub' was not to be despised.

'Hullo, what jolly oranges! I wish I had some money, I know. What are you going to do with them?'

'I'll be taking them home, sir; not likely to meet with any more customers now. You're welcome to one. I've had a stroke of luck this afternoon. Look there! A gentleman gave me this waistcoat and a couple of half-crowns.'

'I say, you're a lucky chap. I wish I was you. But, I say, when you cut that string, it let a bundle of things I was carrying go to the bottom of the pond. D'you think you could fish them up?'

'I don't know. One good turn deserves another. Lend me the umbrella, sir. The pond isn't deep. I think I could reach them.'

The shabby individual proceeded cautiously to the edge of the hole, and lying down full length upon the ice, he began rummaging with the umbrella, immersing his arm nearly up to the shoulder.

'I can feel 'em! I'll have 'em in a minute.'

The Dumpling watched the operation from the bank. The man was supporting himself with his left hand resting on the ledge of ice across the hole. He had just succeeded in raising the saturated bundle, and was pushing it into safety with the umbrella, when suddenly, without warning, the ice beneath him gave way, and he subsided into the water. He clutched frantically with his left hand, and as he grounded on the soft mud at the bottom of the pond his head and shoulders were above water. He gasped out the words, 'Oh dear, oh, it's mighty cold!' and tried to raise himself, but the ice was now so insecure that it kept breaking away as his weight bore upon it.

The Dumpling speedily got hold of the bundle and umbrella, and shuffled off the ice the moment this was accomplished. When on safe ground he called out :—

' Hullo, you've tumbled in, old chap! What a go! Never mind, you were wet through before, and now you're wet through behind! Ha! ha! I'm sorry I can't stop to drag you out, but you're all right. I shall be late if I don't hurry on. Sorry I can't stop. I'll take that orange you said you'd give me.'

So saying, he coolly filled his pockets with at least eight oranges, shouldered the bundle on the end of his umbrella, and hurried on to the washerwoman's cottage. There he delivered the linen, with a facetious remark about its having been half-washed already, and so he should claim half the payment. And without a thought for the man whom he had left wallowing in the icy water, the Dumpling made the best of his way back by the road to Highfield House.

CHAPTER III

HOW it fared with the Dumpling when he got back an hour late for school ; how he shuffled out his excuses, saying that he had gone an errand for the matron and got wet and had to change his things ; how Mr. Fields was constrained to admit his excuses with the assurance that he should ask the matron for further particulars, and how these seemed to tally fairly with the boy's version—are items which may be dismissed without more remark, as not bearing with any importance upon the course of our story.

Next day, after dinner, when Dr. Porchester was transacting his bank business in the schoolroom, he

was surprised at the Dumpling's requesting to deposit
half a crown.

'Why, Bertram, this is the first time you have
patronised my bank this term. Whence comes this
sudden influx of wealth? I hope it will remain in
my safe keeping longer than the last. If I remember
correctly, last term you put in the same sum on the
Ides of September, and, like the usurer Alphius,
asked to have it out again on the Kalends of
October.'

The Dumpling grinned as though he understood
the allusion.

There was nothing very extraordinary in the fact
that any boy should put half a crown into the school
bank. But there was something about this particular coin which evidently interested Dr. Porchester.
While talking to Bertram he had been turning it over
in his hand, and suddenly he stopped and looked in-
tently at the half-crown, and felt its edge. Then he
looked at the boy with a puzzled expression, and
seemed on the point of asking him a question. But
he refrained, and finding there was no further business to be done, he shut up the cash-box, closed the
book, and proceeded with them out of the schoolroom.
The general din of boyish mirth and frolic soon
obliterated any uncomfortable sensations that might
have been aroused in the Dumpling's mind by his
monetary transactions with the doctor.

That evening after prayers, when the boys were all
in bed and most of them asleep, in the hour when a
master likes to throw himself into a very easy chair
and snatch a few moments of well-earned repose
after the strong labours of the day, Dr. Porchester
was sitting with his sister in the drawing-room. She
was busy with the needle. He was dozing over the
current number of the *Quarterly Review*. Jinks
entered with two cups of coffee, and when our revered
chieftain had drunk his quota of that refreshing
beverage his somnolent inclinations were partially

allayed; and after reading a page or two, he addressed his sister thus :—

'By the bye, Rachel, a curious thing happened this afternoon. Bertram put half-a-crown into the bank. That in itself is a circumstance of no small singularity; but a still stranger feature about it is, that the half-crown was the identical coin that I gave to a poor man.'

'Really, John? This is indeed odd. How can you be convinced of the identity?'

'Well, it happened to be the very half-crown I used last Tuesday, when I showed you that trick of spinning a coin and predicting the issue of head or tail by the sound. You remember my explaining the secret of cutting a notch on the edge, and raising a small tongue of the metal. You also remember scratching a small cross upon the coin. Bertram's half-crown presented both these marks, and I am curious to know how it can have come into the boy's possession. The man is lodging at Stringer's cottage, and I shall walk that way to-morrow and try to clear up the mystery.'

So the next day Dr. Porchester visited the cottage in his afternoon's walk. The mistress received him with respectful deference; and in answer to the doctor's inquiries about his new acquaintance, she said, 'He's in a turble bad way, sir, and this is how it was. We were just sitting down to tea about six o'clock last evening, when Joe Smith, who works at the Knap Farm, came in, and said there was a chap half frozen to death in Higham's Pond. William went out at once, and between 'em both they managed to pull the poor fellow out, and found him to be the same as is lodging with us. They carried him here, and I got him to bed and tucked him up warm in the blankets. But, oh! sir, he was raving mad all night, and coughing his heart out, till it was pitiful to hear him; and neither William nor me got a wink of sleep.'

Dr. Porchester's brow contracted. 'It is a very sad

business, Mrs. Stringer.   Have you any idea how he managed to tumble into the pond?'

'No, sir; it's impossible to make anything of what he says. He was quite insensible when he came in last night, and as cold as ice. And when he had been in bed about an hour, the warmth seemed to revive him a bit, and he began muttering and rampaging, and William had to hold him down. He said once clearly enough, "Oh, it's mighty cold; I've got 'em; you can have an orange." We heard those identical words distinctly. Then he said something about "half-crowns," and that seemed to set him off raving worse than ever. He seemed to want to get up, and waved his arms about in a wild way, sure enough. It was horrible to see him.'

'Did you send for Dr. Clark?'

'Yes, sir; Joe Smith went round for him, and he said we must keep him warm, and he gave him some physic, and said he'd come and see him this afternoon.'

The master of Highfield House went upstairs and found the unfortunate man dozing in a troubled sleep. His breathing was painful and spasmodic, interrupted often by a short, distressing cough. Dr. Porchester could not stay long, but on his return walk he called at Dr. Clark's, and ascertained that the man's condition was very dangerous. He was suffering from fever and acute inflammation of the lungs. There was nothing to be done but keep him warm, and give him milk and broth to sustain his strength; but his constitution seemed weak, and Dr. Clark had the gravest doubts of his recovering.

Jinks was dispatched that evening to the cottage with a plentiful supply of liquid nourishment. Meantime preparation went on as usual in the schoolroom of Highfield House.

Hiding his face deep down behind the lid of his open desk, Thomas Bertram was devoting his entire energies towards consuming the juicy contents of his last orange. He had softened it previously by a course of gentle pressure. He had then with his knife removed a circular disc of peel at the spot where the fruit once adhered to its parent tree. And having thus prepared the orange, Bertram was feeding on its luscious substance by suction. He who knew how to 'suck up' to his companions when expediency demanded was not ignorant how to 'suck down' the flesh of an orange. So carefully was the operation performed that the entire contents of the fruit were removed without any rupture of the peel. The Dumpling then blew the hollow globe of peel full of wind.

He now cast a glance at Mr. Fields, who was superintending our studies that evening ; and seeing that his attention was apparently absorbed in correcting exercises, the Dumpling reached forth his hand and took from its hole a gallipot of ink, and very cautiously poured its contents into the phantom orange, and replaced the disc of peel without allowing any trace of ink to be visible on the outside. Having concluded this operation, Bertram put the prepared article in a corner of his desk, shut the lid, and made a pretence of applying himself to the lesson which had so far been neglected.

But as he sat drowsing over the book and lolling over his desk, his thoughts were deeply working upon what he should do with the transformed spectre of his orange. First of all he said within himself that he would present it to Buffles, and enjoy the discomfiture which would ensue when that deluded youth should put it to his mouth and give a scrunch and a squeeze to get at the inside. Then he thought it would be better fun to take it out of his pocket with feigned caution during the French lesson next day, and provoke Monsieur Delamere to confiscate it. He thought that would be a fine joke, especially if he took the other fellows into confidence.

But his meditations were prematurely cut short by a voice from the magisterial throne.

'Bertram, as usual you have been idling the greater part of preparation. Just bring me that orange which has so occupied your attention.'

This was indeed an unexpected surprise. The Dumpling thought he was as wary as most boys in acquainting himself with the bent of a master's observation; but he had obviously been outwitted this time. He looked round with a start, and turned red in the face, and said, 'What, sir?'

'Bring me that orange—can't you hear?'

There was no evading this command. With slow and shambling steps the Dumpling advanced towards Mr. Fields' desk, bearing the phantom fruit in his hand. The eyes of all the boys were centred upon him with keen anticipations of sport. Few things are appreciated by boys with greater relish than the humiliation of a coarse and vulgar bully at school; and Mr. Fields, to judge from his countenance, was not less interested in circumventing the fat boy. His face expressed a comical mixture of disgust and severity, and his words were winged with lightning.

'You're the idlest fellow in the school, Bertram. I'm weary of speaking to you. Bad marks and impositions are wasted on you. Stand on that form and eat that orange at once, and try and feel ashamed of yourself!'

'Oh, sir!'

'*Oh, sir!* No nonsense; do as you're told without a word! I am on the point of reporting you to the doctor for incorrigible idleness. Don't provoke me further!'

The Dumpling 'reared himself upon his hind legs,' to quote an expression from a famous writer of school stories, put the orange to his mouth, and pretended to obey the master's order. Mr. Fields' piercing eye was upon him, like a cat glaring at a rat.

'No shamming—bite it and squeeze it—you're fond enough of orange-juice, I know. You need not be shy.'

The Dumpling knew that he was in for it, and was thoroughly cowed. His hands trembled as the boys were beginning to laugh. He looked round, but the menace of his look was eclipsed by his confusion. Mr. Fields brought his hand smartly down upon the desk. The Dumpling started, and gave a spasmodic squeeze to the orange without intending it. There was a spit and a sputter, and the ink came squirting out over his face and hands. He let the orange drop with a groan of dismay, and rubbed his hand and arm over his face to clear away the obnoxious mess. This only made matters worse, imparting to his rubicund cheeks the complexion of a dissipated negro, while explosions of laughter re-echoed through the room.

Let us draw the curtain, and leave this ill-starred youth till the next chapter, to evaporate from his ridiculous position.

CHAPTER IV

WHEN Dr. Porchester took an interest in any one he was not a man to do things by halves. Like Cyrus the Younger, of whom we read in the history of Xenophon, he made it his first concern to surpass all men in acts of princely munificence to those who rejoiced in his friendship. For three days in succession had the worthy master of Highfield House paid visits to the cottage at the other end of the village, taking with him such remedial and strengthening necessaries as his kind and wise heart suggested.

But it was a battle on unequal terms. Disease had clasped its icy fingers firmly round the lungs and heart of the sick man, and seemed determined to defy all the gentle opposition of warmth and medicine and good nourishment. The cough did not abate ; the temperature did not fall ; the pulse grew more uncertain ; the outlines of the sufferer's face grew sharper and more deeply drawn from day to day. Dr. Clark seemed less hopeful after each visit, and pronounced the symptoms to be so serious that life seemed overbalanced in the scale, and outmatched in the struggle against death.

Dr. Porchester had not said anything to Bertram about the matter, nor made any attempt to solve the mystery of the half-crown. It was just a week after his first interview with the shabby individual. Dr. Porchester had called as usual at the cottage in the afternoon, and for the first time found the sick man in clear possession of his senses. It seemed as if life was suddenly called back from the verge of death. Hitherto he had lain in a dull stupor, not seeming to recognise any one. But that afternoon there was a change. A smile crept over the emaciated features, and the thin hand was feebly outstretched in welcome. Dr. Porchester took it in his mighty palm, and cold, bony fingers pressed warm, vigorous flesh. The sick man faintly murmured, 'God bless you, sir, for all your goodness ! I shan't trouble you much longer ; I'm done for this time.'

'Well, my poor fellow, you're better to-day than you were yesterday ; able to talk for the first time. I've been often to see you, and you haven't seemed to know me till to-day.'

'I have seen you in my dreams, sir ; terrible dreams —such rumblings in the head—wheels and fireworks.'

'Ah, you must not talk much ; I will say a prayer for you, and then you must try and go to sleep.'

Dr. Porchester knelt down and said a few fervent words. He then wrote on a large sheet of paper in bold imitation of printing, 'God is my Father ; Christ died to save me; for His sake, O merciful God, pardon my sins ; into Thy hands I commend my spirit !' This paper he pinned on the wall, so that the eyes of the sick man might rest upon it without effort.

And in the silent watches of the night that followed

a change for the worse drew rapidly on. The breathing became a series of short, quick gasps ; the lungs seemed choked ; and after a long, laboured struggle the lamp of life flickered and fell, and the wearied spirit left the poor wasted body of the sick man.

Two days after this Dr. Porchester told us there would be no lessons in the afternoon, as he had to attend a funeral. He said we might have walks instead of football. He gave this out after dinner. None of us made any demonstration, as is usually the case on such a remittance of work. The Dumpling alone seemed inclined to express satisfaction ; and those near him heard him whisper, ' Hi, cockolorum, there's a half ! ' But there was a look in the doctor's eye which instantly repressed his further utterance.

Dawson and I went out together that afternoon. We passed the church as the funeral came up. The coffin was carried by William Stringer, Joe Smith, and two other men whose names we did not know. Dr. Porchester and Mr. Fields were the only persons following it. We went into the church, and heard Dr. Porchester read the service, and felt very white ; and I don't think we could help crying somehow. The doctor's voice was so solemn, and often faltered ; but the way he read the lesson I shall never forget. When he came to the words, ' It is sown in dishonour, it is raised in glory ; it is sown in weakness, it is raised in power ' ; and when he prayed that, ' when we shall depart this life we may rest in Christ, as our hope is this our brother doth,' his voice sounded as I never heard it sound before ; and a sort of faintness crept over me.

And then we slipped out and walked on, neither of us saying a word till we got back to school.

*   *   *   *   *

The next day, at bank-time, the Dumpling was among those boys who wished to transact business. There were several fellows standing round the doctor ;

I think most of them were in the schoolroom. The
Dumpling came forward.

'A shilling, please, sir.'

The doctor put down his pencil, and turned one of
his keen glances full upon the red cheeks of the fat
boy. It was a glance calculated to make any one
quail who had an evil conscience. The Dumpling's
eyes could not meet it. He stood in a sheepish
attitude, kicking one foot against the form and
fidgeting with the lowest button of his waistcoat.

'How dare you ask me for money!'

'Me, sir? I put in half a crown the other day;
I haven't had it out, have I, sir?'

'No, you haven't. I am not going to ask you any
questions about that money, for fear of tempting you
to tell an untruth; but I must find out how you
came to get possession of that half-crown.'

The boys in the schoolroom had crowded round.
Rumour soon spread that there was a row. From
the playground and library contingents gathered, so
that all the boys must have been present.

'Now, Bertram, fetch me a sheet of school-paper.
Now sit at your desk and write down full particulars
of all that happened on that afternoon when you took
the bundle of clothes to the washerwoman; and if I
detect the semblance of a falsehood, I shall punish
you with the utmost severity.'

'Oh, sir, please, sir! Oh, sir, I didn't mean to;
I'll never do it again, sir! Oh, please let me off this
once!'

The Dumpling had thrown himself upon his knees.

'Get up! don't drivel and blubber there! Do as I
tell you instantly.'

The fat boy got up sobbing and quaking. He took
the paper and went to his desk, and began to write,
though his hand trembled so that he could scarcely
get the pen to form the letters. At the end of some
minutes he stopped.

'Have you finished?'

'Yes, sir.'

'Then bring me the paper.'

The doctor read what was written out loud, amid breathless silence. 'I went to Higham's Pond, and skated, and tumbled in, and a man helped me out, and gave me an orange, and I took some, and got wet, and came home, and was late for school, and changed.'

'Is that the whole truth?'

'Yes, sir, I think so.'

Whenever a boy is obliged 'to think so' about such a matter, it is a bad sign. It is a very lamentable thing when a boy says anything to shake a master's confidence in his word. A breach of confidence is like the breaking of water through the barrier of a dyke. The breach widens, until all hope of repairing the mischief is ruined.

'You *think* so!' said the doctor. 'Before saying what *I think* upon the matter, I shall do my utmost to find out more particulars. Until then I defer passing sentence upon you. But you have not told me how you got the half-crown.'

With face ashy pale, and in a husky voice, the Dumpling answered, 'My uncle sent it to me, sir.'

Dr. Porchester sprang from his seat, and lifted his hand as if to smite the Dumpling to the earth. Two small boys, who had been standing very near, disappeared under the desk. The Dumpling hid his face in his arms, and backed through the crowd. I never saw the doctor strike a boy with his hand the whole time I was at Highfield House; but I thought he was going to then.

'You dare to tell me a deliberate lie! I tried to save you!'

So saying, the doctor snatched up his cash-box and banking-book, and rushed out of the room.

This *was* an excitement! We gathered round the Dumpling, and some of the boldest began to ask him questions; but he glared at us like a savage bull-dog, and said 'he'd lick us all round if we didn't shut up bothering.' So we drifted away by degrees, and went into the playground, and were soon hard at football.

The Dumpling sulked by himself in the schoolroom. I wouldn't have been him for something! We did not interfere with him any more. Our curiosity was not to be satisfied for the present; and there was not a boy who cared to have more to do with him than he could help—not even Buffles and Guzzling Jim.

The doctor had gone to his study, where he had left Mr. Fields reading the *Morning Post*. The doctor had thrown himself into an arm-chair to recover from his agitation; and then he said, 'Fields, Bertram has just told me a horrible lie. It's the last straw; I must write to his father to remove him at once. But we must clear up the business somehow. The boy seems to have been at the bottom of that poor fellow's getting into the water. Mrs. Towels tells me she let him take a bundle of my shirts to the washerwoman's that afternoon. Bertram says he skated on Higham's Pond and fell in, and the poor fellow helped him out. Then from what the poor fellow hinted in his rambling utterances to Mrs. Stringer, it would seem that the bundle had something to do with it; and I feel sure that Bertram somehow managed to rob him of the half-crown. Shall we go to the washerwoman, and see if she can add any evidence?'

'Certainly, doctor; I think it is the best thing we can do.'

So the two masters walked to the washerwoman's cottage. All that they could ascertain from her was, that the bundle was soaked through, and 'in a turble scurmage of black mud, so that she hadn't never seen the likes of it, and thought as how she should never get the shirts clean again.'

'Black mud,' said the doctor, as they walked home. 'Where could the black mud come from? There is no black mud about except at the bottom of the pond. The linen must have been dragged along the bottom of the pond; eh?'

'It looks like it,' answered Mr. Fields.

I know not what further conversation the two masters had about the matter. But when four o'clock came, instead of going to the classrooms, we were all told to sit at our desks in the schoolroom.

Dr. Porchester came in and called up Bertram, and said, 'I am resolved to settle this matter at once, Bertram. When you took that bundle for Mrs. Towels, you skated on Higham's Pond and fell in; and a poor man helped you out?'

'Yes, sir.'

'How did the bundle come to get into the pond and covered with black mud?'

'It tumbled in, sir.'

'And the man got it out for you, and fell in during the operation, didn't he?'

'Yes, sir.'

'Now tell me this, Bertram. When you saw the man in the water, why didn't you try to help him out, or, at least, tell some one he was there?'

'I thought I should be late for school, sir.'

'If you ever thought about anything in your life, why didn't you think that it was little short of murder to leave a poor fellow up to his neck in icy water, without any effort to save him? Are you aware that your miserable recklessness has caused his death? Are you aware that you may be tried for manslaughter?"

The fat boy looked deadly pale, and did not speak.

'I have one more question to ask you,' proceeded the doctor, in a voice of solemn authority: 'How did you rob him of that half-crown?'

Dr. Porchester had risen from his chair and taken hold of Bertra s shoulders with his two hands, and held him as in a vice in such a position that the boy's

M

face should be fully presented to the doctor's gaze. And as he uttered these words the doctor looked into the boy's eyes as though he would read the very thoughts of his heart.

The fat boy could not help meeting that gaze for a moment. It seemed to shrivel his soul. He turned his head uneasily as if in mortal pain. And then in a weak and wearied voice he hoarsely whispered, 'I took it from his purse in the basket, sir.'

Dr. Porchester took his hands from Bertram's shoulders, and drew back a foot, and stood looking at him in awful silence. The wretched boy slowly lifted his arms and buried his face in them and staggered to a seat.

We were told to get our books and go to the classrooms. And that was the last we ever saw of the fat boy. Dr. Porchester wrote to Bertram's father that afternoon, and two days after Mr. Bertram came down and took his boy away from Highfield House.

A Smuggling Adventure

CHAPTER I

N OW, then, Jack Spratt, what are you doing up
there ?'

'Hsh! cave, you ass!'

This reply was whispered with considerable emphasis, and its immediate effect was to make old Hercules
squat down on his haunches like an overgrown frog.
He had come round a corner to a portion of the playground where for some time past builders had been
busy with bricks and mortar. The new wing, destined
to be studies for the senior boys, was in course of
erection, and it was only natural that we should take
a lively interest in the operations.

It was good sport to climb up the perpendicular
scaffold-poles, and then circle the horizontal ones ; it
was pleasant to get into the bucket used for raising
materials to the upper storey, while some willing hand
hauled you up by the rope which passed round a
small wheel above ; and when you got to the top it
was exciting to push and struggle till the basket
began to rock like a pendulum ; and then, when the
oscillation was sufficient, to clutch hold of the frame
of a window or the angle of a wall, and so gain a
standing-place. All this was sport enough, but it had
to be indulged in cautiously, for in one quarter such
recreations were by no means regarded with approval.

The doctor did not much mind our extemporising
gymnastic feats upon the scaffold-poles. He liked us
to be active, and said it was good practice to climb

the long pole in the gymnasium. Neither did the workmen offer any objection. They were friendly disposed, and we used to cultivate their favour by bits of cake, or apples and oranges—not to say an occasional pot of jam when some hamper of unusual dimensions had arrived. We used to call them by their nicknames. One, I remember, was known as 'Yorkshire Pudding,' and another as 'Gooseberry Jam,' and a third as 'Irish Stew.'

It was Miss Porchester whose motherly regard for our necks and limbs made her tremble whenever she happened to see any of us suspended in mid-air, and 'risking our precious lives,' as she was pleased to term it. That good lady would sometimes emerge from a doorway in the house communicating with the upper storey of the new wing. She would gird up the folds of her dress and pick her way along the temporary platform, and venture as far as possible among the skeleton walls; and if haply she espied any boy engaged in the exercises which caused her alarm, she would call upon him to desist—as anxious for our safety as an old hen who sees her brood of ducklings take their first paddle in the pond.

On this particular occasion Jack Spratt was comfortably seated in the basket, his head and shoulders protruding on one side, and his legs hanging over from the knee downwards on the other. He had the rope in his hands, and being a youth of active habits, he was hauling himself up into the aërial regions.

Just as Hercules came round the corner Jack had caught sight of Miss Porchester, treading the plank causeway above; and he was meditating rapidly what course to pursue in prospect of the near approach of the enemy. Therefore, he was by no means pleased at hearing himself accosted in a loud voice, which would certainly draw more attention to his person than he desired. Hence his ungracious reply.

Miss Porchester came on, and in less than ten seconds she would be in full view of Spratt. But he was equal to the emergency, for he slackened the rope, and before our lady-superior caught sight of him, his descent was accomplished, and he had alighted with a solid flump on firm ground. Then, turning over on his hands and feet, with the basket on his back, like the carapace of a tortoise, he executed some rapid movements on all-fours, much to the amusement of the workmen.

Hercules wanted to speak to Spratt on a matter of importance, so without much ceremony he soon put an end to these frolics. He caught hold of the basket and pushed it over, so that Spratt was laid upon his side, and crawled out without more ado.

Miss Porchester seemed to be satisfied that danger was averted, for she did not appear as the two boys sauntered off with occasional glances upwards.

'I say, Jack,' said Hercules, taking him by the arm, 'I actually asked the doctor yesterday if he would mind my training Cacus to ride on. It was rather cheeky, but he did not seem to mind; in fact, he was rather jolly about it.'

'Well, did he say you might?'

'He said he would speak to Miss Porchester about it. That was the worst part of it. She's sure to think I shall be kicked off and break my neck. But I wrote home first, and they don't mind. The gover-

nor says it does boys good to be kicked off and break
their necks—it hardens them—so perhaps she will let
me try.'

Miss Porchester was certainly reluctant to give her
consent; but when the letter was produced, and her
brother said there was not any serious risk, she finally
consented to the proposal, on condition that she and
the doctor should witness the first performance, and
if she considered that the proceedings were likely to

be dangerous, they should
be discontinued at once
and for ever. Cacus was
to be bridled, and Dr.
Porchester was to be close
at hand, to render assistance if required.

Two days after this con-
ference, during the first
lesson after breakfast, Hercules was sent for out of
school. He found the
doctor and Miss Porchester
waiting to attend him to
the paddock. Miss Por-
chester stood outside the
railings, while the doctor
and the boy entered the
enclosure.

The result was satisfactory. For some unexplained
reason Hercules had an influence over the great
donkey which no one else could claim. The animal
was generally pronounced to be vicious and vindic-
tive. Probably that opinion was a libel on his true
character, and accounted for by the fact that those
who had dealings with him often teased and bullied
him.

On this occasion Cacus proved as tractable as even
Miss Porchester could wish. Far from resenting the
prospect of servitude, the great donkey trotted up to

Hercules and rubbed his head on his shoulder. Then
followed a little coaxing, and the ass found the halter
round his neck and the boy on his back; and then,
as if conscious of the honour conferred on him in
being permitted to support the person of his friend,
Cacus moved off with stately paces, and walked and

trotted round the field as if he had been accustomed
to such exercise from the cradle.

Miss Porchester's expression of alarm gradually
gave place to one of comparative assurance. The
doctor said, 'Bravo, my boy! you certainly understand the animal. I hope it is not because he recog-
nises in you one of his own kith and kin under

disguise. Jupiter himself once took the form of a bull. The Weaver in the *Midsummer Night's Dream* wore a donkey's head. Can it be that the transformation has ever been reversed? I will not make invidious insinuations, but sometimes in class, you know—well, never mind. You had better get back to your lessons.'

Hercules dismounted and set free his steed, rewarding him with a large carrot which he had pocketed beforehand.

After this there was no objection to the course of training. Every day, when fine, Hercules found opportunity to exercise the donkey, who never showed any tendency to vice or obstinacy under discipline. Sometimes the halter was discarded, for a tuft of mane was found to answer the purpose; while a stroke of the hand on the right or left side of the neck sufficed for steering his course, and a gentle application of the heels was enough to accelerate the speed when desired. Verily the poet was right when he said that by gentleness even fierce bulls are made submissive to the yoke, and he might have said the same of donkeys.

Now before Cacus could be considered to have completed his education, it was necessary to instruct him in the art of jumping. This proved also to be merely a matter of patience and practice. At first a branch of a tree was the obstacle; then a fairly respectable hedge was extemporised; until at length Hercules felt confident of being able to follow the harriers on the back of his steed.

Dr. Porchester was wondrous pleased at the success of his ass-trainer, and promised Hercules that some day, when the hounds met in the neighbourhood, he should join the glad throng. But the promise was never destined to be fulfilled.

Chapter II

THERE was a rule at Highfield House concerning hampers, which (on looking back) I am bound to admit was an excellent rule, though, at the time, it was far from meeting with favour among the boys. All hampers were to be brought to the storeroom, to be unpacked in the presence of Miss Porchester. The storeroom was a commodious apartment well furnished with cupboards and drawers, in which the various eatables were deposited ; and at set times in the day Miss Porchester was 'at home,' and prepared to receive such of her young friends as might happen to possess property therein, and might wish to enjoy its use. Furthermore, she would only deal out pots of jam, etc., on certain nights, and then only permit a limited number to appear on each table. And there were other details in the working of that rule added from time to time, as experience might suggest or expediency demand ; for example, a clause was inserted to the effect that not more than one species of jam was to be seen on any plate at tea-time ; which clause was necessitated by the fact that on one occasion Miss Porchester was horrified to see a boy gloating over his plate, which contained no less than three separate strata of jam — black currant, apricot, and gooseberry — with a sardine floating on the top.

This was too much for Miss Porchester's nerves, hence that clause.

Now this law, though intended to be as vigorous as those of the Medes and Persians, was not always obeyed to the letter. There were occasional evasions of it practised with more or less cunning and success. A species of smuggling was carried on at times, and not every hamper found its way into the store cupboard. Sometimes one might be secreted in the box-room or in the boot-house. I remember one being buried in the ground, and most of its contents were ruined by a thunderstorm. The boy Jack Spratt was performing the acrobatic feat recorded in the first chapter with reference to a hamper which he had good reason to expect would shortly arrive.

He had formed the bold project of raising it by wheel and pulley to the upper storey of the new wing, and secreting it in one of the future studies under a pile of boards intended for the floors. He was nearly floored himself by the sudden appearance of Miss Porchester. For had that lady caught sight of him suspended in mid-air, she would have put pressure upon him to exact a promise never again to risk his life in that way. And had he been liberated on *parole* from the fatal consequences of being reported to the doctor, he would have had to keep his word and find some other hiding-place for his hamper.

However, although he was not caught, yet none the less did circumstances arise to prevent his carrying out his scheme, as the subsequent pages of this veracious history will explain.

The fact was that Spratt had been promised a hamper from home as soon as ever he should be at the top of his class by a week's marks. He was doing his best to achieve that grand distinction, and reap the promised reward. The other boys in his class were quite astonished at the change which had lately come over him. Till now he had been more or less of an idle scapegrace, getting kept in to do impositions almost every half-holiday, because he would not exert himself to work at the proper time.

But now he had changed all that. He ground at his translations, and made 'word-lists' which gladdened the master's heart. His exercises were models of care and neatness; his fingers habitually ached with rapid penmanship in the weekly examinations; in fact, it was clear to every one that Spratt had turned over a new leaf. The other boys could not understand it until he told them, with a grin, one day, and then they were amused right royally.

I need not insinuate that this sordid motive was the only inducement which prompted Spratt to work harder than usual. It certainly was the fuse which ignited the powder of his energy. But when he had once tasted the pleasure of rising above the dull drudgery of impositions and detentions, then ambition added influence, and he stuck to his work, because it gradually became a habit which brought him more genuine satisfaction than he had ever realized under his former course of idleness.

But this condition was not matured until a period rather beyond that covered by this story. Then he was only in the first stage, working and striving to amass marks with a view to earning the promised hamper.

The progress of his enterprise was far from discouraging, and its final success seemed within measurable distance. He had started 9th at the beginning of term, and gained three places the first week. The second week found him 5th, and the third found him actually 2nd.

On the morning when the marks of the third week were read out, Spratt was in a high state of excitement. He felt sure of his hamper at last. He thought he must be top next week, and that very afternoon he wrote home announcing his place, and begging that the hamper might be got ready without delay, as it was almost certain to be wanted the following week.

His father and mother both wrote back, congratulating him and commending his diligence; and he was assured that the hamper should be despatched as soon as ever they heard that he was really top for the week.

Two days passed of the fourth week, and Spratt felt that his work was going on at full speed; though at times he found himself allowing a question to pass in class, through the fact that his mind was so preoccupied with thinking of the reward in prospect. In addressing his Sunday letter home he actually wrote 'Hamperia' instead of 'Hampshire,' and said something in class about the 'garden of the Hamperides.' Trust Mr. Fields not to let such a slip of the tongue pass unnoticed.

'Ah, Spratt,' said he, 'a very poetical idea—the Garden of the Hamperides! What sunny vistas and cool glades open to our enraptured gaze! where through the swooning heat of endless summer days the Sons of the Hamper enjoy perpetual bliss. Methinks I see a group of joyous lads reclining under the shade of the barren plane or dark holm-oak. A hamper is before them, towards which with lazy dalliance they stretch forth their arms for tarts and cakes. A limpid stream of raspberry vinegar flows babbling through the glade, from which anon they quaff refreshing draughts. No need for them to pluck golden apples from the tree; no fear of being gobbled up by a sleepless dragon. The golden apples lie safe in the hamper's depths. Oh, thrice and four times blest are those happy youths!'

Spratt underwent this 'roasting' with what good grace he might. He got very red over it, and the merriment was loud and exuberant. Mr. Fields' eye twinkled as he went on, and he concluded by setting as the subject for our weekly Latin verses—'the Garden of the Hamperides.' Following the line

marked out by his facetious commentary upon that
blissful region, we managed to turn out some effusions
which we thought might fain rouse Ovid's ghost to
envy.

One good effect of Spratt's sudden devotion to his
studies was to wake up other members of his class.
More than one was put upon his mettle. The unin-
terrupted upward march of a fellow who hitherto had
been wont to flounder in the mud at the bottom was
not to go for ever unchallenged. There were Giles
and Dodson, who in the first two weeks held undis-
puted possession of the first two places. There was
Phillips, otherwise called 'Popsy,' who ran them close.
(He was a boy with a parrot-like nose, and his hair
had a curious way of curling forwards over his fore-
head, whence his name, since 'Epops' was found in
the dictionary to be the Latin for a hoopoe.) This
trio had never anticipated any serious interference in
their feudal rights from Spratt, and when they found
him bent upon getting top, they were equally bent
upon preventing him. The
consequence was that they
also put on more steam,
and the tone of general
energy thus imparted to
the work gave the master
of our form much satisfaction. He declared it would
turn his grey hairs black
once more, and save him
the expense of chemical
preparations for giving
back the bloom of departed
youth.

The long and short of
it all was, that when the
marks for the fourth week
were read out amidst
breathless excitement,

Spratt, to his inexpressible disappointment, found himself no higher than fourth! Poor fellow! he was woefully crestfallen. *Væ victis!* In a moment his visions of Hamperia faded like the unsubstantial pageant of a dream. All his anxious hopes were dashed to the ground. He could not do anything that day but indulge in melancholy despair. He wrote home in the afternoon to announce his failure. He said it was no use trying, that other fellows were much cleverer than he was; and he begged that the hamper might be sent in spite of his place in class, for he had so set his heart upon it.

But Spratt's parents were firm, and said that he must not despond, that perseverance would eventually be rewarded, and that he must not expect the hamper until he achieved the proud success of being top for the week.

CHAPTER III

A FORTNIGHT passed, during which time Hercules had steadily continued his training of the big donkey. By Dr. Porchester's permission he had extended the range of his rides. The first time he went outside the premises the ass and his rider occasioned no small stir in the rustic world. They had gone cantering across the common, past Mr. Galpin's establishment, where the boy Simon came out and laughed so uproariously that his master had to come and see what was the matter; down Hangman's Lane, taking a few jumps here and there; and it would be hard to say which of the two enjoyed the excursion most. So expert had Hercules become in the art of asinine equitation that he performed this ride bare-backed, without a bridle or even holding the mane. The donkey being stronger than most of his kind, there was no need to sit far back. Hercules sat him as he would sit a horse, and galloped along like a circus artist.

It was just after the return from this expedition.
Cacus had been set free in the paddock, and Hercules
was closing the gate, when he saw Spratt rushing
towards him with the wildest expressions of joy.
He was brandishing his arms and shouting, and behaving generally as if he had just escaped from
Broadmoor. Spratt made for his friend.

'Oh, I say, I'm top for the week! I've just heard
it from Fields! Oh, I'm so jolly glad at last!' And

the poor fellow was so overcome with emotion that
he burst out in repeated explosions of laughter and
tears.

Hercules slapped him on the back.

'I'm awfully glad, old chap! Hamperia for ever!
Now for the deep dim vistas where oft my fancy
sighs for tarts and buns and oranges, and cake and
apple-pies!'

'I've never had a hamper yet,' said Spratt; 'and

it will be so jolly to give the fellows some grub. They're so awfully kind to me always, and I've never been able to return their kindness. But now they shall have a rare feast! They shall all share it, from the senior monitor to the last chap in the lowest class.'

'Ah, but if madam gets hold of it you'll have to keep it in the store-room.'

'Oh, she mustn't get hold of it. We must manage to smuggle it away somehow. It would be too bad if she only let me have a slip of cake once a day and a pot of jam once a week. I think I shall ask her to let me give a grand feast to all the chaps.'

'She would not let you. She's very particular not to let any fellow think he can change her horrid rules about grub. I would not ask her if I were you.'

'Well, then, we must manage to smuggle it safely, and then we can settle how to dispose of the contents.'

The moment Spratt found an opportunity he seized pen and paper to write home, and composed a letter, in his best style, as follows :—

'MY DEAR FATHER,—

'I am glad to tell you that I am at last top in week's marks, so please send off the hamper at once. Please send four large cakes and at least twelve pots of jam, besides Devonshire cream and sardines, and lots of apples. I should like nuts and oranges, and mince-pies and buns, and two tins of mixed biscuits, and three or four potted tongues and sausage-rolls ; and you might put in a ham, to keep the things steady. I hope it will be a real good one, and the sooner it comes the better. Please let me hear when it will be at the station, that I may look out for it.

'I am, your affectionate Son,

'J. SPRATT.'

Before fastening up this important letter, Spratt further consulted Hercules about the hamper.

'How can we manage to get hold of it before Miss P. pounces on it?'

'Well, the only dodge would be to be in the way when the carrier comes.'

'But we are always in school then. How did Brown manage to get his last term?'

'Oh, he asked one of the workmen to tell the carrier to leave it in the laurels; but it was a risky job, and the carrier wouldn't do it until the workman paid him. He said he should get into no end of a row, and he'd never do it again for any one.'

'Well, look here, Hercules, the carrier must have nothing to do with it. The long and short of it is that you must ride to the station on Cacus and fetch it. Now, will you?'

Hercules was astounded at this proposal, and stoutly refused to undertake such a dangerous job. He said he could never carry it on the donkey's back, and if the doctor caught him there would be trouble.

But Spratt said he could manage it perfectly; the hamper would not be very large, and he could easily get to the station and back between dinner and tea on a half-holiday. Even if the doctor caught him he would not say much, and all he could do would be to make him hand the hamper over to Miss Porchester. But with ordinary precaution they need not be caught.

Spratt's eloquence was so overpowering that Hercules at last expressed himself willing to run the risk. He said he would go to the station on Cacus, and, if possible, fetch the hamper back. If that was impossible, he would call and see the carrier, and try and make arrangements with him to deliver it surreptitiously.

'That's all right,' said Spratt; 'so I'll just put in a postscript. Here goes: "I shall be able to send to the station for the hamper, so please put on the address, 'To be left at Deepwells Station till called for,' and be sure to let me know when it is sent off."'

N

Hercules did not reel at ease about the part he had
undertaken in this transaction. There was one ass,
he said, concerned in it, and he hoped the result
would not prove that there were two, or even three.
But he made the most of the time to practise his
part, for he went off and got an old hamper and filled
it with a motley collection of cricket-pads and old
jam-pots and various curiosities, and hoisted it on to

the back of Cacus while he jumped up behind. At
first the ass decidedly objected to the inconvenience
of the extra burden. He turned his head round and
tried to get a look at it, and flapped his ears and
showed his teeth, and strove to bite the encum-
brance. But Hercules spoke soothing words, and
presented to the vicious teeth a carrot as a peace-
offering. And Cacus, who could never resist such a
tempting morsel, accepted it and seemed pacified,
and consented to perform his task with more or less
submission.

The next day the same performance was repeated

with very satisfactory results. Dr. Porchester happened to come out while the exercise was going on, and watched it with amusement and interest.

'You certainly have succeeded admirably in training the donkey, my boy. The next time I feel disposed to ride, I hope to find him more tractable than

I did the first time. I see you are accustoming him to carry luggage.'

'Yes, sir; he goes so well that I think he ought to be of use in fetching things from the station.'

'Well, I wish you would take him to-morrow to the station and fetch a parcel of books for me. The carrier does not go till the day after, and I particularly want the books. They will not be nearly so awkward as that hamper.'

'All right, sir, I should like to go.'

No letter came for Spratt the next day, and Hercules performed his journey without let or hindrance, and much to his own satisfaction. The great donkey attracted no small attention as they passed through the streets of Deepwells, and when the train ran shrieking by, the animal seemed disposed to show alarm. Yet, even under such a trying ordeal, his composure was restored by a few caressing touches and soothing words, and Hercules had good cause to be pleased with his behaviour. It augured well for the conveyance of the hamper.

CHAPTER IV

THE wished-for letter, announcing that the hamper had been despatched, arrived at last, though not till some days after it had been expected. And now for the great question of transporting it to Highfield House.

It was Saturday morning, and Spratt came running up to Hercules after breakfast with a letter in his hand.

'It was sent off yesterday, and it must be at the station now!'

'Well, I do not feel at all comfortable about bringing it back. Do you know at all what size it is?'

'A jolly good big one, I hope. I told them to put in lots of things, and they're sure to do it in style.'

'I shall never be able to bring it if it's too heavy to lift.'

'Oh, it will be all right. You will not have to carry it. The porter will help you to get it up, and you will only have to keep it steady. You needn't go as if a pack of wolves was coming after you. Take it easy.'

'Well, I will try my best, but I don't believe we

shall get it out of the station-yard without a smash. I believe it would be best to tell the carrier to call for it.'

'Bosh! my good man, I don't want it to get into

the storeroom. I would not give sixpence for a hamper if I was only to have a slice of cake out of it a day, and a pot of jam twice a week. I want all the chaps to have a regular jubilification.'

Dinner was over, and Hercules, fully conscious of the gravity of his undertaking, started for Deepwells station. It took him about three-quarters of an hour to get there, and the journey was accomplished without adventure. On his arrival Cacus was tied up in a shed which formed one of the outbuildings of the station, and Hercules, with beating heart, went to the parcels office to inquire for the hamper. There it was, confronting him upon a rack, and a portentous-looking article it was. He was dismayed at the sight. It was a hamper that stood at least three and a half feet high, and he could not possibly encircle it with his arms. Truly the parents of Spratt had followed out their son's request, and done the thing in style.

It did not need two looks to make Hercules feel sure that he could not by any contrivance take it back on the donkey. He stood staring at the hamper with his hands behind him, the picture of blank disappointment.

'What is there to pay?' he asked, for want of something to say.

'Carriage paid to the station, sir,' said the porter. 'Be you going to take it?'

'Well, I wanted to, but it's too big. I don't want it to go by the carrier, but I suppose it must. When does he go?'

'Let's see: this is Saturday; not till next Tuesday. Tuesdays and Thursdays—them's his days, sir.'

'What a horrid nuisance! Couldn't you send it over to-night?'

'Don't know as we could send it before Monday at soonest. The station cart is gone in the other direction.'

'What would a fly cost?'

'Four-and-six, besides something for the driver. Did you walk over, sir?'

'No, I rode on a donkey, and meant to take back the hamper, if it had been a decent size, but it's as big as a small house.'

'Oh, there, you've no cause to complain of the size. Young gents like you wants lots of good things. There's many that wouldn't mind packing you a smaller one for what's over from the big 'un.'

'Jolly likely. But can't you wheel it over in a barrow? I'd give you a bob—that's all I've got.'

'Couldn't wheel it four miles up all them hills. Did you say you came over on a donkey? You could borrow a cart and harness close by, and we could put the donkey to. What would be easier?'

'That will not do; the donkey has never been in harness in his life.'

'Oh, he'd go if he knows you. A donkey as one can ride will draw a shay-cart all right. Let's see him.'

Hercules escorted the porter to the shed, where Cacus was standing half asleep.

'Well, if he ain't a whopper! Talk about pulling a shay-cart, why, he'd pull a wagon. Bring him along, sir; the cart's close by. We'll put him to, and he'll run you over to the school in no time.'

Hercules thought that the experiment was worth making, and it went through his mind that he had spoken to the doctor about utilising the donkey for fetching things from the station, so that, if he happened to meet the doctor on his way back, he could probably pass it all off without disagreeable consequences. So they proceeded to put him to, and he submitted to the operation with good grace. The hamper, which required two men to lift, was put on board, and Hercules, having arranged to bring the cart back on Monday, set forth on his homeward journey.

He thought it expedient to lead the donkey through the streets, and the animal proved very tractable. Perhaps the sultry weather had made him sleepy, or he may have had such confidence in his master that he did not care to dispute the propriety of this new form of service. The extra weight was nothing.

So they trudged on, the ass and the boy, with progress slow but sure. The hamper rode comfortably enough; no fear of the jam-pots being broken. Hercules regarded it with complaisance, and his feelings towards the parents of Spratt mellowed. He no longer wished them to have sent a smaller one—nay, so easily did the shay-cart go, that he would not have minded if the proportions of the hamper had been even larger. He exulted in the fact that never had such a magnificent specimen been seen at Highfield House, and if the contents were at all commensurate in excellence with the size, truly Spratt might be congratulated upon the generous spirit of his race. So the first mile of the homeward journey was successfully accomplished.

The village had now been left far behind, and Cacus had grown so accustomed to the work that Hercules thought he might as well ride as walk the rest of the way. So he brought the cart to a halt and climbed on board, pushing the hamper farther abaft to adjust the trim. Leaving him to jog along over the next two miles of road, we may return to Spratt.

He had seen Hercules start forth upon the journey, and encouraged him to give good heed to the accomplishment of his important mission. Many of the other boys were in the secret, and they also had assembled to see the valiant knight go forth. The excitement was great, and various were the surmises as to the success of the enterprise. Some said it would be all right, others that it would be all wrong. When, however, the donkey's tail had vanished round the first corner, the boys went off to their respective recreations, and soon forgot about the hamper. Spratt only continued thinking about it. He happened to have some lee-way to make up in his Greek, and rather a lengthy imposition to get through, and so he had gone to the schoolroom. As, with ink-stained fingers cramped around his fine-pointed steel pen, he transcribed the weary lines, he constantly uplifted his

eyes to the schoolroom clock, which ticked away the
lagging moments with stolid indifference. It took
Spratt an hour and a half to get through his work,
and when it was ended he hastily put away his
appliances and set out to meet his friend and escort
him on the last portion of his return journey.

Spratt's excitement was intense as he hurried on
towards the common. Such important destinies hung
upon the thread of fate. It was a convoy of provisions for the school-army of juveniles, and Spratt,
the comptroller of the commissariat, felt the full
weight of responsibility with regard to its safe trans-
mission.

It was now about 4.30 p.m., and a blithesome
summer afternoon. Spratt soon reached the common,
and followed the course of the road by a parallel
route over the heathery ups and downs, through
coppices of birch and fir. The road was always more
or less in view, and, while keeping a sharp look-out
for the first glimpse of his friend, Spratt was minded
to keep out of sight as much as possible, in case any
one should be coming whom it might not be agreeable
to meet.

It was now about the time when Hercules had
entered on the last mile of his journey. The donkey
was trotting along at a very respectable pace, apparently desirous of bringing his labour to an end as
soon as possible.

The cart now turned a corner, and there was disclosed to view a stretch of road extending straight
ahead for a hundred yards or more. There was a
hedge on the left side and open common on the right,
separated from the road by a deep ditch. Now, at
the farther end of this straight piece of road Hercules
espied a female figure walking leisurely away from
him. He came on a little nearer, and the view of the
female figure became more distinct. No second sight
was needed to see that it was Miss Porchester. Hercules instinctively tightened the reins, with the inten-

tion of pulling up, that he might give the lady time to get farther out of range.

Miss Porchester was proceeding very leisurely on her way. She had a taste for botany, and paused once or twice to gather some wild flower at the road-side which arrested her attention. Spratt had his eye upon her from behind the friendly shelter of furze-bushes and birch-trees. He heard the sound of wheels, and, craning his neck in the direction of the sound, he saw the donkey-cart approaching, and had his first enraptured glimpse of the hamper, rising in bold proportions behind the driver. It was an ecstatic moment.

CHAPTER V

NOW Cacus was but an ass, and although judicious training had done much towards softening and civilizing the evil traits of his asinine nature, yet he still shared in some degree the obstinacy characteristic of the more degraded mem-bers of his race. Hercules had tightened the reins with energetic hand at the sight of Miss Porchester, and Cacus was startled out of a dreamy trot by the sudden tension of the bit. There smote upon his senses a consciousness of restraint which was offensive when he had fixed his heart upon reaching the cool pastures of freedom. The ass shook his head and turned back his long ears with a flap by way of protest, but his master showed no inclination to take the hint, and only tightened the reins with stronger force. But Cacus was possessed of prodigious strength, and was evidently determined to have his way. He moved his head with violent jerks and took the bit firmly between his teeth, and after a few preliminary kicks and plunges, he pranced forward with a jump and commenced to gallop.

He was a good one to gallop. He had received such frequent practice in that exercise under the grape and canister of fives-balls and other missiles. And now he plunged forward in a wild stampede, with contemptuous disregard of the rein. At the first plunge, crack went one of the traces!

Now Spratt, when he first sighted the convoy, feeling secure of observation from Miss Porchester, ran forward, picking his way among the furze-bushes, and came up to the cart just as Cacus had settled into his stride at full speed.

Hercules was holding manfully to the reins, jolted and bumped till his jaws rattled, the hamper swaying ominously behind, the cart wheels wobbling over the rough road most uncomfortably. The hamper rocked from side to side, and serious sounds issued from its interior of grinding and colliding jam-pots. Hercules saw Spratt close in front, and shouted to him to catch hold of the rein and stop the runaway ass. But it was no easy matter. Spratt made a valiant dash, but Cacus swerved to avoid him, and in a moment the cart was whirling past in a cloud of dust. But Spratt made a successful grab at the hind-rail and got a firm hold with both hands. And now it was a race of life and death. Spratt, taking long strides, hung on behind; Hercules, leaning back with all his weight, tugged mightily at the reins; Cacus, in nowise hindered by their combined efforts, pressed on in his wild career. The cart was an ancient rattletrap, the harness in the last extremity of decay. It was only a question how long things would hold together, for catastrophe seemed certain. And it came quickly enough.

Cacus, beyond all control, chose his own path, and decided to take a short cut across the common. And just as the cart was near enough to Miss Porchester to cause her to look round, there was a tremendous jerk—bump—SMASH! Over went the cart, snap went the other trace, out flew Hercules, heels over head, in a sprawling heap into the ditch. Spratt was whisked off his legs in a trice, the hamper flew past his eyes, ten thousand sparks seemed to flash through his brain, and after a moment of blank darkness he too found himself in the ditch amid a ruin and wreck of hamper and cart.

Miss Porchester was ˉstartled, terrified, paralysed by the sudden alarm. She saw nothing but a cloud of dust, and the heels of an infuriated animal disappearing among the furze-bushes. She would have fainted if she had had time to think, but the noise and confusion were so sharp and decisive that she could not even faint. She was simply petrified with the conviction that some terrible accident had happened.

She took a few trembling steps towards the scene of the wreck, and called out, in a piteous, wailing voice,—

'Oh dear, I hope you are not hurt; are you killed?'

Strange to say, neither of the boys was seriously hurt. The ditch was full of soft black mud, and thickly grown with reeds and rushes. Hercules had not lost his presence of mind, and in the brief fraction of a minute he had resolved upon a bold line of policy. He remembered that he had on a blue jersey cap, and he had pulled it down over his ears during the drive. His right hand and arm had been imbedded up to the elbow in the black mud, and, as he slowly collected himself to rise, he brushed his muddy arm across his face, thereby tinting it with the complexion of a dissipated negro. Then, whispering to Spratt to keep quiet, he laboriously rose upon his legs and presented himself to Miss Porchester in a disguise which prevented recognition.

'Beg pardon, marm, but did yer appen to see the dunkey go by?'

'Oh yes; he galloped across the common. I'm so thankful you are not killed.'

'Thank 'ee, marm. Could yer tell me if oi be var vrum the vullidge?'

' No, only a little way. I hope your companion is not hurt.'

' Oh, 'e's all square, marm. Get up, Jarge, you lout, and speak to the lady.'

Spratt, who had been watching these proceedings with extreme interest and amazement at his friend's audacious imposture, now slowly emerged from the ditch, and contrived, during the process, to assume a negro-like disguise even more grotesque than that of Hercules.

' There, marm, he be all right. Not hurt, are you, Jarge ? '

' Noa, I bain't hurt that I knows of—only a bit mudded up.'

' It's all right, marm. I'll just go and fetch that old ass of a dunkey, and Jarge 'll stay here and mind the cart. Thank 'ee, marm, for your kind inquiries.'

' Well, I am thankful the accident was not more serious. I am also glad to see that you do not seem the worse for liquor. Here's a shilling for you, and mind you do not spend it at the public-house.'

Miss Porchester had taken out her purse and handed a shilling to the blackamoor.

Hercules pulled his forelock ; and telling Jarge to stop and mind the cart, he set off to trudge across the common with the best imitation possible of the lumbering slouch of a country bumpkin. Not till he was well out of sight of Miss Porchester did he quicken his pace to a run, and then he gave vent to his pent-up feelings in explosions of mirth.

But he had some unpleasant apprehensions as to how it would all end. He ran on towards Highfield House, feeling sure that Cacus would make for the paddock. Nor was he mistaken. For as he made the last turn in the lane that led to the back entrance of the school demesnes he saw the great donkey quietly browsing by the gate. He looked through the hedge, and saw the boys leaving the cricket-field to get ready for tea, for the first bell had rung. He waited till they were all gone, and then, quickly taking off the reins and harness and hiding them in the ditch, he turned Cacus into the paddock and shut the gate.

Then with the utmost caution he made his way unperceived into the house and reached his bedroom safely. It did not take him five minutes to change his things and hide his muddy jersey under the bed. And then he left his room, ran down the passage and staircase and out of the house, meeting a few boys on the way, but not stopping to talk.

With all speed he raced off to the scene of the accident, and found Spratt sitting in the cart looking very glum and lamenting over the destruction of the jam-pots. For Spratt had occupied himself during the interval with investigating the condition of the hamper.

Alas! the damage was irretrievable. Five large glass jars of jam and three pots of marmalade had been shivered to atoms, and their contents poured ruthlessly throughout the rest of the eatables. Cakes and pies were saturated in jam.

It was no use crying over spilled milk. Spratt washed his face and arms in the clearest puddle he could find in the ditch. He brushed the mud off his coat as well as he could, and then the two boys hurried back towards the school.

On their way they stopped at a cottage, and enlisted the services of a man, who for the sum of two shillings consented to bring the hamper in a wheelbarrow to the back entrance of the school premises, and take back the cart and harness and settle matters with the owner.

The two boys were late for tea—a very serious offence. They were set a long imposition, and not allowed to go out for a week. And further misadventure attended their attempts at smuggling the hamper. For that same evening during preparation Spratt and three other boys stole out with the in-

tention of fetching in all the provisions that had not
been spoiled. But they were detected in the act by
Miss Porchester, and compelled to deliver up the
goods, which were at once consigned to the storeroom.

In talking over the matter afterwards Spratt
admitted that 'the game was not worth the candle,'
and resolved on the next occasion to let his hamper
arrive in the ordinary way, for a jam-pot at tea once
a week is better than an ocean of jam which cannot
be enjoyed at all.

The Mysteries of Mosterton Marsh

CHAPTER I

IT was a dull afternoon towards the end of May.

Two boys, Frank Pearce and Edwin Aston, who figured in the story of 'The Gold Fish,' had gone out for a walk together, and were now making their way across some meadows through which the stream flowed after leaving Hawthorn Glen. The locality was called Mosterton Marsh.

There had been a great deal of rain, and these meadows were partially flooded. Indeed, at most times of the year the ground was more or less swampy thereabouts. Rushes and reeds grew in rank abundance, marigolds and purple loosestrife and other plants which love a marshy soil luxuriated there; plovers haunted the place in summer; snipe and woodcock in winter. And, as may be supposed, it was a favourite walk for the Highfield boys; though, when the floods were abroad, it was out of bounds.

Pearce and Aston had no business to be there that afternoon. They had been trudging in a straight line through the fields, climbing over hedges and gates where necessary, and evidently they had some purpose in view. Occasionally a few words passed between them in an undertone.

There was a steady west wind blowing; clouds were scudding across the sky, and watery shafts of sunshine shed fitful gleams over the landscape; but shadow soon swept it away, and the sun was fast confessing itself vanquished as heavier clouds came up.

The boys had now reached the borders of a meadow where the swamp was more pronounced. There were frequent patches of tall reeds standing like islands out of rushy pools. It was hard to define the river bed.

The boys surveyed the field from the top of the hedge, and Pearce said,—

'That's the place, and I don't wonder. Isn't it bogeyfied?'

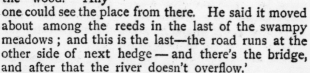

'I should think so.'

'Jem said he saw the light again last night. Of course he could see it from the farm well enough, just up on the hill by the wood. Any one could see the place from there. He said it moved about among the reeds in the last of the swampy meadows; and this is the last—the road runs at the other side of next hedge — and there's the bridge, and after that the river doesn't overflow.'

'How often has he seen it?'

'Three or four times in different fields; but last night he saw it there, and he was in an awful funk. So should I have been.'

Jem was a boy working at Miller's Farm. He had come up to the school that morning with a basket of eggs; and Pearce had talked to him at the back entrance after breakfast, while on a journey to the boot-house.

The conversation between the boys continued as they stood on the hedge.

'They say,' quoth Pearce, 'that a Jack-o'-Lantern always appears when some one is going to be murdered. It may come three or four times, but, sure enough, it never comes so often for nothing. It isn't always the fellow who sees it that is murdered. Sometimes it's a chap he tells about it. I say, Aston, I wish Jem hadn't told me. I wonder if he told any one else? I've told you, mind; so that lessens the chance of its being me.'

'Well, I haven't much to thank you for, if that's why you told me. I don't want to be murdered. But surely, Pearce, you are not such an ass as to believe that bosh?'

'I don't know. Others, cleverer than you, believe it, anyhow. But it's not likely to be either of us. There's an old chap who lives near us at home, and he knows all about these things, and tells me. Well, last year he saw a Jack-o'-Lantern, and told his wife—not that he wanted to get rid of her, for they're awfully fond of each other—but she was in a terrible fright, and went and told the magistrate. And, sure enough, there was a man murdered within a month close by. She says the magistrate must have told him—because it's always sure to come. She told my father about it, and he asked the magistrate.'

'Well, what did the magistrate say?'

'Oh, he didn't like to say he did; so he said he didn't; but I know he did.'

'But magistrates don't tell lies; my father's a magistrate out in India.'

'I never said they did; only it looks very odd.'

Well, I think the best thing we can do is to tell

all the chaps, and then there will be very little chance of its being any of us.'

'Oh, I don't know.'

'Well, I know that we had better be going back if we don't want to get into a row.'

'All right, jump down. We can cut across to the road just the other side of the field, and then we can run.' So off they went.

This conversation had not been so private as Pearce and Aston supposed. It had been overheard by the boy Jem, who was just the other side of the hedge. He had seen the two Highfield boys coming across the field, and recognised Pearce, and being of an idle turn, he had slipped out of the barn-yard and ran down to waylay them. Then he thought he

would dodge behind the hedge and suddenly
surprise them. So stealthy were his movements
that he had crept up under the hedge to where they
were standing ; and when he knew what they were
talking about, he thought he would listen a bit before letting himself be seen. So he heard all they
said, and then decided not to let himself be seen at
all.

Pearce and Aston got in just before roll-call ; and
Jem on his way back drove the cows into the yard.
So no questions were asked by the authorities on
either side.

Jem was not a bad sort of a boy, and had worked
for Farmer Miller more than a year. He had a
younger brother called Jack, who sometimes worked
on the same farm when there was an odd job to
be done. The two boys were fond of fun and such
sports as came within their reach.

Whenever the hounds met within easy distance,
Jem and Jack were always certain to be at the meet,
if they could get leave ; and they would follow on
foot with a good wind, and sometimes contrive to
keep the field in view till the end of the run. They
knew where the jackdaws, owls, wood-pigeons and
hawks built, and though they never took eggs, they
were keen enough to get hold of the young birds,
and showed much skill in rearing and taming them.
They often caught a fine trout in the river, and knew
generally as much practical natural history as any
boys in the neighbourhood.

Now as Jem finished up his work that evening
at the farm he thought over what he had heard the
boys say ; and if he had talked to himself as boys
sometimes do (in stories) he would have said something of this sort :—

'That young gent Pearce is in a scare about the
Jack-o'-Lantern. I think I might have a bit of fun
against him. Of course I saw the light in the
meadow last night, 'cos we'd got the guv'nor's lantern,

Jack and I, and went down to look after the plovers.
And Jack hung the lantern on a long stick and
waved it about; and if ever there was a Jack-o'-
Lantern to be seen, there he was, as large as life,
ha, ha!'

And then Jem wondered how it could possibly
have anything to do with murder. He scratched his
head and was puzzled, and resolved to consult Jack
about it some day, but not that evening, because he
was sleepy. So when he got home he ate his supper
and went to bed.

CHAPTER II

'I SAY, Frank, my aunt says you may come home
with me after school on Saturday till Monday, if
old Poco will allow you.'

'Hurrah! Aston, you're a brick, and your aunt's a
jolly chap—or the other way on, perhaps, would be
more polite. How jolly! I'm awfully obliged. The
doctor's sure to let me go. I haven't had a bad
mark this term.'

And Frank chucked his cap into the air, and gave
it a kick as it came down, just by way of expressing
his delight.

That invitation fitted in nicely with another which
followed later on in the day. Frank had a second
interview with Jem after dinner, and the conversation
as before had reference to the mysterious light in
Mosterton Marsh.

Jem had begun in this way:

'I say, master, be you afeard about that light?
Have you ever heard what some folks say about it?
Awful things, I can tell you—nothing less than
murder!'

'Oh, I have heard some bosh of that sort, but I'm
not such an ass as to believe it. Do you, Jem?'

'Well, I can't say as I do or I don't; leastways, I
heard a gent say the other day that he believed it.'

'Did you? Then he must have been a fool. I had a look at the meadow. Have you seen the light again?'

'No, sir, I haven't looked for it; but I dare say it might be about. I shouldn't mind going with you some evening, say about eight o'clock, and perhaps we could find out what it is.'

'Well, it wouldn't be bad fun. Let me see, I could manage it next Saturday. I'm going to spend the afternoon with a friend, and their house is not half an hour's walk from the meadows. Would that suit you?'

'Yes, sir; shall I meet you at the cross roads — you know, Tippet's Corner — say about a quarter to eight?'

'All right, if it does not rain.'

So Jem went back to the farm, and Pearce told Aston of the plan. Aston thought it could easily be managed. They would take the butterfly-net. Miss Davis liked to encourage her nephew in the love of natural history. Under her supervision a glass case had been erected in the hall of Chesterton House, in which reposed the mortal remains of sundry butterflies and moths, not arranged in any attempt at entomological order, but regarded with pride by the aunt, who never let a visitor pass without drawing attention to the refined tastes of her nephew.

A nocturnal ramble in quest of moths was often allowed to Edwin in company with some trustworthy escort. Miss Davis had great confidence in Frank Pearce, and told Edwin how glad she was that he had found such a steady companion. So there was not likely to be any hindrance to the proposed expedition.

Jem walked back to the farm with thoughts moving in his mind which made him chuckle now and then. He enjoyed a bit of harmless fun as much as most young gentlemen do ; and it seemed to him likely to be one of the best jokes he had ever known, for his experience was limited.

He found Jack in the yard, greatly excited at having just caught a rat. Eggs and young chickens had lately been disappearing, and rats had been suspected of theft. Jack had tried for a rat with the old trap a dozen times, but the old rats knew the old trap, and possibly cautioned the young ones, so that there had been no success. Jack, however, had at last circumvented one of the marauders by a trap of his own contrivance, simple and effective. As it is not patented, I may describe it for imitation in case of need. Jack stood perfectly unmoved for two hours watching a hole near the hen-roost ; and when at last a rat came out, and possibly mistook him for a heathen idol, Jack promptly overwhelmed the animal with a brick.

As Jem entered the yard, Jack came up grinning from ear to ear, and holding the mangled monster by the tail ; and then he threw the rat at Jem, and told him the tale of the stratagem.   Jack was so excited that Jem could not edge in a word about next Saturday evening until he had listened to three distinct versions of the rat-hunt.   When at last he had a chance, Jem said :

' I say, Jack, that young gent I told you about wants to look for the Jack-o'-Lantern on Saturday night. D'you think he would be likely to see it, Jack ? '

' P'raps he might, Jem.'

' Down by the big patch of reeds, eh, Jack ? '

' Likely enough, Jem.'

''Bout eight o'clock, Jack ? '

' Ay, sure, Jem.'

' All right, Jack—I'll show him the way.'

And so the services of Jack-o'-Lantern were bespoken for the Saturday evening.

Frank Pearce walked round the field with Edwin Aston before dinner next day, which was Friday. They talked over the proposed visit to the swampy meadows, and the possibility of their seeing the mysterious light.

Aston said :

' It's all bosh about murder, and greater bosh still about the light, I believe.   The old buffer who lectures on chemistry once talked about marsh gas spontaneously combusting ; but I don't see how it can go on burning so as for a chap to see it dancing about, as they say it does.   When the gas escaped in the schoolroom last term, and some fellows exploded it, it made a great flame and noise, but it didn't go kicking about like a nigger in a hornpipe.'

'Well, Jem's in a funk about it, I can tell you. He said he heard a gentleman say the other day that there was sure to be a murder, so it isn't only me who has heard about it.'

Aston was silent for a minute, and then he said :

'I think we could get some fun out of this business. Let me think—I know—that was it ! Oh, we'll scare that chap Jem out of his seven senses. Of course it's all bosh about there really being any ghostly light. It isn't the sort of place to be haunted—not like Hawthorn Glen. An open field with the road running alongside ; who ever heard of anything ghostly in such a place ? No ; but if I don't invent a Jack-o'-Lantern that will make Jem's hair stand on end, you may call me bread-and-cheese and eat me, as our old one-legged national schoolmaster at home used to say. Look here, Frank, do you remember old Stinks telling us how to make phosphorised oil ? I've got a bottle of it at home, and I'll get a bladder from Galpin and blow it up, and pour a dose of the oil into it, and tie it by a string to a long stick, and when it's swished about it will make a glorious Jack-o'-Lantern.'

'That's splendid, and no mistake.'

'Then I'll go with you, and just before we get to Tippet's Corner I'll slip off into the fields and dodge down behind the hedges and get among the reeds, and when I see you and Jem coming along, I'll set my lantern dancing. You must pretend to be in an awful funk, and see if Jem doesn't cut and run for bare life !'

'Oh, that would be a joke ! But wouldn't you mind going about the fields in the dark ? Suppose you fell into the river or stuck in the marsh ?'

'Oh, it will be all right—it will not be dark at eight ; and the floods must have gone down since last week—there's been no rain. Besides, for the matter of that, I needn't go down to the swamps. I could hide in the hedge or in the furze—there's plenty of furze in the higher part of the field. It would terrify him all the more if it wasn't actually in the swamp. You leave it to me, and I'll raise such a bogey-light as will make Jem's hair stand up like quills upon the fretful porcupine.'

And Aston danced with excitement at the mere thought.

That afternoon, on his way back from school, Edwin went to the butcher's and purchased a bladder for threepence ; and, on reaching his aunt's house, he experimented with the luminous oil with a success that surprised him. It was a dark evening, and tea was an hour later than usual, so he had plenty of time to practise. And this is how he went to work.

He poured some of the oil into the bladder, and inflated it by means of a quill. He then tied it tightly, leaving a long end of string to dangle it by. Then he shut himself with the bladder inside the large cupboard which stood in his room ; and when he swished the bladder about to circulate the oil over it inside, he found it filled with strange, unearthly light. This half frightened him, and he was glad to get out of the cupboard into comparative daylight. He hung the bogey-light (as he called it) from a hook in the roof of the cupboard, and then peeped at it through a chink of the door. Then he thought he would convert it into a ghost. So he slipped his night-shirt over the bladder, buttoning the neck-button so that the bladder half-protruded through the opening. Next he drew eyes, nose, and mouth with burnt cork, and then he hitched up the right sleeve on another hook, and so created a most uncanny-looking goblin. Then, shutting the cupboard-door, he went down to tea.

CHAPTER III

MISS DAVIS and her nephew sat down to tea, and in the course of conversation Edwin said :

'Aunt, do you believe in ghosts?'

'No, Edwin, certainly not, in the vulgar acceptance of the word.'

'What's that, aunt?'

'Don't speak so abruptly, Edwin; you startle me.'

Miss Davis, as she spoke, looked towards the door, as though she fancied her nephew's question might possibly refer to an apparition entering the room. Of course her evenly balanced mind was not really betrayed into such a foolish idea; still, the sudden question, 'What's that?' asked in the gloaming, immediately after an allusion to ghosts, might suggest a furtive glance towards the door even to a person of stouter nerves than Miss Davis.

All that Edwin meant to imply, as a matter of fact, was that he did not clearly comprehend what his aunt meant by 'the vulgar acceptance of the word.' But he did not explain, and went on:

'Well, aunt, a chap came up to the school this

morning who said he had seen a strange light hover-
ing about the meadows below Tippet's Corner, and
he thinks it will be followed by a *murder*.'

Edwin spoke the last word in such an impressive
voice, that his aunt's nerves again sustained a shock,
and she answered :

' Edwin, your conversation this evening is not so
agreeable as usual.   I have often told you to be very
particular about the topics you select at the tea-
table.   I must add, however, that I am surprised that
Dr. Porchester allows you to converse with such
persons.   An ignorant mind is often prone to indulge
foolish superstitions, like the Athenians in the days
of St. Paul.   You must be on your guard against
lending a ready ear to the idle conversation of the
uneducated classes.'

' Well, aunt, I don't believe in it ; but he said that
he heard a gentleman say he did.'

' You cannot be too careful, Edwin, about choosing
your associates.   And I do hope you will not form
a vulgar acquaintance with the village boys.   They
can only teach you harm.'

' Oh, aunt, it was only a fellow from Miller's Farm,
a very harmless sort of chap, who brought some
eggs up to the school.   Frank Pearce happened to
be by at the time, and he told him about the
light.'

' Well, Edwin, I am glad it was nothing worse.
It is bad enough that your young minds should be
tainted with foolish notions.'

' What d'you think the light was, aunt ? '

' That I cannot say, Edwin, as I did not see it.'

' Do you think Jane believes in ghosts, aunt ? '

' No, Edwin, I am sure she does not.   Jane is a
sensible young woman, and I took care to convince
myself that she had no such silly fancies before en-
gaging her.'

' I like the science lectures awfully, aunt.   I know
you like me to try and work out at home what we

learn at school; and I was making an experiment before tea.'

'Yes, Edwin, it gives me great satisfaction whenever you show genuine interest in your lessons. Scientific experiments are of the utmost value in advancing knowledge; and even boys may make important discoveries by dint of patience and perseverance.'

By this time tea was finished, and Edwin was in the act of opening the door for his aunt, when suddenly the habitual repose of the house was broken by a series of violent screams upstairs; then followed a heavy sound as of some one falling, and then all was still.

'Oh, bother!' said Edwin; but the remark was drowned by the agitated exclamations of his aunt.

'What is it? what is it, Jane? what is it?'

The hapless Jane was incapable of returning answer, having collapsed in a dead faint upon the floor of Edwin's bedroom.

But the gallant footman had hurried to the rescue, and now stood in front of his mis- tress, ready to do and dare the ut- most in her service.

'Oh, James, something dread- ful must have hap- pened! Go up- stairs and see what it is. Oh, my poor nerves! I think the sound came from Master Ed- win's room.'

James flew up- stairs three steps at a time, and Miss Davis herself followed slowly
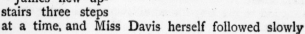

The footman made for Master Edwin's room, which was at the farther end of the gallery facing the hall. The door was open, and he entered.

There was a faint light apparently from nowhere, which disclosed to view the prostrate form of the housemaid. James, never a laggart in deeds of gallantry, was in the act of stooping down to raise her up when his eye gravitated towards the fatal cupboard, attracted by the light which issued from it.

Now had he been standing erect and faced the phantom in the ordinary attitude of a man, he would no doubt have at once recognised the absurdity of the thing. As it was, he only got a sidelong glance from an angle of vision not often employed; and the result was that a most hideous distortion of the grim occupant of the cupboard fell upon the retina of his eye. This conveyed such a ghastly impression to his brain that he lost his presence of mind for the moment—nothing more—and found it convenient to stagger into a chair. There he sat with arms hanging loose, and legs outstretched, and mouth wide open, staring at the grim bogey.

Meanwhile Miss Davis was making progress towards the room, and heard the flump with which James settled into the chair. So did Edwin, who was following in the wake of his aunt with feelings in his soul 'like mixed pickles,' as he afterwards reported. He did not wish his aunt to be alarmed; but as she did not believe in ghosts there was no fear. Indeed, he had had no intention of alarming any one: he wanted to test the experiment before embarking on the expedition to the marsh, and never dreamt that the results would be so disastrous. He had wanted to explain his experiment to his aunt at the tea-table, and was leading up to it when the meal came to an end. So that no blame must be attached to the boy for mischievous and thoughtless conduct.

Edwin followed close behind Miss Davis, and as she entered the room his conscience troubled him, and he began to say :

'It's all right, aunt; it's nothing at all—only the experiment I told you of, with phosphorised oil——' But he had not time to finish the sentence. Miss Davis, who had not her spectacles on, and consequently saw only dim and imperfect outlines of objects, had come point-blank upon the open cupboard. She was completely unnerved, and gasped out, 'Goodness, gracious! What is it? Oh, how horrible!' and she subsided over the ruins of Jane.

It has taken longer to describe these several effects upon the three persons concerned than it actually took to enact them. Edwin was now the only member of the quartet in possession of his rational faculties, and he felt the predicament to be decidedly awkward. He eyed the three unfortunates, two of whom lay apparently dead. James was evidently alive, and Edwin turned his attention to him.

He began by charging the dumbfoundered footman as he might have charged an adversary at football; and supplemented deeds by words to this effect :

'Get up, you old duffer! What are you gaping at? Get up and get cook to come. She'll know how to bring round the ladies.'

James, being thus brought to his senses, retreated with crestfallen countenance to fetch the cook.

Meantime Edwin struck a match and lighted a candle, and proceeded to dismantle the bogey. He disrobed it of his night-shirt, smoothing out that article and folding it up. He let the wind out of the bladder, and decanted the phosphorised oil into the bottle. He hid the bladder in a drawer and shut the cupboard. And when cook arrived he was able to lend his undivided assistance in reviving his aunt and the housemaid.

Jane received a good scolding from the strong-minded cook, so soon as the former was in a condition to appreciate the force of words; and Miss Davis, as might be expected after such a shock to her poor nerves, retired to her room; and by the time Edwin was in bed, peace and quiet once more reigned in Chesterton House.

CHAPTER IV

WHEN school was over next day, Pearce and Aston did not take long to run down the lane and across the fields to Chesterton House. I can never think of those lanes and fields without emotion. I went down to Deepwells last autumn, just to wander about and refresh old memories, and came to a particular stile, on which I cut my name one day with Harry Dawson. The letters were just visible, almost obliterated by the influences of a quarter of a century. The two boys vaulted over that stile, and then walked slowly the rest of the way, so as not to arrive too hot. Edwin had been giving Frank a vivid description of the tragical events of the previous evening, and they decided that it boded favourably for the success of their proposed expedition that evening.

Edwin had not seen his aunt since the fracas, and was rather apprehensive of meeting her, but he did not think she would lecture him before Frank. And he was right. They found dinner awaiting them, and Miss Davis greeted Frank with motherly affection. She was as kind-hearted an old lady as ever lived.

It so happened that Miss Davis made no allusion at all to Edwin about the matter on his mind. Possibly she forgot; possibly she thought well to let it pass; for after the protestations she had made in behalf of herself and housemaid, she might have found it difficult to give a satisfactory explanation of the behaviour displayed by both.

The afternoon passed merrily. There was no lack

of amusement in the garden. The boys fed the gold
fish, and they rowed about the lake and fished; and
if such a programme was not sufficient to entertain
two boys for an afternoon, I should be sorry for
them.

Some of my boys said to me the other day, 'Oh,
sir, we should like to have been at your school; you
had such jolly fun there!'

I suggested that there is probably just as much
fun in other schools, but it does not always find an
historian. Where would have been the fun of the
Trojan War, if 'the blind old bard of Scio's rocky
isle' had not relieved the blank of his sightless life
by song?

While tea was going on, Edwin said,—

'Aunt, I hope you will allow us to go out afterwards ; we can take the butterfly-net, and we want to have a look round those meadows by the bridge ; perhaps we shall see a Jack-o'-Lantern !'

Miss Davis smiled, and gave consent, telling the boys to be back in good time.

So the butterfly-net and other appliances, including a bamboo fishing-rod, were got hold of, and the boys set forth.   They dawdled about and caught some moths, and then hid the net in the hedge ; and as the time for meeting Jem drew on, they walked more quickly towards Tippet's Corner.   Aston made sure that all was in readiness for kindling the bogey light ; and he coined another name for it—the *Bamboogey*—since it was to be suspended from the end of a bamboo fishing-rod.   Then he branched off into the fields, leaving Frank to go on alone.

Frank did not much like the solitude.   It was a dark evening, and the hedges were high ; so he hurried on to the cross roads, where he found Jem.

'Well, master, you be come, then.'

'Yes, Jem, it's all right ; let us go on.   How dark it is !'

'We'd best keep down the road to the bridge, and then turn into the fields.   I saw the light last time in the field by the bridge.'

'Come on, then ; let's go.'

They hurried on and soon reached the bridge. They got over a gate and walked under the hedge, keeping a sharp look-out over the field.   Jem pointed towards the large patch of reeds where he had seen the light, but it was too dark to distinguish anything.

They had gone about a hundred yards up the field, when Frank put his hand on Jem's arm, and said, in a low whisper,—

'Look there—I saw a light !'

'Where ?'

'Up there ! I'm sure I did.   There—look !'

Jem, who had been peering hitherto towards the river, now looked in the opposite direction, and there, just above the hedge at the farther end of the field, hovered a mysterious globe of pale phosphorescence, now swaying gently to and fro, now whirling rapidly round in fantastic gyrations, now jumping up and down. Jem shuddered and said,—

'Oh, maister, I never seed it like that before—it's an awful goblin!'

'Oh, come on, and let's see where it is. Don't be afraid, Jem!'

Frank walked on boldly, but Jem clutched his arm, and said,—

'Don't go on, sir — it's certain death. That be one of them corpsy dancers, what come from graves as haven't yet got skeletons in them. Let's get back. Oh, mercy, don't leave me!'

Jem's language sent a creepy shiver through Frank's marrow, and his great desire was to get to Aston. So he shook off Jem, and said,—

'Come on; what a funk you are! I thought you said you'd try and find out what it was.'

'Maister, maister, don't leave me! I shall die of fright! Oh, look, there be another of them! Oh, the bogeys are about to-night, sure enough!'

Frank looked, and saw another light moving between him and the bamboogey. It rose and fell, and swayed backwards and forwards, and shed a fitful glimmer, and looked to Frank's excited imagination like an illuminated skull and crossbones. It was Frank now who was smitten with a deadly panic. He dared not go after Aston, for he would have to run the gauntlet of this appalling phantom. A strange moaning sound, dying off into a heartrending wail, now struck fresh terror into the hearts of the two boys. It was only a sheep-dog howling far away, but Jem declared it was the death-shriek in some murderous assault.

This additional horror fairly scared Frank out of his senses. His one idea was to run for his life. And this he did, plunging madly through furze-bushes and reeds, scrambling over the gate, across the bridge, and along the road as hard as he could go in the direction of Chesterton House.

Jem, when he saw Frank Pearce take to his heels, would have laughed, if only it had been broad day-light. But he was strongly inclined to follow his example ; for he was as fully persuaded that the first light was a supernatural manifestation as Frank was about the second. Jem now thought the best thing to be done was to make for his brother and get home as soon as possible. But there was the river and an ugly bit of swamp between them, so that he would have to go round by the road over the bridge. Cir-cumstances, however, now rendered that course un-advisable. For the first light was becoming active to an extraordinary degree. It had ceased its manœuvres above the hedge, and was travelling at a rapid rate high in the air, sweeping and swirling down the swampy meadow in the direction of the bridge. If it continued this course, Jem's retreat would be virtually cut off ; for he could never dare risk a close encounter with such an appalling visitant. Jem was verily in an ' awful funk.' There was nothing for it but to reach the road and run for his life to the cottage, and get his father to come and rescue Jack, who beyond doubt would be no less terrified than Jem was. Therefore, without further reflection, Jem took to his heels and made tracks for home.

The four boys now resembled four pawns upon a chess-board engaged in executing a gambit and a counter-gambit.

Aston's course has already been indicated. He had seen no signs of Pearce and Jem as he sheltered under the hedge and upraised the bogey light above it. The bamboo rod reached twelve feet into the air, so that the light was high above the hedge while he was below. Nor had he seen the other light, which was not visible from his position. So he resolved to have a brisk run down the meadow, and its result was, as we have heard, to scare Jem from the scene of action.

Suddenly, in the full course of his rapid career, Aston caught sight of the other light down among the reeds. Jack had already seen the bamboogey, and his heart was quaking with terror, for never in the wildest freaks of fancy had he imagined the existence of such a lively goblin. In manipulating his lantern Jack had paid strict attention to the orthodox rules of the game. Now he saw before him a light that entirely disregarded such rules—a lawless and reckless goblin, and withal apparently making for him! What could an ignorant lad do under such circumstances but shiver with fright? None too warm was Jack before; his feet were wet and the evening was chill, and his natural warmth burned low. Lucky for him that he was on the side of the river nearest the farm, separated from it only by a couple of hedges, which were as nothing to him. Therefore, without loss of time he was minded to make what haste he could to gain the hospitable shelter of the farmyard. As a soldier who leaves his arms on the field of battle when seized with panic, so did Jack put down the lantern and turn to fly. Six steps only had he gone, however, splashing through pools in the darkness, when he found himself hopelessly sinking in the squashy swamp. Deep down in the mud and ooze his legs descended, even to the knees; nor even then did his feet find firm ground. Oh, how he struggled to extricate them! but the tenacious mud held him fast. It was impossible to lift his knees, and there he must have stuck till now, if no one had come to his rescue.

As for Aston, his course had been arrested by the sight of what he supposed to be the genuine Goblin of the Marsh, around which hovered vague mysteries of dread, and in whose train lurked grizzly murder. Should he dare to approach and discover its nature?

Ah! if he only had Frank by him, he might then command the necessary courage; but alone in the darkness—ugh! He shuddered at the thought, and turning at right-angles, fled to the hedge. He must get out of the field at all cost, and the cost was not small.

The hedge was high, the bank steep, but Aston scrambled up, and began forcing his way through its obstruction. Whoever planted that hedge must have done so on an unlucky day, like the planter of that 'sorry log' which nearly killed Horace. Aston shoved his best and got into the middle of that hedge, but he could get no farther. He tried to break away the tangled branches, but the thorns

stung and tore him in all directions. He tried to
work to the right, he tried to the left; he tried to
wriggle out backwards by the way he had entered.
But fresh branches seemed to have sprung up behind
him, and by no contrivance could he succeed. The
Caudine Forks seemed a playground! To add to his
distress there now smote upon his ear the sound of
weird and dismal wailings. For Jack's terror of being
sucked down into the abyss of mud overcame for the
moment his supernatural fears, and he was blubber-
ing and moaning in such plaintive and agonised
tones, that Aston, as he listened, bethought him of
all the horrible things he had ever heard of—hounds
of war let loose and hastening to gnash upon him
with their ravenous jaws—demons and ghosts, goblins
and vampires and furies huddled together to sweep
through his mind and paralyse his senses.

Chapter V

FRANK PEARCE made desperate haste back to
Chesterton House, and reached it long after
ten o'clock. He rang at the bell, and James
appeared. Miss Davis had retired for the night.
Frank poured out his tale of woe to James, saying
that he had lost Edwin, and been frightened by a
strange light in the marsh, and wanted to know what
had better be done. James, who had been waiting
up for the young gentlemen, and was sound asleep
in the cook's armchair when the bell awoke him, was
too sleepy and bewildered by the announcement to
know definitely what course to recommend. He
could not leave the house to search for Master Aston;
Miss Davis was gone to bed; it was a bad job.

'Well, James, something must be done to find him;
I must see Miss Davis. It wasn't my fault; there
was a real ghostly light that came after me. I tried
not to be afraid, but somehow I couldn't help running
away. Wouldn't you have run, too?'

James, remembering his late experience, did not give any decided answer to this question; and the conversation was interrupted by the appearance of Miss Davis upon the scene. She had heard the bell and the sound of voices in the hall, and felt it incumbent upon her, as mistress of the house, to ascertain that the boys had returned safely. She therefore donned a stately dressing-gown, and from the gallery above inquired if all was satisfactory.

'Oh, Miss Davis, Edwin has not come back yet. I'm very sorry, but I lost him in the meadows; and, please, what had we better do?'

'You lost Edwin? How was it possible, Frank? Did he fall into the river? Tell me, is he *drowned*?'

'Oh no, Miss Davis. He's all right, I hope; but we got separated, and I saw a ghostly light which came at me, and I was obliged to run away—I could not help it.'

'Oh, Frank, how could you leave my precious nephew, when I trusted him to your care? Oh dear, how dreadful! I must dress at once and come downstairs. James, go and tell Jane to come to my room immediately.'

The operation of dressing was accomplished by Miss Davis more quickly than had ever been thought possible before; and she came down to the hall in a state of undisguised anxiety, but filled with resolution.

'Oh, this is too dreadful! My poor boy lost in the marsh at midnight! Ring the alarm-bell, James. Order the coachman to get the carriage immediately. We must drive at once to the place and search the meadows. At once, James.'

The footman proceeded to execute the orders, and in less than half an hour Miss Davis was bowling along the road at a rapid pace, attended by Frank and James. When they reached the bridge the carriage was stopped, and Miss Davis directed the coachman and James to take the carriage-lamps and go into the meadow and shout for the lost Edwin,

while Frank mounted the box and held the reins. The coachman had assured her that the horses would stand perfectly quiet, if Frank did not fidget them.

There is a well-known story in the classical mythology which relates how Phaethon once prevailed upon his father, Helios, to grant him permission to drive the Chariot of the Sun for one day across the heavens, with the result of direful mischief to the universe in general, and himself in particular. For hardly had his unaccustomed hands grasped the reins when the horses became restive, and, leaving their usual course, careered madly over the heavens, spreading a conflagration which no fire-engine could extinguish. Whereupon Zeus killed the rash youth with a flash of lightning.

Frank was soon reminded forcibly of this legend. He experienced a sensation of pride at handling the ribbons with a pair of thoroughbreds at the ends. He tried to sit still and obey the coachman's injunctions, but somehow he could not prevent his hands from twitching the reins. The horses recognised the unfamiliar movement, and seemed nervous and excitable. They pricked their ears and pawed the ground and shook their heads, and seemed to feel that something was wrong. Perhaps they shared in the ghostly terrors that seemed unduly active that night. Perhaps they were indignant at being expected to stand still in the cold for no apparent reason, when they might have been slumbering peacefully in their stalls with plenty of good straw to keep them warm. At any rate they grew restive, and, after fretting and blowing their noses by way of preamble, they finally clenched the bits between their teeth, and set off at a brisk trot.

Miss Davis put her head out of the window and screamed to Frank, who was tugging at the reins with all his might.

And then she screamed for the coachman and James ; but the wheels rolled round and the hoofs clattered upon the sounding road, and Miss Davis sank back exhausted on the cushions of her carriage, and resigned herself as best she could to the prospect of sure and sudden catastrophe.

Smoothly and rapidly the carriage rolled on in the darkness. The road was level and the horses knew their way, for it was a frequent drive with Miss Davis.

They trotted smartly on, being evidently aware that in due time they would reach home. And, guided more by their own instinct than by any direction of Frank's hands, they accomplished the first of the two miles without mishap. Frank was devoutly thankful, and hope burnt strong in his heart that after all no mischief might arise. He was on the point of raising his voice to encourage the lady inside, when his ear caught the sound of other wheels ahead, which were evidently approaching. He had not a notion which side of the road he ought to take. It was too dark to see anything—no—a turn in the road suddenly showed him two bright lamps glaring like the eyes of some supernatural monster possibly bent upon his destruction. It was a moment of desperate excitement. Frank set his teeth hard. He had a rein in either hand, and tugged first at one and then at the other with all his strength, and without partiality.

There was a confusion of noise and light, a sudden shock of collision, a clamour of voices, but somehow the thoroughbreds did not stop nor plunge, nor appear to take any notice. The obstruction was past, neither carriage was overthrown. Frank turned his head for a moment, and the glimmer of the lamps was retreating. Whatever had happened? At any rate no lives were lost. Frank heaved a deep sigh of relief, and hope revived in his heart.

And now they were entering the village. A friendly light shone here and there from a cottage window. A flare of light and sounds of merriment issued from the doors of the Spotted Dog, and more than one nocturnal carouser came out with somewhat unsteady step to see who was driving by at so late an hour. Frank might have called for assistance, but, having come unscathed out of the ordeal so far, he ventured to risk the brief portion of the journey that remained. For by this time he had gained experience and confidence, and felt that the horses were paying more deference to his hand. He even believed he could guide them safely through the gates of Chesterton House, if only they were open. What would happen if they were shut he dared not contemplate!

Onwards a little farther and the gates were reached. To Frank's unspeakable relief they were open. With perfect precision the horses took the curve, and the carriage rattled up the drive. Frank's heart beat with wild excitement as at last the carriage drew up in front of the door. And there was Edwin Aston on the steps, with James on one side holding a carriage-lamp and the coachman on the other side holding a carriage-lamp.

'Hurrah, Edwin! That's all right!' and Frank jumped down from the box. The coachman stood in charge of the horses, and James made haste to assist his mistress. Brave old lady that she was, with all her nervous vagaries, when it came to a crisis of real danger she showed most praiseworthy endurance. She alighted from the carriage with a smile, and throwing her arms round Edwin's neck, she kissed him, and said, 'Thank God, my dear boy, you are safe!'

*　　*　　*　　*　　*

I learnt afterwards that Jem and his father had gone out and rescued Jack, and he was the only one of the party who suffered any serious consequences from the night's adventure. Poor boy! What with the fright he endured, and the soaking of the swamp, he was ill with a feverish cold for a fortnight, though he afterwards regained his native vigour.

The four perpetrators of these ghostly mysteries were careful to preserve the secret of the particular part they played, with this result—that there were four centres disseminating to their four respective circles of friends and acquaintances the firm conviction that Mosterton Marsh was haunted. And as each of those friends and acquaintances became the centre of a fresh circle, a regular chromatrope of evil report was set going with reference to the unlucky swamp; which, revolving after the manner of that familiar mystery of the magic lantern, kept perpetually turning out new ideas of goblin lore, to brood over the place like its own vaporous mists, and probably never to be separated from it even to

THE END.

Suckling & Co., Printers, 88, Fleet Street, London, E.C.

STORIES FOR BOYS.

By TALBOT BAINES REED.

The name of Talbot Baines Reed will always be associated with fascinating, healthy stories for boys, dealing with public school life, and early business careers. No writer has been able more skilfully to give his characters a real personality, or to portray more faithfully their failures, sharp struggles and final successes.

THE ADVENTURES OF A THREE-GUINEA WATCH.

With Seven Full-page and Sixteen other Illustrations in the Text. Large crown 8vo, cloth gilt, 3s. 6d.

A straightforward story of school-life, and of the duties and temptations of young men entering upon the work of life. The kind of book to rejoice the heart of the boy who gets it as a Christmas or Birthday present.

THE COCK HOUSE AT FELLSGARTH.
A Public School Story.

With Seven Full-page Illustrations by ALFRED PEARSE. Large crown 8vo, cloth gilt, 3s. 6d.

A splendid story of school life. The rollicking fun of the juniors, the rivalry among the seniors, the school elections, the football match, are told in such a forcible manner that the tale will prove a source of delight to all boys—young and old.

THE FIFTH FORM AT ST. DOMINIC'S.
A Public School Story.

With Seven Full-page and Eight other Illustrations in the Text. Large crown 8vo, cloth gilt, 3s. 6d.

A lively story, abounding in stirring incident and in humorous descriptions. A thoroughly healthy tale to place in the hands of a boy. It ought to become popular both as a gift and prize book.

A DOG WITH A BAD NAME.

With Seven Full-page Illustrations by ALFRED PEARSE. Large crown 8vo, cloth gilt, 3s. 6d.

The story of a big ungainly youth who seemed fated to be misunderstood and to be made the butt of his comrades. His trials at school, and as a tutor, and the unsympathetic treatment by his guardian are delightfully told.

THE RELIGIOUS TRACT SOCIETY, LONDON.

STORIES FOR BOYS.

By TALBOT BAINES REED.

ROGER INGLETON, MINOR.

With Seven Full-page Illustrations by J. FINNEMORE, R.I. Large crown 8vo, cloth gilt, 3s. 6d.

The Guardian says:—"Mr. Talbot Baines Reed knows how to tell a story, and he does himself justice in 'Roger Ingleton, Minor,' in which he makes an excellent book out of the return of a long-lost half-brother who had gone out alone into the world, many years previously, after a bitter quarrel with his father. The discovery of the missing brother is not accomplished without many exciting incidents, out of which Mr. Reed weaves his plot."

The Aberdeen Free Press says:—"This story has a modern atmosphere. The plot is very skilfully constructed and the interest is maintained up to the last page."

SIR LUDAR: A Story of the Days of the Great Queen Bess.

With Eleven Full-page Illustrations. Large crown 8vo, cloth gilt, 3s. 6d.

The Guardian says:—"This stirring tale, which is played in the days of Queen Elizabeth, and tells of the wonderful adventures of a sturdy prentice-lad who contrived to crowd into a few years as much danger and fighting and hairbreadth escapes as would have lasted an army of ordinary folk for their whole lives. It is a capital book for boys which those who begin reading will have to finish. Mr. Pearse's illustrations, too, are very good."

The Aberdeen Free Press says:—"This is a stirring tale of adventure with plenty of fighting."

PARKHURST BOYS, and other Stories of School Life.

With Seven Full-page and many other Illustrations. Large crown 8vo, cloth gilt, 3s. 6d.

In this volume are brought together a large number of the miscellaneous stories written from time to time for the *Boy's Own Paper* by Talbot Baines Reed. The collection is prefaced by an appreciation of Mr. Reed as boy and man, and it contains some of his best work and his brightest wit. There are seven sketches of life at Parkhurst School; eleven character delineations of "Boys we have known"—such as "The Bully," "The Sneak"; twelve representations of "Boys of English History"; and seven other short stories of boy life and interest.

THE RELIGIOUS TRACT SOCIETY, LONDON.

STORIES FOR BOYS.

By TALBOT BAINES REED.

THE MASTER OF THE SHELL.

With Seven Full-page and Five other Illustrations in the Text. Large crown 8vo, cloth gilt, 3s. 6d.

A thoroughly interesting story of public school life, dealing with the pranks of schoolboys, bubbling over with love of mischief and fun, and the trials of a young House-Master.

MY FRIEND SMITH. A Story of School and City Life.

With Eleven Full-page and Eight other Illustrations in the Text. Large crown 8vo, cloth gilt, 3s. 6d.

It deals with the temptations and difficulties boys meet with when entering upon business life, and is a first-rate book to give a boy who is just leaving school.

REGINALD CRUDEN. A Tale of City Life.

With Seven Illustrations by ALFRED PEARSE. Large crown 8vo, cloth gilt, 3s. 6d.

Depicts in Mr. T. B. Reed's excellent style the last days at school of Reginald Cruden, who then, through the death of his father, and consequent loss of money, has to start in business at the bottom of the ladder.

His work and adventures in a City printing office, and how he became the innocent victim of a fraudulent company promoter are skilfully told, and open a chapter in the business life of a boy which is full of interest and excitement.

TOM, DICK, AND HARRY.

With Fifteen Full-page Illustrations. Large crown 8vo, cloth gilt, 3s. 6d.

This story first appeared in the *Boy's Own Paper.*

It exhibits in the highest degree the author's knowledge of schoolboy life, his humour, and his power of carrying the reader along in fullest sympathy with the experiences of his different characters.

THE RELIGIOUS TRACT SOCIETY, LONDON.

THE BOY'S LIBRARY OF ADVENTURE & HEROISM.

An attractive series of books for boys, well printed and illustrated, and handsomely bound. Large crown 8vo, cloth, full gilt, 3s. 6d. per volume.

ALLAN ADAIR; or Here and There in Many Lands.

By Dr. GORDON STABLES, R.N., author of "In the Land of the Lion and the Ostrich." With Ten Illustrations by ALFRED PEARSE. Large crown 8vo, cloth gilt, 3s. 6d.

The Examiner says:—"Allan Adair, the only son of his widowed mother, distinguishes himself as a lad in helping to save a vessel in distress, and in return is offered a berth by the owners in one of their ships. Of course he accepts, and a life of world-wide travel and incident is the result. Among many exciting episodes may be mentioned shooting 'rattlers' in the Sierras, encounters with narwhals and bears in the Arctic regions, a hairbreadth escape on the terrible ice-river of Spitzbergen, and adventures among the savages of Patagonia."

A HERO IN WOLF-SKIN. A Story of Pagan and Christian.

By TOM BEVAN. With Seven Illustrations by J. FINNEMORE, R.I. Large crown 8vo, cloth gilt, 3s. 6d.

The Morning Leader says:—"Here we get a young Goth, a very notable fighting-man, who performs feats of valor against the Roman legions, and eventually dazzles a huge audience with his prowess in the Coliseum itself. He is beloved by Floria, a noble Roman maiden, who leads her young barbarian to Christianity and happiness after he has rescued her from the lions in the arena. Full of combats and escapes, 'A Hero in Wolf-skin' should be very popular in the world of youth."

The Sheffield Independent says:—"Boys will delight in it hugely."

The Primitive Methodist Leader says:—"The book is full of thrilling episodes and is just the kind to kindle in boys and in youths the stuff that true men are made of."

THE ADVENTURES OF VAL DAINTRY IN THE GRÆCO-TURKISH WAR.

By V. L. GOING. With Seven Illustrations by FRANK FELLER. Large crown 8vo, cloth gilt, 3s. 6d.

The Sidney Daily Telegraph says:—"This is a fine stirring book for boys."

The English Churchman says:—"Mr. Going has got off the beaten tract in selecting the last Græco-Turkish War as his subject, and he has produced an uncommonly good book, which boys will appreciate."

THE RELIGIOUS TRACT SOCIETY, LONDON.

THE BOY'S LIBRARY OF ADVENTURE & HEROISM.

THE HEROES OF MOSS HALL SCHOOL.

By E. C. KENYON, author of "Little Robin Grey," etc. With Seven Illustrations by ALFRED PEARSE. Large crown 8vo, cloth gilt, 2s.

The Glasgow Herald says:—"Is full of exciting incidents, some of the old conventional type—snowballing, cricket match, paper chase, and so forth—others of a more unusual kind, as for instance the attempted Fenian Raid on the Armoury of the Cadet Corps. They all go to make up a very readable book, which there can be no harm in asking mother to slip into one of the boxes with a view to meeting possible emergencies."

The Aberdeen Free Press says:—"The narrative abounds in incident, and is marked by a vigour and brightness of style which cannot but prove attractive to young lads, while appealing strongly to all healthy and manly instincts."

THE LOST EARLDOM: A Tale of Scotland's Reign of Terror.

By CYRIL GREY, author of "For Crown and Covenant." With Three Illustrations by RAYMOND POTTER. Large crown 8vo, cloth gilt, 3s. 6d.

The Northern Whig says:—"This is a thrilling tale of Scotland's reign of terror, with scenes laid on braeside, in mountain passes, and in the courts of kings. The interest is strongly sustained."

The British Weekly says:—"A workmanlike and well-expressed tale which will be perused by its possessors more than once."

A TROOPER OF THE FINNS: A Tale of the Thirty Years' War.

By TOM BEVAN, author of "A Hero in Wolf-skin," etc., etc. With Three Illustrations by J. FINNEMORE, R.I. Large crown 8vo, cloth gilt, 1s. 6d.

The Schoolmaster says:—"A new book for boys full of excitement and adventure. Young Conrade's noble and courageous nature will awaken the most generous sympathies of the fascinated boy readers."

The School Guardian says:—"Mr. Tom Bevan is rapidly improving in his story-telling, and is likely before long to be in the front rank of writers of books for boys. In 'A Trooper of the Finns,' he gives us a spirited picture of military life on the Continent in the times of Gustavas Adolphus, and of the adventures and perils passed through by a Scottish youth who takes service under the famous Swedish King. The full page pictures by J. Finnemore are deserving of a special word of praise."

THE RELIGIOUS TRACT SOCIETY, LONDON.

THE BOY'S LIBRARY OF ADVENTURE & HEROISM.

WILD LIFE IN SUNNY LANDS. A Romance of Butterfly Hunting.

By GORDON STABLES, M.D., R.N., author of "The Shell Hunters." With Seven Illustrations by ALFRED PEARSE. Large crown 8vo, cloth gilt, 3s. 6d.

The Scotsman says:—"A lively story of adventure in butterfly-hunting, fighting bears and penetrating trackless jungles in various Oriental regions and some undiscovered parts of Africa."

The Daily Telegraph says:—"It is illustrated with seven vivid pictures by Alfred Pearse and is full of adventure all over the world with savage tribes of more or less appalling ferocity and hideous habits."

THE VOYAGE OF THE BLUE VEGA.

By GORDON STABLES, M.D., R.N. With Six Illustrations by ALFRED PEARSE. Large crown 8vo, cloth gilt, 2s. 6d.

"The Voyage of the Blue Vega," by Dr. Gordon Stables, is a yarn which all boys and many "old boys" will delight in. It is a tale of adventures in the Arctic regions, a quarter of the globe which has not been "overdone" in the way of fiction. The style of Dr. Stables—brisk, vivid, chatty, almost confidential, we might call it—carries the reader along as on a flood. There is plenty of adventure in this story, and there is also a romantic mystery pervading the whole. Everything comes all right in the end, as ought to be the case in a book for boys, but a great many threads have to be straightened out before that takes place. There lies the enthralling interest of the story. It shows convincingly that the hand of Dr. Gordon Stables has by no means lost its cunning.

COMRADES UNDER CANVAS. A Story of Boys' Brigade Life.

By FREDERICK P. GIBBON. With Seven Illustrations by ALFRED PEARSE. Large crown 8vo, cloth gilt, 3s. 6d.

A story quite likely to become the classic one of Boys' Brigade Life, just as "Tom Brown's Schooldays" and "The Fifth Form at St. Dominic's" are now confirmed favourites as stories of school life. "Comrades under Canvas" deals with the adventures of members of three Boys' Brigade companies during their annual camp. The interest of the story never flags for a moment, its style is breezy and healthy, and while there is nothing "preachy" about the book, the moral tone is keen and bracing. Boys have their characteristic temptations and failings, and this book, the sale of which ought to be encouraged by every Boys' Brigade officer and everybody interested in boys, will show lads how they may overcome their perils, and live noble, self-sacrificing, Christlike lives.

THE RELIGIOUS TRACT SOCIETY, LONDON.

THE BOY'S LIBRARY OF ADVENTURE & HEROISM.

BOB MARCHANT'S SCHOLARSHIP.

By ERNEST PROTHEROE. With Seven Illustrations by ALFRED PEARSE. Large crown 8vo, cloth gilt, 2s. 6d.

The School Guardian says:—"A very readable tale with plenty of 'go' in it."

The Manchester Courier says:—"An attractive story of schoolboy life."

The Spectator says:—"Here we have a story of adventure, the scene of action being what is called the educational ladder. Bob Marchant wins a scholarship . . . . which takes him to Orville College, a first-grade school. . . . . The subject is worth treating and should not be less interesting than the perils by flood and field which commonly form the themes of these stories."

THE BOY SETTLER; or, The Adventures of Sydney Bartlett.

By H. C. STORER. With Three Illustrations by J. FINNEMORE, R.I. Large Crown 8vo, cloth gilt, 3s. 6d.

A story of Sydney Bartlett's school days, and adventures in New Zealand. Leaving England as a boy, he joins the Mounted Police, sees something of the Maori War, meets with an old settler and throws in his lot with him. The story is full of life and interest.

FROM SCAPEGRACE TO HERO; or, The Adventures and Triumphs of Jem Blake.

By ERNEST PROTHEROE, author of "Bob Marchant's Scholarship." With Seven Illustrations by J. MACFARLANE. Large crown 8vo, cloth gilt, 3s. 6d.

Jem Blake, a wild, unmanageable village boy with an inveterate taste for mischief, by his pranks and practical jokes keeps the country-side in a continual ferment. Led into betting by an older lad, for a time it seems as though nothing can stay his progress along the downward path. Jem, however, is led to see the error of his ways, and commences to atone for his past indiscretions. Thanks to circumstantial evidence, Jem, though innocent, is convicted of being concerned in a poaching affray. Sent to a reformatory for three years, by his courage and presence of mind at a trying moment he attains a remission of his sentence. Entering the Army, Jem, out on the South African veldt, wins the Victoria Cross. In the meantime, his innocence concerning the poaching incident has been proved, and the hero returns home to enjoy his well-merited honours. The author of "Bob Marchant's Scholarship" has here given us a story full of movement, skilfully and vigorously told.

THE RELIGIOUS TRACT SOCIETY, LONDON.

THE BOY'S OWN SERIES.

UNTRUE TO HIS TRUST; or, Plotters and Patriots.

By HENRY JOHNSON, author of "Turf and Table," "A Book of Heroes," etc. With Five Illustrations. Large crown 8vo, cloth gilt, 2s. 6d.

The Times says:—"A tale that is well-conceived and interesting."

The Sheffield Independent says:—"A piece of masterly historical painting."

The British Weekly says:—"A well written and readable book that conveys a great deal of instruction. The period of Charles II. has been very carefully studied."

THE VOYAGE OF THE STORMY PETREL.

By W. C. METCALF. With Three Illustrations by LANCELOT SPEED. Large crown 8vo, cloth gilt, 2s. 6d.

The Glasgow Herald says:—"Possesses all the qualities which young readers for whom it is intended can best appreciate. These are narrow escapes and strange experiences, and adventures full of excitement both on land and sea. The volume has some exciting illustrations.

The English Churchman says:—"A good story of adventure."

The Liverpool Courier says: "This is a stirring tale of an adventurous voyage in which exciting incidents follow one another in rapid succession."

DUCK-LAKE. Stories of the Canadian Backwoods.

By E. RYERSON YOUNG. With Seven Illustrations by J. MACFARLANE. Large crown 8vo, cloth gilt, 2s. 6d.

The Sheffield Daily Independent says:—"It is a spirited story of the Canadian backwoods, in three sections. The characters include Canadian settlers and North American Indians. A number of well-drawn illustrations assist the young reader to realise the physical type of the people who move in the story."

The Dundee Courier says:—"A sectional story of the Canadian backwoods and admirably told. The bush life of the settlers is pictured with a graphic pen, and there are a number of sensational episodes, a bear hunt among the number.

THE RELIGIOUS TRACT SOCIETY, LONDON.

THE BOY'S OWN SERIES.

KORMAK, THE VIKING.

By J. FREDERICK HODGETTS. With Fifteen Illustrations by J. FINNEMORE, R.I. Large crown 8vo, cloth gilt, 2s. 6d.

The School Guardian says:—"This is certainly one of the best of the season's books, full of adventure, and written in crisp, good English. The hero is a Swedish boy who, after many adventures, comes into contact with King Alfred, becomes a Christian, and marries the king's granddaughter. We warmly commend it as a good boy's book."

The Methodist Times says:—"This is a fine, healthy book which is bound to appeal to every lad into whose hands it falls."

CYRIL'S QUEST; or, O'er Vale and Hill in the Land of the Inca.

By ANNIE GRAY. With Three Illustrations by ALFRED PEARSE. Large crown 8vo, cloth gilt, 2s. 6d.

The Manchester Courier says:—"'Cyril's Quest' is a capital tale of adventure, bright spirited, and healthful in tone. Cyril and Hal Hazelton were two brothers trying to work profitably an old farm left to them by the father when he was dying. An offer comes to them from an Uncle John in Argentina, but Cyril is true to his promise, and stays at home with the younger children. Hal goes, and being disappointed with Argentina, proceeds to Peru in search of treasure and is lost. Then Cyril goes in search of him, and the adventures of the twin brothers and their final success are well depicted."

THE BRIGANDS' PREY; A Strange Story of Adventure.

By A. M. JACKSON. With Five Illustrations by G. E. ROBERTSON. Large crown 8vo, cloth gilt, 1s. 6d.

The Manchester Courier says:— "There is no lack of variety in the adventures of Philip and Dick, the two boys who play the *rôle* indicated in the title of the story. From an English school they go to Italy for the holidays. Dick's father having incurred the wrath of the Brigand chief, the boys are captured. They attempt to escape, are sold into slavery, and transported across the seas; they share in a slave's rebellion and escape into the interior of a savage country. Here they come across Dick's pretty sister, previously kidnapped—attired in a Robinson Crusoe costume; and after fighting with savages and man monkeys all three escape in a boat and are rescued when at the last gasp."

THE RELIGIOUS TRACT SOCIETY, LONDON.

THE BOY'S OWN SERIES.

THE SETTLERS OF KAROSSA CREEK,
and Other Stories of Australian Bush Life.

By LOUIS BECKE, author of "Tom Wallis," "Wild Life in the Southern Seas," etc., etc. With Three Illustrations by J. FINNEMORE, R.I. Large crown 8vo, cloth gilt, 2s. 6d.

"The Settlers of Karossa Creek" is a rattling yarn which proves conclusively that the right hand of Louis Becke has not lost its cunning. It is a book that all healthy-minded boys will revel in, full of stirring adventures relating to the bush life of Australia and the islands of the Pacific. "The Settlers of Karossa Creek" will stir the blood of every lad and stimulate the impulses to patience, endurance, brave daring, and true knightliness. The health-giving fragrance of the sea and the free, glad, open life of new lands are in it from first page to last.

THE SPECIMEN HUNTERS.

By J. MACDONALD OXLEY, B.A., author of "North Overland with Franklin," "Archie Mackenzie." Illustrated. Large crown 8vo, cloth gilt, 2s. 6d.

Mr. Macdonald Oxley, who knows so well how to tell a story of adventure and peril—here takes his young heroes out to India and the Far East, with a learned Professor whose duty it is to obtain specimens of beasts and birds. Their ramblings and the Professor's tasks bring them into a succession of highly critical situations, in which their lives are often in extreme peril. The qualities of self-control, manliness and courage are in constant demand. Boys and girls—more especially those with a taste for travel and natural history—should find the book "irresistible."

THE ADVENTURES OF TIMOTHY.

By E. C. KENYON. With Four Illustrations. Large crown 8vo, cloth gilt, 2s. 6d.

A story of adventure during the great Civil War, when King Charles I. and his Parliament resorted to the arbitrament of the sword to decide who should have the mastery. The hero is a Round-head, and the heroine is a charming young person, whose hand a hard-hearted guardian seeks to dispose of in a manner to which her heart consents not. The author is not carried into any excess of partisanship, though his sympathies are obvious, and we can confidently recommend the story as a very good specimen of grand historical romance. The air resounds to the clashing of swords—so to say—but the love element occupies the place of supreme interest throughout, and will hold the interest of the reader without fail.

THE RELIGIOUS TRACT SOCIETY, LONDON.

STORIES FOR BOYS.

THROUGH FIRE and THROUGH WATER.
A Story of Adventure and Peril.

By T. S. MILLINGTON, author of "Straight to the Mark," etc. With Sixteen Illustrations. Large crown 8vo, 2s.

The School Guardian says:—"To boys who like plenty in their books and that of a decidedly stirring order, 'Through Fire and Through Water' may be highly commended. Jack Smith's ambition to be a sailor and how it was finally gratified notwithstanding the obstacles that intervene, his capture by Algerian pirates, and his subsequent rescue. . . . . The story never flags for a moment; it goes with a swing from start to finish."

The Story of Chalmers' Adventurous Life told for Boys.

TAMATE: The Life and Adventures of a Christian Hero.

By RICHARD LOVETT, M.A., author of "James Chalmers: his Autobiography and Letters," etc. With Two Maps and Fifteen Illustrations by J. FINNEMORE, R.I., printed in double tone ink. "Christian Heroes" Series, No. 1. Large crown 8vo, Cloth gilt, 3s. 6d.

The Christian Leader says:—"The story of the great New Guinea missionary and explorer cannot be told too often. Here it is told to boys, and it will be strange indeed if it does not at once prove a real success. James Chalmers was as brave a man as ever lived. His exploits and hairbreadth escapes were legion, and it is practically a series of these that are narrated in the present volume, with all the rapidity and spirit that the boyish temper loves. The writer has to some extent made use of the materials already drawn up for his biography, but he has had access also to letters and diaries hitherto unpublished, and from these vivid pages we gain a clearer idea than ever of his hero. A lion-hearted soul! The boy reader will find him irresistible."

CONDEMNED TO THE GALLEYS. The Adventures of a French Protestant.

By JEAN MARTEILHE. With Seven Illustrations by E. BARNARD LINTOTT. "Christian Heroes" Series, No. 2. Large crown 8vo, cloth gilt, 3s. 6d.

The Expository Times says:—"Let the boy who wants authentic history and excitement combined read 'Condemned to the Galleys,' by Jean Marteilhe."

The Northern Whig says:—"It is a most interesting and reliable work, giving a story which reads like the most fascinating fiction, but is really the genuine history of the sufferings and adventures of a young Protestant."

THE RELIGIOUS TRACT SOCIETY, LONDON.

THE BOY'S OWN SERIES.

THE DOCTOR'S EXPERIMENT; or,
The Adventures of One of Dr. Reade's Pupils, as narrated by Himself.

By H. FREDERICK CHARLES, author of "The Boys of Highfield," "Gentleman Jackson," etc. Illustrated. Large crown 8vo, cloth gilt, 1s. 6d.

Scotsman says:—"A capital story for boys, which will interest them from the first page to the last."

Saturday Review says:—"Another wholesome story of schoolboy life. All is told with great skill and power of delineating character. There are many episodes in the main narrative, some of them extremely amusing."

GENTLEMAN JACKSON.

By H. FREDERICK CHARLES, author of "The Doctor's Experiment," "The Boys of Highfield," etc. Illustrated. Large crown 8vo, cloth gilt, 2s. 6d.

The story of a boy who starts in life heavily handicapped by a drunken father, but succeeds by hard work in attaining an honourable position in life.

TOM WALLIS. A Tale of the South Seas.

By LOUIS BECKE, author of "By Reef and Palm," "Admiral Philip," etc. Illustrated. Large crown 8vo, cloth gilt, 1s. 6d.

A stirring story of the multitudinous adventures by land and sea of an intrepid young Australian, and it literally teems with exciting episodes. Mr. Louis Becke's knowledge of life in the Islands of the Pacific is a matter of common repute; he knows what he is writing about, and tells his tale with a rugged simplicity and naturalness which will charm all readers.

THE STORY OF A CITY ARAB.

By G. E. SARGENT, author of "Frank Layton," "Boys will be Boys," etc. Illustrated. Large crown 8vo, cloth gilt, 2s. 6d.

In every large city there is beneath the surface of general society an alarming mass of ignorance, immorality and crime. Mr. G. E. Sargent has drawn from his experience, observation and opinions of others, an exciting story, well told, full of adventure and interest to boys.

THE RELIGIOUS TRACT SOCIETY, LONDON.

THE BOY'S OWN SERIES.

THE SHELL-HUNTERS: Their Wild Adventures by Land and Sea.

By GORDON STABLES, author of "Allan Adair," etc. Illustrated. Large crown 8vo, cloth gilt, 1s. 6d.

This is one of Dr. Gordon Stables' stories of adventure. A middle-aged man and a couple of boys make a voyage of discovery in the South Seas. The tale is full of exciting incidents and hair-breadth escapes so dear to the heart of all boys; and it has the advantage of being cleverly illustrated by ALFRED PEARSE.

HAROLD, THE BOY EARL. A Story of Old England.

By J. F. HODGETTS, author of "Kormak the Viking," etc. Illustrated. Large crown 8vo, cloth gilt, 2s. 6d.

ILDERIM, THE AFGHAN. A Tale of the Indian Border.

By DAVID KER. Illustrated. Large crown 8vo, cloth gilt, 2s. 6d.

David Ker, the author of "The Lonely Island," has here written a stirring and highly imaginative tale of India and the North-West Frontier. The heroes are men of high character, and a bright, healthy moral tone is maintained throughout.

ADVENTURES IN THE SOUTH PACIFIC.

By ONE WHO WAS BORN THERE, author of "Annie Carr," etc. Illustrated. Large crown 8vo, cloth gilt, 2s. 6d.

The Guardian says:—"The pictures of the South Sea Islanders are evidently drawn from life, and the accounts of the kidnappers, both cannibal and slave-hunting, are well told and full of grim interest."

The Methodist Times says:—"The book is a true record of the adventures of the son of a South Sea Island Missionary. The writer begins at the beginning—at his earliest whippings—and goes on through escapades by land and sea. He narrowly escapes poisoning by *carea* and is in an awful tornado. Perils by famine, by murder, by heathen superstition, by sharks, by pestilence, by white slave-traders, bring before the reader vividly, life as it is in the savage islands of the South."

THE RELIGIOUS TRACT SOCIETY, LONDON.

THE BOY'S OWN SERIES.

THE STORY OF A POCKET BIBLE.

By G. E. SARGENT, author of "The Story of a City Arab," "Frank Layton," etc. Illustrated. Large crown 8vo, cloth gilt, 2s. 6d.

NORTH OVERLAND WITH FRANKLIN.

By J. MACDONALD OXLEY, author of "Archie Mackenzie," etc. Illustrated. Large crown 8vo, cloth gilt, 2s. 6d.

A book of adventure for boys. It gives the many stirring incidents of an Arctic journey, made by Lieutenant Franklin before the great expedition in which he and his crew lost their lives.

THE CAPTAIN'S STORY; or, Jamaica Sixty Years Since.

By Captain BROOKE-KNIGHT. Illustrated. Large crown 8vo, cloth gilt, 2s.

CAPTAIN COOK; His Life, Voyages, and Discoveries.

By W. H. G. KINGSTON, author of "Little Peter the Ship Boy," "Ben Hadden," etc. Illustrated. Large crown 8vo, cloth gilt, 2s. 6d.

Among all those Englishmen who, from a humble origin, have risen to an honourable position, Captain James Cook is especially worthy of record. His life and labours are graphically described by the late W. H. G. Kingston. His boyhood, his first voyage on a collier, then his volunteering for the Navy, his many voyages and discoveries, his various adventures among the South Sea Islands, are full of interest to boys.

THE HEIR OF BRAGWELL HALL.

By ALFRED BEER. With Seven Illustrations by J. FINNEMORE, R.I. Large crown 8vo, cloth gilt, gilt top, 2s. 6d.

The Record says:—"A powerful story, full of adventures, such as appeal to healthy-minded boys. The young 'heir' is a very objectionable young person when we first meet with him; but the disasters he encounters on his tour round the world—including a shipwreck, and a few other troubles of that sort—greatly discipline his character."

The Glasgow Herald says:—"The story is cleverly conceived, well written and high-toned."

THE RELIGIOUS TRACT SOCIETY, LONDON.

THE BOY'S OWN SERIES.

THE WALLABY MAN.

By Dr. A. N. MALAN, F.G.S., author of "School Days at Highfield House," etc. With Seven Illustrations. Large crown 8vo, cloth gilt, 2s. 6d.

The Sheffield Telegraph says: "A book over which schoolboys will enjoy a hearty laugh. The 'Wallaby Man' keeps a tame kangaroo which attracts the notice of two schoolboys. Through it, the boys get mixed up unwillingly in two robberies. One of the boys, however, is an admirer of Sherlock Holmes, and aspires to emulate the great detective's methods. For the results the reader must consult the book itself."

The Primitive Methodist says: "This is as fine a story for lads as we have read for many a long day."

GEOFF BLAKE: His Chums and His Foes.

By S. S. PUGH. With Three Illustrations by LANCELOT SPEED. Large crown 8vo, cloth gilt, 2s. 6d.

The School Guardian says:—"This is a new edition of a good story of school life in a somewhat old-fashioned school. There is a wholesome tone throughout the book, and it deserves the circulation it has secured."

CAVE PERILOUS.

By L. T. MEADE. With Seven Illustrations by S. T. DADD. Large crown 8vo, cloth gilt, 1s. 6d.

A very brightly written tale, full of incident and adventure of English life nearly a century ago. It is very fully illustrated, and forms a handsome gift book.

FOR CROWN AND COVENANT.

By CYRIL GREY, author of "The Lost Earldom." With Three Illustrations by ALFRED PEARSE. Large crown 8vo, cloth gilt, 1s. 6d.

A stirring tale depicting the struggle for Christ's Crown and Covenant in Scotland during the reign of Charles II. By the adventures of the chief characters, the reader is carried from scene to scene with ever-deepening interest.

THE RELIGIOUS TRACT SOCIETY, LONDON.